# The Accidental Highland Hero

## The Highlanders

## Book 2

### TERRY SPEAR

The Accidental Highland Hero
Published by Terry Spear

Copyright © 2010 Terry Spear
Cover Copyright © 2010 Rene Walden of BG
Designs

Discover more about Terry Spear at:
http://www.terryspear.com/
ISBN-13: 978-1-63311-051-9

# DEDICATION

To Karen White who loves my wolves and gives my
other series the chance to fall in love with! Hope you
enjoy these wickedly fun Highlanders!

# PROLOGUE

*Cala na Creige, Scotland, 1103*

'Twas the first time since her father's death in a fortnight, Lady Eilis Dunbarton had managed to sneak out of her uncle's castle without escort. She'd so longed to see the beach below the cliffs where her father and she had spent many a day talking about the sea and his journeys. Only here could she find a gift for her cousin that she would truly treasure.

Eilis unfastened her brooch and pulled off her ariasaid. After attaching the brooch to the plaid, she tucked it behind a crag on the grassy ridge so as to keep it dry.

By the time Eilis traversed the steep, natural steps cut into the cliff by wind and rain and reached the rocky beach, the tide was coming in. She couldn't tarry long and hurried to sort through the sea-polished stones when she spied a glint of purple crystal a few feet away, the water already washing over it. The stone would be the perfect gift for Agnes's day of celebration as much as she loved the color. Eilis hurried forth, her foot slipping on the wet, mossy rocks. She nearly took a tumble. Her heart leapt in her throat.

then the small, narrow cave where the incoming tide had drowned two laddies last summer caught her eye. Were their spirits still trapped there? She shuddered, remembering how she and Agnes had sneaked into the forbidden cave only a day before and found a dagger and silver brooch. She swallowed hard. 'Twas best she kept her mind on the incoming tide and be quick about her business.

Elated to find such a treasure, she took a deep breath of the salty, fishy smelling air, grabbed the shimmering purple crystal, and dropped it into her pouch. It clunked against her other precious stones.

Drawing closer to the tidal waters, she spied an amber stone. As disconsolate and imprisoned as she and her wee brother had been since their father's death, she knew Ethan would love yet another gem to add to his collection. 'Twas a shame she could not bring him along for a brief respite, but she'd had a difficult enough time slipping out on her own without taking him with her.

Wending her way over the rocks, she attempted to reach the glistening stone, the tidewater already rushing in to claim it. Nay, it would be hers this day. There was no telling when she could sneak out alone again. Mayhap never.

She only wished her father's youngest brother living in Ireland could have taken her and her brother in. But she could wish all she liked and naught would change. Soon she feared her Uncle Ceardach would give her in marriage to some chieftain to tie another clan's loyalty to his. Ethan would then be at her uncle's cruel mercy.

The sea soaked her to her ankles, the water icy cold, and she slipped again. Her skin prickled with unease. The deeper the water, the harder to see her treasure and to make any progress against the flow. Och, just a few more feet. The tide threatened to wash her back onto the diminishing shore.

When she reached the spot where she thought she'd spied it, she crouched, wetting her kirtle, and dug at the stones with her fingers. Lifting one after another, she tossed them aside. Where was the pretty amber stone? The water tugged at her, trying to topple her as she fought its strong push. Heart racing, she stood, shielded her eyes from the sun peeking through clouds, and peered into the water. She thought she glimpsed it farther out than she'd first imagined.

She hesitated. 'Twas not too far to go if she hurried. Mayhap she would not get too much wetter, although the cold was already making her feet ache. She thought of Ethan and how he would react when she brought him the gem. His face would light in glee. Aye, she had to get him the treasure.

She waded deeper, the cold icing her legs, her skirts soaking up the water, weighing her down. when she thought she stood in front of it, she peered into the water and smiled. *Aye, there it is.* She leaned over and thrust both hands into the water and grabbed the treasure, but the stone was wedged tight. Larger than she thought also.

The water had risen too high, was moving too fast, and now even her chest was immersed as she—

The rock began to give, and her heart did a little

skip for joy.

A man's youthful voice, shouted, "Nay, lass!"

'Twas too late for a warning.

The tide pulled her off her feet, tugging her like a hundred wet hands toward the cave into the dark and jagged rocks. Her breath let out in a whoosh. Grasping for purchase on the ragged rocks in her path, she swallowed a mouthful of briny sea and choked.

"Hold on!" the man shouted again, but his voice was still a goodly distance away.

Searing pain ripped through her torn palms and fingers while she clung on, the tide threatening to drown her as it attempted to pull her into the cave. She couldn't give in, not when she had to look after Ethan.

Was the man coming? She couldn't hear him for the roar of the water crashing along the cliff face and the seagulls screeching high overhead. Another wave roared over her, soaking her to the skin while she held her breath against the onslaught. The wall of water yanked her from her tentative hold on the slippery rocks.

Just as the sea was pulling her under, hands grasped her wrists and tugged her away from the entrance to the cave. The man held her tight around the waist and kicked his legs, drawing her farther from the deadly menace.

Coughing to expel the seawater that gagged her, she tried to open her eyes. The saltwater stung, and she couldn't see anything more than a blur and closed them again.

"Are you all right, lass?" The man dragged her from the water and onto the first of the steps leading back up the cliff. The water lapped at the rocks just below them and would rise even higher.

All she could think of was how angry her uncle would be if he saw her clothes and hair wet. And if he knew a man had touched her, despite the best of intentions, he'd kill him. Beyond that, the man who held her so intimately, did things to her she never had imagined—sent a strange heat through her body when she should have been chilled to the bone. His strong arms secured her against him, lean and hard, his lips so close even his eyes took in her appearance with too much familiarity. 'Twas more than scandalous. Yet, she clung to him with all her strength—loving his warmth, his protectiveness, his noble endeavor to save her when he could have died.

He pulled a strand of kelp from her hair and threw it back into the sea.

"I am...I am all right," she sputtered, her throat raw from swallowing the seawater.

He raised his brows. "Aye, you are a hardy one that. Although what the devil you were doing, I cannot fathom."

He would not understand. 'Twas not more than a foolish lass's whim he would think. But to revisit the place her da and she used to come, and what the stone would have meant to her little brother—these things meant the world to her. Except she had lost her brother's treasure. Her eyes filled with tears.

The man half carried, half dragged her up the steep incline. Several feet above the tidewater broiling in a frenzy against the rocks, he helped Eilis sit.

"Here, drink this." He pulled a flask from his belt.

The honeyed mead helped soothe her throat, the sweet wine washing away the salty grit. She tried to wipe the biting salt from her eyes, but her wet sleeves irritated them even more.

"Here." He pulled a dry cloth from a pouch. "Where do you live?"

After wiping her eyes, she opened them, although they still burned, and she squinted against the pain. When she was able to see more clearly, she noticed the man's hair, the color of freshly turned earth, rich and glistening with water, hanging loosely at his shoulders. His brows were furrowed with concern. But his dark brown eyes swallowed her up, held her hostage. She didn't think she'd ever seen such a handsome man in her life.

"Lass, where do you live? In yonder castle, mayhap? You will catch your death. Even now you are shivering. Shall I take you there?"

"Your name, sir," Eilis whispered, her bloodied hands burning, tears pricking her eyes.

"James." He tugged at her to get her to her feet.

Her gown laden with water, she could barely stand.

"Concentrate on taking one step at a time, lass. We need to get you to the top of the cliff." He wrapped his arm around her waist and helped her to the next step. "You weigh as much as my horse, I fathom. What is that you are carrying?"

She couldn't tell him 'twas a collection of rocks. He would think her daft. Inching up between his pulling her and her climbing, she felt a new pain, this in her right hip. Hopefully, she had not broken anything or her uncle would be more than angered.

By the time they neared the top of the ridge, Eilis felt like she'd been climbing cliffs on an all-day hunt.

"We are almost there, lass. Just a wee bit more, and

I should be able to pull you up."

The next thing Eilis knew, she was on her back, and the youth was lying atop her, his head between her breasts, his legs between hers, his breath rasping.

"James," she gasped, her chilled body instantly heating as if she'd been immersed in cook's boiling soup. The tingling in her stomach renewed and spread to the tips of her breasts and between her legs. She'd never felt anything akin to this before, and the sensation both intrigued and alarmed her.

He lifted his head, and his mouth curved upward in the most devilish manner. "You are alive."

Her legs bared to the warm breeze, she tried to wriggle free, shoving his shoulders with her hands, but pain jolted through her hip, her palms burning, and she groaned.

"You are hurt, lass," James said, his eyes widening as he eased off her. "Where do you ail?"

"Beg pardon, sir," she cried, scooting away from him, yanking at her kirtle to cover her naked legs. Her uncle had thoroughly warned her about men, of any age—young and old, how easily they could compromise a lady's affections, then leave them in a bad way, heartbroken and alone.

"Your dress, lass, was too sodden. When I finally managed to get us to the top of the cliff, we collapsed, and you fainted, pulling me on top of you. I listened for your heartbeat to make sure you had not died."

"I am quite alive, sir." Verra much so, if the way her body had reacted to his was any indication.

What was worse, she missed his intimate touch, the heat of his body, his protectiveness. Yet the image of him between her legs reminded her of the kitchen maid

Eilis had spied with a stable boy in the barn and with another man she did not know. Both times the maid's kirtle was above her waist, the rest of her naked to a bare-arsed lad—och.

Eilis would think naught more of the matter as she had told herself so many times before. Besides, this was not the same. James was noble for having risked his life to save her.

Until she looked into James's eyes and saw a hint of the devil in them. Or mayhap it was his lips curved up in such a roguish way that intrigued her like no other.

\*\*\*

"Aye, I see you are verra much alive." James smiled at the bewitching lass. As soon as he'd spied her on the rocky beach, he wondered what she was doing. When he saw the danger she was in, he'd had to stop her and nearly broke his neck in his rush down the slippery stone steps.

Now her green eyes held his gaze, boldly, unlike how a serving girl or even one of the ladies of a manor would react, looking away demurely, trying to draw him in with her subtle female ways. The lass more than held his gaze, assessed his looks—twice already, stirring his loins like no other.

He assumed from the quality of her gown, she was a lady of some means. Although he tried not to look at it overmuch, the way the wet fabric clung to all her soft curves, revealing way more than he should have seen. Just observing her like this, for once, he was at a loss for words.

What was she doing without a chaperone, risking her life with the tide coming in?

She was daring, adventuresome, and even half drowned—the prettiest lassie he'd seen with fiery red-gold curls in wet straggles down to her hips and cheeks full of color. Although when he'd listened to her heart, her cheeks had been quite pale.

None of the shy, retiring girls he'd met would have left their castles without proper escort. And none of them would have been caught dead doing—well, he wasn't sure what she'd been doing. Looked to be fishing without a net.

Although she'd spoken barely a few words, her speech was as honeyed as his mead, not shrill like cook's voice, or harsh as the kitchen staff. Even though he'd startled her with his actions, she had not screamed for someone to rescue her.

She more than intrigued him. He thought he intrigued her a little also.

"Your name, lass? And from where do you hail?"

Just then a man shouted from the road some yards beyond, "Where are you? Da will have your hide!"

The girl's eyes widened. "Hide. Hurry! Beyond that crag. If my cousin finds you alone with me, he will slay you."

"I just saved you."

"He will kill you! I beg of you, if you value my life and your own, leave."

Her eyes misted.

With great reluctance, James would do as she bade. He took her arm, realizing then how cold she was and berated himself for not going for help sooner. "I will wait over yonder to see that your cousin finds you."

She licked her lips as if preparing them for a kiss. Without further thought, he pressed his mouth against

9

hers and tasted the honeyed mead and her own sweetness.

Her lips parted in surprise, and he pushed harder. Soft, yielding, perfectly innocent. 'Twas with the utmost difficulty he broke the kiss. "Lass, your name."

He knew then he had to see her again. Somehow. Although he hoped she was not of an enemy clan.

She shook her head and pushed him away. "He will kill you, fool. Go." She pressed her finger to her lips as if cherishing his touch. She tried to sit up, but she groaned, and James hesitated to leave her. Again, she shoved at him. "Go," she whispered, her word angry, but her eyes sad.

He ground his teeth and dashed off to the outcropping of rocks, hating that he had still not learned her name. Irritated he would have to hide when he had only the lass's best intentions at heart—well, except for the kiss—chaste as it was.

His younger brother slipped in beside him. "I have searched for you for miles," Malcolm whispered, then peered around the rocks to see what James was watching.

Malcolm let out his breath. "What is going on? Da is calling for you. Who is the lass? What is she doing there, soaked from head to toe? And what were you doing kissing her?"

James groaned inwardly. How long had his brother been watching them? "Little brother, her cousin comes for her. Hush."

'Twas not much longer when a strapping young man, red blond hair like the girl's, came into view astride a roan, a scar across his face, giving him a surly look.

"There you are. God's wounds, cousin, my da will take a strap to you for running off. Why are you soaked to the bone? Get up."

"I...I hurt myself."

Her cousin jumped from his horse, leaned down, and grabbed her wrist.

James would have leapt from his hiding place and protected the lass if his brother hadn't seized his arm and shaken his head.

The girl's cousin yanked her to her feet, and she screamed out.

'Twas more than James could bear. He fought against Malcolm, furious he would stop him from rescuing the lass.

"Och, Da will be more than displeased." Her cousin grabbed her by the waist.

"My bag." Her face pained, she motioned to the leather pouch on the ground.

He glanced at it. "Your rocks?" He grunted. "Da needs to find you a husband without delay."

"But—"

He threw her over the saddle, and again she cried out. Before she could protest or James could get loose from Malcolm, the lass's cousin remounted and galloped off.

"Who was she?" Malcolm asked as they rose from their crouched position.

The most foolish lassie James had ever met, and the only one who had ever heated his body to a fevered pitch, stolen every reasonable thought in his mind, and left him yearning for more of her touch.

He frowned at his brother for stopping him from rescuing the lass from her brutish cousin. Malcolm leaned down and lifted an ariasaid from the ground, hidden by the shadows of the rocks. "Is it hers?"

James took the plaid from his brother and smelled it. "Aye." 'Twas the sweet lassie's scent. He tucked it into his plaid and traversed the rocky cliff. When he reached her bag, he hoped to discover more about who she was and where she was from. He peered inside and stared at the contents. Rocks? No wonder the lass weighed as much as his horse. Well, that, and her wet kirtle. He tied the pouch to his waist, hoping to learn who the lass was and return her treasures. "Is Da drunk again?"

"Aye. When is he not? But he says you must wed soon, and he wishes you to choose from one of the lassies he has in mind for you to marry."

"I will not be laird until he is gone. 'Tis time to take up my sword in the Crusade." Mayhap James could redeem his father's sins. Or mayhap not. He glanced in the direction the lass's cousin had ridden. "Time enough later to find a lass to wed."

When he could find one who made him feel like the girl in the green kirtle did, with silken hair and sea green eyes, who challenged him with her sweet innocence, aye, then he would wed.

# CHAPTER 1

*Dubh Linn, Ireland, 1107*

Eilis hastily brushed away tears and kissed her beloved cousin's cold cheek. Now with Agnes dead, 'twas only her wee brother and her against the world.

"Hurry, Lady Eilis," her cousin's maid, Wynda, scolded. "You must not keep your uncle waiting. He has an audience with the king after he speaks with you."

The fact Eilis's uncle had summoned her right before he spoke with Muirchertach did not bode well.

"I am afraid of Uncle Ceardach," Ethan whispered, her brother's small hand squeezing Eilis's to death, and she knew no matter how much she wanted to protect him from her uncle's harsh ways, she had no power here. "He is verra angry that Cousin Agnes died," Ethan added.

Looking up at Eilis, Ethan took a hesitant breath, his green eyes wide with trepidation, his windswept

1

curly blond locks tangled over his forehead and the rest hanging down to his shoulders—a miniature version of their deceased father.

Eilis's heart shrank with distress. "Aye," she said softly, wishing she could allay her wee brother's fears, wishing she could steal away with him and live with some other kinsmen. But there were none who would go against her uncle's will and provide them shelter.

She had seen her uncle terrorize his brother's servants and even his own this verra morn. She had hoped once Agnes married Laird Dunbarton, their uncle's temper would settle. Now with Agnes dead, their uncle's hopes to secure peace along their clan borders died with it.

Ethan's hand squeezed Eilis's again when they saw Broc, their uncle's only son, also headed in the direction of the great hall, shoving a servant out of his path. An old scar cut against Broc's brow, a mishap when fighting a neighboring clansman, giving him a perpetual scowl, now deepened as he spied Eilis with her brother.

"He is angry also," Ethan whispered to Eilis.

"Aye." She imagined Laird Ceardach MacBurness had taken his anger out on Broc as much as he did anyone else in the clan this morn. Soon, her uncle planned to return to Scotland, leaving his brother's castle in Ireland after but a brief visit, meant to secure concessions from him, no doubt. She wished Ceardach would leave Ethan and her behind to live in Ireland. But Ceardach was the elder of the two and despite her prayers and wishes, she knew he would not give them up to be wards of his younger brother, Maddock. Ceardach would train Ethan to be a warrior, loyal to his rule. She feared her uncle would soon offer her to some minor chieftain to gain special considerations as well. What she wouldn't give to raise her brother of six summers until he reached manhood.

They entered the great hall where Uncle Ceardach sat, his red beard streaked gray, making him appear older than his forty summers. He gave her only a cursory glance. Then Broc entered the hall, a smug smile fixed to his lips.

Uncle Ceardach rose to his full height, which made Eilis all the more uneasy. His green eyes pinned her as if to say she would not object to the disagreeable news. Immediately, her heart beat irregularly.

Her uncle folded his arms across his broad chest. "I have weighed this matter with the utmost concern, and my decision will stand."

She scarcely breathed, and Ethan's small hand was cutting off the circulation in hers.

"You will marry Laird Dunbarton." His cold eyes fixed on her, challenging her to object.

Her heart took a dive, her knees went weak, and she could scarce believe his words. Her uncle couldn't mean for her to wed the old laird in Agnes's place. Would the laird even be agreeable? "But—"

Her uncle waved her objection aside. "You will do as I bid. Since your mothers were twins, lassie, you look enough like your cousin, the same red gold curls, the same height, same green eyes. Laird Dunbarton has never seen either of you, and no one there will ever know the difference. The fighting along our clan borders has to stop, and he agrees to halt the conflict with this marriage."

Her thoughts swirled with confusion.

"You will take her place."

She grasped at any hope to make him change his mind. "But, my laird, will Laird Dunbarton accept me since I am but your niece not your daughter?"

"I will not have my plans laid asunder because of Agnes's death. I cannot afford for him to say no. You will be Agnes from this day forth."

Her heart stopped beating for an instant. He could not be serious. Ethan looked up at her, his mouth agape. They had always been taught not to tell falsehoods. How could she explain to him their uncle was forcing her to live the biggest lie of their lives?

"But, my laird," Eilis pleaded, knowing her entreaties would fall on deaf ears but praying her uncle would listen to reason while he paced back in forth in his brother's castle overlooking the coast. "He will know I am not your daughter. Agnes—"

Laird MacBurness came to an abrupt halt and glowered at her. "The agreement has already been signed and witnessed."

"The marriage agreement says Laird Dunbarton will marry Agnes, my laird. Not me," Eilis implored, her heart sinking in despair.

As the clan chief's only daughter, Agnes had had everything Eilis ever wanted, a father and mother to take care of her every whim, a clan who treated her like a princess. Eilis had loved Agnes like a sister. Knowing she'd never see Agnes's smiling face again brought tears to her eyes.

Taking a heavy breath, Eilis remembered the way her mother had looked, flushed with fever, then pale as death, the same way Agnes had appeared on her deathbed. Only in Eilis's mother's case, the fever was due to birthing Eilis's baby brother who was born stillborn, and her mother died shortly thereafter.

Eilis was certain that's why her father, so distraught over her mother's death, had fought against the raiding MacIntosh clan with no care for his own safety and lost his life.

Eilis's thoughts shifted again to poor dear Agnes. For once, Eilis had been grateful not to be the clan chief's daughter when her uncle made arrangements to marry Agnes to the Dunbarton chief, who was sixty summers in age. Although Eilis had fretted enough for the both of them that poor Agnes would have to marry the old chief.

How could a twist of fate be so cruel?

Now, there was no one to console Eilis in her grief. Worse, she could not protect her little brother if her uncle made him stay with him.

Leaning against the south wall, Broc considered her as if she were a peace offering, his blue eyes ice cold.. He wouldn't voice a word to save her. Truth be known, he wanted her to marry the old laird just as much as his father did, to keep the peace, to ensure their plans were not interrupted.

"I am not any good at feigning the truth. I will say the wrong thing and Laird Dunbarton will want my head and yours also," Eilis tried again.

"He would not be successful."Ceardach MacBurness smiled heartlessly, the look of a battle-hardened Highland warrior. Her father had always warned her his older brother had eaten lesser men to break his fast. She was certain her uncle wouldn't be swayed by her entreaty.

He gave her a stern look, his red hair hanging

loosely about his haggard face, made harder from the strain of losing his only daughter. He cared not about Eilis nor Agnes for that matter. They were only pawns to be used wherever it suited the clan best. But losing his daughter had created the latest angst during his long years of embattled rule.

"If I don't resolve this matter at once, I'll have another fight on my hands," he growled to Brock. "God's wounds, couldn't Agnes have waited to fall ill until *after* she'd wed Dunbarton?" he roared.

Instantly, Eilis felt feverish and wondered if she was coming down with the same sickness her cousin had died from. 'Twould serve her uncle right.

MacBurness's beady green eyes seemed to shrink even smaller in the tanned seasoned lines of his face. "'Tis not my fault my daughter died of fever early this morn. You will do this for the sake of our clan. If you tell Laird Dunbarton otherwise, it will go badly for you. Your own people will deny you are Eilis."

"What about Ethan?" she asked in a small voice, already knowing what would happen to her little brother. Her uncle would not want her influencing her brother any more than she already did, and Dunbarton probably would not want her attention diverted from him to a sibling either.

Her uncle gave her a sly smile. "He stays with me to learn to be a man." He motioned to a servant. "The lady is ready for her journey." Turning to Eilis, he said, "Do well by us, my niece, and your clan will speak only praise of you. Try any bit of trickery, and you will live to regret it. Now go and fulfill my promise to Dunbarton."

'Twas not what her uncle had promised Dunbarton

at all! 'Twas the most despicable of lies, and somehow she had to steal Ethan away and find someone who would shelter them. But she couldn't even begin to think of anyone who might aid them who wasn't afraid of her uncle.

Agnes's maid, Wynda, stiffly walked toward Eilis, as dour as usual, her gray eyes clouded with hate, her lips pursed in complaint. Did her uncle intend Wynda to attend her in her new life? Och, the woman had treated her with contempt ever since Eilis's da had died.

"Come." Wynda's petite stature and older age gave the illusion she was weak and easily manipulated, but the bony fingers gripping Eilis's arm told the truth. "The ship awaits." Wynda jerked Ethan's hand away from Eilis's, and her brother wailed.

Her heart in her throat, Eilis grabbed for his hand, but Laird MacBurness commanded, "Take him away!"

One of her uncle's men strode forth, seized Ethan, and hauled her crying brother off toward his chamber.

Her uncle gave Eilis a look like she better not disobey him. With a nod of his head directed at Wynda, he signaled to the woman to yank Eilis out of the hall and through the keep toward the waiting ship and her fate.

***

James MacNeill, laird of Craigly Castle, surveyed the sheep pastured in the glen, and seeing no sign of the raiding Dunbartons, he motioned for his men to continue the sweep south. He would string every last one of the raiders by his neck if he didn't put them to the sword first, he swore.

To think he was supposed to be concentrating on wedding the fair Catriona, not dealing with troubles at his clan borders again. The thought of her creamy soft skin beneath his, the way she moved her hips, hurrying his thrusts, and mewed her pleasure stirred him all over again. Although it had been a year since he had been with the widowed lass, it seemed like yesterday.

*Catriona.* He could not wait to see her on the morrow, although he was tired of pretending they had a chaste relationship in front of his clansmen, whilst burying himself deep inside her when she stayed in the chamber adjoining his. She had to agree to be his this time. She had to. He would allow her no other answer.

Movement in the woods stole his attention. 'Twas a Dunbarton! *The murdering thieves.* With a war whoop, James targeted the bearded, heavy-set man, his tangled red hair hanging about his shoulders. He responded by charging toward James with a hearty war cry of his own. James's own men had scattered in search of the Dunbartons and those who were allied with them, so he was on his own. James would not let the whoreson out of his grasp. Either he killed him, or he took him hostage. Those were the only choices he would allow.

The redheaded beast seemed of like mind and with murder in his eyes, swung his sword at James. But James had fought valiantly in the Crusade and for his father until his death, ensuring the MacNeill lands were free from poachers and brigands. The man would not best him.

Yet the sheer force of the Dunbarton's blows sent a jarring vibration through James's sword arm every time steel met steel. The mountain was unmovable, and the strikes James dealt seemed to have no effect.

The beast gave a sly smile, his blue eyes narrowed with despise. "Laird MacNeill, you will taste my sword afore long. Why do you not give up? Make it easier on yourself. You know Laird Dunbarton will send us to plague you until you give your life for his nephew."

"'Tis I who should be seeking Laird Dunbarton's head for the death of my dear sister," James said dryly.

Yet he knew the fault partly lay with him. Had he let his sister marry the Dunbarton's nephew, would they still be alive today? Mayhap not. But he couldn't tamp down the feeling he was the reason for his sweet sister's death.

The battle between the clans had gone on for over a century. They killed a MacNeill, and the MacNeill evened the score. It would go on for several more centuries, no doubt.

Just when James thought he had struck a decisive blow, cutting the brigand clean across the chest, blood spilling from the fresh cut, the giant retaliated. Striking James's readied sword with such force, the brigand knocked James from his horse.

On foot against the big man, James was sorely disadvantaged. Crippling the Dunbarton's horse might have worked to even the odds, but even in battle, James could not injure a good horse. Instead, he danced like some Sassenach fool, moving himself out of the path of the rider and his horse, feeling the whoosh of the beast's steel but missing the cut of its blade. Then swinging about as if readying himself for the final battle, only with him on foot and his opponent mounted, he waited for the Dunbarton to make a mistake.

With their eyes staring each other down, the Dunbarton kicked his warhorse forward.

James swung his sword first and made a deep cut

across Dunbarton's thigh. With a howl, the enemy missed striking at James, who nimbly jumped away.

The Dunbarton whipped his horse around and charged again. Except this time, he swung first, and the impact of his sword against James's knocked him off his feet. With a thud, James landed hard on his back, knocking the breath from him.

'Twas not a good position to be in during a fight.

He tried to jump to his feet, but weariness cloaked him in a shroud of refusal. Staggering, he unsheathed a throwing dagger. He barely had time to aim it when the Dunbarton swung his sword at James's head.

Whack! The dagger hit the Dunbarton in the temple.

The man teetered on his horse for a moment, then plummeted to the ground. *Dead.* Meaning to take the beast alive, James cursed under his breath.

Noting a missive in the man's belt, James reached down to remove it.

*Meet the ship at the aforementioned time and bring the precious cargo here post haste.*

James smiled wryly. He would send his cousin and seneschal with several of his men and intercept this precious cargo before Laird Dunbarton could get his grubby hands on it.

***

An icy wind tugged at Eilis's plaid brat cloaking her head while she held onto the ship's railing with a death grip. Her brother's cries still echoed in her mind. His rounded green eyes filled with tears of terror still held her hostage. He was all she had left in the world, and she wanted more than anything to free him from their uncle's tyranny. But what could she do?

A woman set upon the Irish Sea, bound to marry a man she didn't love, pretending to be her cousin? She feared she was destined to fail, and all she could hope for was the creaking ship sailing across the frothing sea from Ireland to Scotland would sink.

The wind howled, black clouds boiled into mountains above, lightning flashed, casting jagged bolts of light into the rising waves, and she threw up her morning meal over the ship's railing.

"You must come back to the captain's quarters, my lady," Agnes's maid clutched the railing and commanded Eilis, although her brusque manner revealed a hint of fear. Could the maid of steel be afraid of the storm?

Eilis hoped so, as much as her own insides quaked.

The waves lifted the ship toward the heavens then dropped it, crashing it into the next black trough. The elderly woman shrieked, her face as gray as her eyes.

"I am sicker down there than I am up here. Leave me be and go inside with you."

"Nay, I cannot leave you alone with the crude men on this ship."

The woman had to be daft. "They will have naught to do with me! They are too busy trying to keep the ship afloat!"

"I order you, my lady, come back inside."

*Command this!* Eilis heaved the last of her oatcakes over the side, tears splashing down her cheeks, mixed with fresh rainwater and the salty sea. If she fell overboard, she would not have to marry the old Dunbarton chief. She would not have to lie about who she was and forever fear he'd find out.

But she was a coward, and the small nagging voice

in her head said she had to return for her brother and rescue him some day. Staring into the angry waves capped with white foam, dashing into the ship's hull, beating it with horrible vengeance, she couldn't jump.

"My lady—"

"Nay, go away. Leave me be." Mayhap a wave would wash Eilis overboard when she hadn't the courage to do it herself.

"You cannot mean to throw yourself over the side. Our clan will be punished for it, and you will be hated for all eternity." The maid curled up her lip. "Besides, your uncle kept Ethan as an added bargaining tool in case you get other notions."

Eilis glared at Wynda, her pasty face angry and determined. How could Eilis hope to survive Dunbarton's scrutiny when she could keep no secrets from even Agnes's maid?

The woman's eyes bored into her like icy gray daggers. "Think you I do not know what you are planning." She grabbed Eilis's arm, her fingernails digging into the flesh through the long-sleeved kirtle. "Come with me, my lady, or I will fetch the guard. He will not be as gentle as me."

As if the woman had ever treated her with even a wee bit of gentleness. But thank God he was just as seasick as Eilis, and she was sure he couldn't deal with her at the moment.

Early this morn, she'd overheard Wynda speaking with the personal guard, poised to protect Eilis, when in truth he served as a spy for her uncle to ensure she did as she was told. Agnes's maid accompanied Eilis for the same purpose. To instruct her, to keep her in line, to monitor her every move.

At some time or another Eilis feared she must have offended God, although she did not know when. It had to be the reason her life was in such dire straits. Yet she wondered, mayhap Dunbarton would not be as bad as she dreaded.

She shook her head and fought being dragged from the railing. Dunbarton was ancient and had buried two wives already, both who had died in childbirth and their bairns along with them. She would be next.

She caught a glimpse of a wave rising like a mountain, growing higher and higher. Her mouth dropped open, and the cry she would have made, died on her lips. Cresting, the wall of seawater buried the ship as if it were dunking a small wooden toy.

Crushing cold water, no air, total darkness, cries of alarm, the cracking and splitting of wood filled her with mute terror. Swept off her feet, she slid across the deck. Something struck her shoulder, her head, her legs, the sharp pains cutting through to the bone.

Then silence.

Eilis knew she'd died until men's ragged shouts brought her to full consciousness. Clinging to bits of ship that floated up and down the massive waves, she held on tight. Her head pained her something fierce, and the chill from the water seeped into her bones. She was only vaguely aware she was no longer on the ship. Although in the dark she could not see any signs of it.

Even more frighteningly, the men's shouts died away. Rain splattered across the top of the sea, thunder grumbled, waves splashed into each other, and the wind cried in the darkness. But no sound of a human soul penetrated the black night, and sheer panic rose in her breast. 'Twould be easy to let go and end the misery she was sure to face, but she couldn't do it. Coward, she chided herself. No, not a coward. Somehow, she had to save her little brother.

Left to shiver endlessly, she gritted her teeth to prevent them from clattering, the ship's remnant keeping her afloat. Fervently, she listened for any human groan or cry, but there was none but the storm and the sea's harsh melody.

They had left her behind, she fathomed. When would they discover she was missing? Too late, she suspected.

The waves settled into a choppy rhythm, up, down, up, down, with no long lulls in between, making her head ache and her stomach roil with new upset.

Near morn, the rain and wind died down to a gentle patter and whisper.

Worrisome thoughts plagued her. Would her appearance anger the Dunbarton chief? *Aye.* Would the sailors be able to salvage her wedding gown? Her other gowns?

She would not look like the MacBurness's precious daughter but her half-drowned cousin. She lifted her head. The motion sent streaks of pain across her skull while she attempted to observe any signs of land. Still too dark to see anything but the cold, black water.

How far out to sea was she?

It didn't matter that it was the middle of summer, except that the sun would rise early. The water was as frigid as a loch in winter. Watching the sky for the beginning of light, her eyelids grew heavy. Worse, she could no longer feel her fingers or toes, but better, she was not feeling so cold. In fact, she was feeling rather warm.

And for the moment, she was free of Agnes's nagging maid. The sound of waves crashing on a beach quickly quashed her weary relief. The tide yanked her perilous perch into the rocks farther out, but she couldn't avoid them, nor leave the safety of her floating home. Her energy spent, she clung to the ragged piece of wood with as much strength as she could manage, her arms aching.

Men shouted in Gaelic from the direction of the beach, and she lifted her head to look. Thinking someone had sighted her and were bound to rescue her, she saw instead six men attacking two others. The two fought valiantly against the onslaught, their swords slashing against their enemy's.

She stared at the sight, barely believing the irony. Clinging to life, she couldn't fathom how others would kill each other when she was in such dire straits and needed rescuing.

Unable to resist admiring the bearded man and the slighter built one fighting overwhelming odds, she prayed they would survive. But when the two men finished the last of the brigands off, she reconsidered. Were they the brigands? Which clan had set upon which? Worse, would they find her one of the enemy?

The younger man shouted in her direction this time. "Yo, there! Hold on!"

Then he and the bearded man commandeered a small boat. Resting her head against the wet splinters of wood, Eilis tried to concentrate, but her mind drifted. They would rescue her and then where would she be?

If they were not from an enemy clan, it would only be a matter of time before they set her upon a horse and sent her to Dunbarton to seal the lie her uncle had forged. If he should discover her uncle's deceit, Dunbarton could very well be angered enough to end her life for the treachery.

"Hold on!" the young man shouted again, closer this time. "We will rescue you! Just do not let go!"

Her floating home lifted on a sharp swell, drawing her closer to the jagged rocks. Then the wave bashed her against the boulders. Her arms too numb to hold on, she lost her precious driftwood and was delivered atop a ragged rock.

"God's teeth, hold on!" the young man hollered.

Another wave crashed into her, and she choked on salty water, fell against the boulders, and hit her head hard. Sharp pain radiated through her skull, and the sun instantly vanished from the sky.

# CHAPTER 2

"'Tis a sweet lassie near drowned," a gruff man said. He wrapped her in a blanket while the boat tossed about in the rough breakwater. "Lass?"

"Is she dead?" the other man asked, his voice not as aged as the other's but just as concerned.

She heard the men's voices, understood their language but couldn't open her eyes for the life of her. Her temple throbbed with such pain she could barely think straight.

The boat rose and fell with such a terror, she knew it would soon break up in the surf. No ship would ever be big enough again to protect her from the sea. Then the waves and the boat crashing in the turbulent water, the smell of the salty sea, and the feel of the sun on her cheeks faded away.

A short while later, she heard a smileding noise, and the boat quit rising on the swells. 'Twas sitting on the beach now, she thought. Her stomach began to settle, although she felt she was still rolling with the waves. One of the men lifted her out of the boat and held her close. Instantly, she felt a wee bit warmer, although her body trembled without end, and she clenched her teeth lest she jar them loose from her head.

"Lass, your name? The name of the ship you were on?" he asked, his voice harried, but coated with warmth and reassurance.

Her name? Panic rose in every bit of her. Her name? Why could she not remember her name?

"She is half drowned, Eanruig. She will never make it to Castle Craigly," the younger man said.

Eanruig snorted. "She is a Scotswoman, Niall. She will make it."

"Are you thinking what I am thinking?"

"Aye, if you are thinking the comely lass would be a good offering for your cousin James."

Nial laughed. "'Twould be something, would it not, if she were not betrothed or wed, to fish the half-drowned lass out of the sea and present her to the only clan chief in the region who refuses every offer of a wife, and he accepted her? Except we have no idea which clan she hails from nor if we are at war with them. And as choosy as my cousin is..." His words dropped off, and he said no more.

Was she betrothed? She could not recall. She could not remember anything, and the panic returned with a vengeance. Opening her eyes, she squinted at the brightness of the sun, saw the tanned face of the dark bearded man who carried her, his black hair hanging loosely about his shoulders, dripping wet like she was. Wet and cold.

"But bonny Catriona will catch James's eye, and

that will be the end to this madness. 'Tis not fair he has had four offerings and has turned them all down." Niall glanced down at her. "She is awake." His voice was tinged with hope. "Lass, your name?"

She looked at the younger man, his dark brows furrowed with concern, his brown eyes wide. He stood tall and lean, his posture straightening as if to impress her of his height. She *was* impressed. High cheekbones and an angular face were covered in a shadow of a beard running along his chin and jaw, giving him a slightly roguish look. A steady breeze tugged at his wet, tangled auburn hair. He seemed familiar somehow. Was this good or bad?

His lips curved up slightly. Was he amused at the way she so boldly considered his attributes? She only wished to consider the men more closely who had rescued her. Would they soon place her in a dungeon?

Mayhap they would, if she was one of the clan who had attacked these two. Beaten by the waves and wind and rain and rocks, she was too weary to care what happened next.

The older man, Eanruig, the other had called him, stared at her for a moment, then watched again where he was going, his long stride carrying her farther away from the waves crashing against the beach. "No other survivors. But the lass does seem a wee bit familiar."

No, not him. She didn't recall having seen the older man before.

"It was God's will we found her when we did, or she might not have made it."

"Aye, if Dunbarton's men had not set upon us, we might not have paused at the beach and seen the lass. Which makes me wonder what they were doing there in the first place. Although our men are still trying to learn about the ship that Dunbarton was interested in. I am wondering if their cargo was on the same ship the lass was on." Eanruig smiled. "If so, he has lost his precious cargo at the bottom of the sea." He gave a shake of his head. "As for your cousin, he rejected the last four lassies, Niall. Think you he will not reject Catriona also? He is a hard man to please."

"Aye, my aunt has always said so."

The two men laughed.

"Catriona will be here on the morrow to catch James's eye," Niall said. "Think you I will have a chance with this one?"

Eanruig considered her further. "She is a bonny lass, lad. You stand a chance if she is not from an enemy's clan. Unless she is already betrothed."

She closed her eyes, wishing she could sleep then wake and know who she was and where she was bound, whether she was wed and if so, had she lost her family aboard the ship? Her heart sank even further into a pit of despair. But she could conjure up no feelings about the matter, no sense of what had been, and it was more than terrifying.

"James will be enraged when he hears of this latest attack against us."

"On his own cousin, no less," Eanruig said.

Then the sun, the smell of the man's fishy woolen clothes, or even her own, the touch of his warm body, and the smell of the horse he lifted her onto, all faded into nothingness.

Sometime later, although she was not sure how much except the sun hovered high above, the rhythmic clip-clops of the horses woke her. She observed the inner bailey of a sandstone castle that appeared golden in the sun's rays. Several men, women, and children ran to greet the two men and stare at the stranger in their midst. Worse, she was as much a stranger to herself as she was to them. Yet something deep inside her begged her to keep her identity secret as if it was best no one ever knew her. What evil had she done to warrant feeling in such a manner?

"Who is the lass, Niall?" an older woman asked, her brown eyes warm and kindly, her equally dark brown hair tinged with a light smattering of gray, braided down her front.

The ends wrapped in silk, and metal tassels extended them even farther for the longest, most beautiful tresses. Having her hair adorned with expensive trinkets and fabric indicated she was the lady of the castle. She had the same eyes and mouth as Niall. A relation, no doubt.

"Half-drowned in the sea, my lady, and the ship carrying her lost forever," Eanruig said. "As fiery colored as her cheeks are, I fear she has taken a fever."

The woman placed ice cold fingers on her temple, and she shivered. "She is burning up. Take her into the guest chamber next to the laird's."

Niall's brows rose. "Aunt Akira, I thought you bid the servants prepare the chamber for Catriona."

The woman huffed, her eyes narrowing. "Think you she arrives on time? Nay, the willful lass sends word she is coming in a fortnight."

"You have told James?" Niall asked, his voice dark.

"Nay. Mayhap a miracle will occur, and Catriona will arrive on the morrow as she had promised. No

21

sense in borrowing trouble. Who is the lass, Niall?"

Their words echoed off the massive stone walls of the keep.

"She has not spoken a word, my lady."

"We have no idea which clan she comes from?"

"Nay, Aunt," Niall said. "And naught from the wreckage to identify the ship."

"Verra well. I will be right up to see to her. And Niall?"

"Aye, my lady?

"You and Eanruig, no word to His Lairdship concerning the lady."

"Because we know not who she is?"

"My verra thoughts, nephew. 'Tis best James not know who she is until we do. He has had his own battle this morning with more raiders and is not in a verra good mood."

"And if she is from the enemy's clan?"

"We will deal with that when we have to."

Then the interrogation would truly begin, and her deepest worry beset her. Who was she truly, and was she from an enemy clan? Was she in league with those who had attacked her rescuers? She would die if she was, after the kindness these people had shown her.

\*\*\*

In his solar, James listened intently to what his seneschal and his cousin had to say about the attack at the beach, both looking a little worse for wear. "Have you no idea what the precious cargo was they were seeking? The ship would have docked at the seaport. Why would the brigands be so far away from the docks? And why were you not with the rest of our men?"

Niall cleared his throat and glanced at Eanruig as if waiting for him to explain. His seneschal didn't seem to have an answer any more than his cousin did, but then Niall spoke. "The ship had broken up in the storm. 'Tis our guess they were searching to see if anything survived. Our men were still trying to find records of a ship coming in at the docks. We had not thought Dunbarton's men would be at the beach and not at the docks, but they must have seen the debris as well, and gone to investigate."

James rubbed his chin, his thoughts dark. "I have to know what the cargo was that Laird Dunbarton deemed precious." He considered Niall's bloodied sleeve. "Your blood or theirs, cousin?"

"A wee bit of both."

"Have Tavia see to your injuries." James turned his attention to Eanruig, the man as big as the one he had bested earlier in the day and the perfect choice as a bodyguard for his cousin.

Although neither Eanruig nor he would ever let on to Niall that was the purpose Eanruig served whenever they left the castle. With his three brothers gone to seek their fortunes, James was not about to lose his cousin, who had been raised as their brother, to a band of rogues. Beyond being incensed Dunbarton's men attacked him and James's seneschal, the business of a shipment coming to port that carried some goods for Dunbarton's clan, intrigued him. Good that the ship sank and left them without. But he had to know what precious cargo the ship had held. No doubt Laird Dunbarton would pay for another shipment, and James would have to stop that one next.

"The men on board the ship all drowned, I take it?"

"Aye," Eanruig quickly said.

James stared at him, feeling as though something was not right. His cousin and Eanruig were much more subdued than they normally would be after a clash with Dunbarton's warriors. Although they were now dry, he could smell the saltwater on their skin, and a residue of the white powdery sea salt clung to Eanruig's beard and both men's hair.

"You took a dunk in the briny sea?"

"Aye," Niall said, then his lips lifted a wee bit, but the result looked insincere.

A servant carrying a bucket of water hurried to pass him, but as soon as James caught his eye, the man quickly lowered his gaze and rushed toward the stairs.

This matter concerning choosing his betrothed had to be decided quickly. 'Twas making his people ill at ease whenever they saw him, but he did not think he was to blame.

***

A hoard of women pulled off her wet gowns and though a fire burned in the hearth, she was even colder than before. Then some time between that horrendous effort and the next, she, who couldn't remember her name, was washed, then dressed in a dry gown. Lying buried beneath blankets in a huge bed and smelling of sweet lavender, she stared up at the face of Niall's kindly aunt.

"Lovely lass, may we know your name?" the lady asked. Large concerned brown eyes and lips curved upward slightly as if trying to set her at ease, greeted her.

Niall walked into the room, and his aunt frowned at him.

"Did you learn her name? Which clan she is from?" he asked.

"She is barely able to stay awake. She has had a bad bump on her head. I fear 'tis hopeless until she is better."

"James is asking again about Catriona. Would it not be better if we told him the truth? That the lass will not be here on the morrow?"

"Nay, you know how he is. He must have a wife by winter, or give up the clan to his brother, Malcolm. So leave him be. For a fortnight, he has behaved like a bear. 'Tis better he knows naught about Catriona until the morrow. Mayhap she has changed her mind and will still arrive by then?"

"Aye, like the remnants of the ship we plucked the lassie from will suddenly become whole and emerge from the bottom of the sea."

His aunt smiled at him. "'Tis not that you have some interest in the lass, is it?"

He shrugged. "I will need a wife one of these days, especially should James's brothers not be interested in being laird. Then I would be next in line. I am not as choosy as my cousin." He smiled. "This one suits me fine."

His aunt shook her head. "Impulsive as always. You have no knowledge of who the girl is. What if she is married? With child even?"

Niall drew taller and furrowed his brow. "Is she?"

"She doesn't appear to be. But you have no idea who she is. What if she were a Dunbarton?"

Folding his arms, Niall's already dark eyes grew black. "You have a point, my lady. As to James, I will engage him in a bout of archery before the meal. If I let him beat me, mayhap his mood will improve."

"Aye, 'twill be good when he has chosen his bride and mopes no more about it." His aunt motioned to the bed. "We will call her Marsali until we know her name."

"Pearl. Sounds appropriate since we plucked her from the sea. Until the meal." He glanced at the healer. "If you have a moment, you might take a look at the nick or two I received in battle."

Tavia tucked a loose dark curl back into her braid, glanced at him and gave him a funny, wee smile. "'Tis naught more than a scratch, I fathom, but aye, I will have a look at them if Lady Akira gives me leave."

Lady Akira nodded.

He gave a bow to his aunt, then smiled at Tavia, whipped around, and took his leave with the healer hurrying after his long stride.

His aunt faced the shipwrecked lass. "Niall had better not beat James at archery, considering the foul mood James already is in, but knowing my nephew, he will not give in a breadth of a hair. I must see to the meal, Marsali, and will check on you afterward. Your own will be brought to you shortly." The lady patted her shoulder in a motherly way, and she imagined her own mother being as kind.

Which brought a wave of grief crashing over her. Had her mother been on the ship? Drowned with the others? If not, would she worry that her daughter had been lost at sea and grieved for her? Her head pounded with the new concern.

Marsali, for want of her own name, closed her eyes, unable to keep them open any longer. They burned like they were on fire, as did her skin, although a pretty maid attempted to cool her forehead with a wet cloth. When she tried to shove the blankets aside, the maid thwarted her time and again. The struggle wore her out, and before long, she dreamed of a glen and mountains, of the blue waters of a tranquil loch, and heather blooming.

She could almost smell the sweet floral fragrance when a woman shrieked outside her chamber, making her heart jump.

"Quit tickling me. The chamber is not occupied by fair Catriona, you knave, but by another young woman."

"The room was to be readied for the Lady Catriona. Who ordered it otherwise?"

"Lady Akira. She still runs the castle until Laird James chooses a wife, ye know." She giggled, and the footsteps scurried away.

The healer had returned and was tending to Marsali. Her long brown braids dangling over Marsali, Tavia leaned over the bed and placed another cold wet cloth on her feverish forehead. Marsali tried to push the clammy cloth away. 'Twould make her cold again.

"I think you be a Dunbarton," Tavia finally said, her dark brows raised, her tone of voice accusatory. "You looked quite stricken when Master Niall mentioned it. Are you from the enemy clan, a Dunbarton, lady?"

\*\*\*

So many concerns wormed their way into James's thoughts. Although he had little stomach for it, he tried to make the most of the afternoon meal. The boar seemed too dry, the brown bread too hard, even the butter slightly rancid. Naught appealed.

The news Eanruig and Niall brought him about being waylaid by Dunbarton's men made his blood run hot. And where were his brothers and their Viking friend, Gunnolf, when he'd asked for their assistance? 'Twas unlike them not to send word. Unless they'd had more trouble escorting Lady Anice to her castle than they could manage. James shook his head.

This business with Lady Anice and the misfortunes that had befallen her staff worried him. 'Twas not like he and his brothers could not handle the sword play if that's where it led. But he wished them home to help him with his border squabbles. When Dougald sent him a missive warning Malcolm was growing overly fond of the Scottish lass, James could not believe it. King Henry desired her wed to a Norman baron loyal to his rule, since she was his wife's favorite cousin. James hoped Malcolm's head would not be on the chopping block next if he took his relationship with the lass too far.

Sighing deeply, James reminded himself it was Dougald that got into the most mischief with the ladies. Malcolm would not get himself into trouble.

With all his heart, James had given his younger brothers his enthusiastic thanks for all their support when he became the current laird of Craigly Castle and best wishes to make their way in the world, but...

He missed their hearty wit, their rows, the way they fought together, watching each other's backs in the thick of battle.

He glanced at his cousin Niall, who'd been raised like a brother with the rest of them, when his parents had died of the fever. Niall smiled back at him. Except that James beat his cousin fair and square at archery, that was the only good thing that had happened this day. The feat was not easily accomplished, and as usual, Niall tried his hardest to best him. James's seneschal caught his eye.

Eanruig had been curiously avoiding him all afternoon. Even his mother had managed to stay clear of James. He snorted under his breath. He had heard the whispered rumors, that he was acting like an ogre, but who would not under the circumstances? 'Twas a trying business, choosing a wife...

Sometimes he wondered if it would be easier to let Malcolm, the next oldest of his brothers, run the clan as chief, and let *him* choose a wife from the insipid choices he had. Only Catriona sparked James's interest. The others had been too young, or too boorish, or too timid.

What he needed was a hardy Scotswoman like his mother, who could bear his bairns and survive the harsh winters. Someone who had not just come from the cradle or acted too afraid to speak in his presence. He tossed the chunk of dry bread back on the plate. And his clansmen had the gall to wonder why the lassies did not appeal?

They were all pretty, aye, but there had to be more to them than that.

The times he'd been with Catriona, he found her attractive, willing in bed, and able to carry a conversation without being overwhelmed by his position. He thought she would do.

"You say the chamber is ready for Catriona," James said to his mother, unable to get his mind off Catriona's impending visit.

His mother's eyes widened a bit.

James leaned back in his chair. What was the matter with everyone? Did they fear he would reject Catriona also? There were no others, save a distant cousin he could inspect in a month or so afterwards if circumstances were such that he had to. "My lady mother?"

"Aye."

The worried look on her face said otherwise. "Are you certain?"

"Aye, aye, you need not fash yourself over it. 'Tis my business to manage the household, my laird." She quickly looked to her meal.

"I agree, although you seem uncertain." He frowned at her. "You seem bothered about something. Even Eanruig, who normally pesters me throughout the day, has avoided me." He turned and slapped Niall's shoulder. "Even my cousin asked me to try and best him at a game of archery, and he has not asked that of me in ages. Whatever troubles everyone?"

Tavia hurried into the great hall, her face ashen, her brown eyes as round as the goblets sitting on the trestle tables. She wrung a wet cloth between her fingers and headed straight for his mother, who was getting ready to bolt from the table when James caught her wrist. "What is going on, Mother?"

"A lady is ill. Tavia was taking care of her. She must be worse. I will return soon."

"*Tavia* serves as our healer. Why would you need to see to the matter?" He frowned. "Which lady is ill?"

His mother looked from him to Niall. James grew increasingly suspicious. "Catriona has not arrived early and is ill?" he asked, his heart thundering.

"Nay, nay, my son. 'Tis naught like that. I will be

but a moment."

"I will attend you." James rose and motioned to his people. "Eat."

"I will go with you," Niall said, also rising.

James shook his head and strode out of the great hall with his mother and Niall, but the maid seemed even more distraught than before. Tavia wrung her hands, her eyes cast downward as if she were inspecting the rushes littering the floor.

"Out with it, Tavia," James said, wondering why Niall wished to see the woman, but suspecting he knew all about her already. The latest of his string of conquests?

"I wished to speak to Her Ladyship alone first, my laird," Tavia demurely said.

James stopped and faced the petite woman. "Why?"

"I...I said something I ought not, and she left."

"What?" His mother's word was stricken with concern.

"Who is the lady, where was she staying, and what is this all about?" James ground his teeth, his face hot with annoyance.

Niall cleared his throat like he always did when he'd been up to mischief. "Eanruig and I found her on the rocks after her ship sank. We saw the sun glinting off a brooch she was wearing and after nearly wrecking the boat on the rocks, we managed to pull her from the sea, slightly battered."

James stared at him in disbelief. Normally it was his good fortune his clansmen always kept him informed no matter how trivial the concern. So what was the problem now? "Why did you not already say so? I asked if there were any survivors."

"Nay, you asked if there were any men who survived," Niall corrected him, but his tone was conciliatory.

James raised his brows. "Man or woman, I would not think I would have to be so explicit. Why did no one think to mention this to me? Was the lass the only one who survived?"

Niall nodded. "She was thrown upon the rocks in a bad way. When Eanruig and I reached her, she was unconscious. She is staying in the chamber next to yours where Catriona was to reside."

In utter disbelief, James glanced at his mother, now seeing why she had been nervous when speaking of the chamber.

She shrugged a shoulder as if it mattered not. "Catriona delayed her journey for a fortnight."

James clenched his teeth and controlled his language, then stormed toward the chamber. "And what, pray tell, Tavia, did you say to upset the woman?"

"I called her a Dunbarton. She got out of bed, and when I tried to confine her, she fought me. I could not stop her and came to tell Lady Akira at once."

James's blood instantly boiled. "You gave Catriona's chamber to a Dunbarton?" James asked his mother, unable to curb his angry tone of voice. "Our staunchest enemy?"

# CHAPTER 3

Unable to find her own plaid brat in the guest chamber, Marsali dashed into the adjoining bedchamber. Grabbing a green and blue plaid from the foot of a massive bed dominating the room, she threw the wool over her shoulders. With naught to fasten it, she held tight to the cloth, hiding the thin chemise she wore beneath it. Would be unseemly to dash through the unfamiliar castle barely dressed, yet her only concern should be to escape from the enemy's midst.

Was she a Dunbarton?

She couldn't remember, only the name seemed too familiar, and she feared she was. Not that it was a bad thing, only that these clansmen thought so.

The men constantly squabbling over their borders was not her fault. If she were King Alexander's queen, she would rule there would no longer be any fighting amongst the clans. Although he reigned only over the land between Forth and Spey while the land south of Forth was entrusted to his younger brother David—so

James did not come under either's rule. Not even King Alexander could stop the continuous bickering between the clans in his dominion nor could the clan chiefs elsewhere. Which brought to mind a stranger question. Why did she know her king's and his brother's name and not her own?

No doubt she had done something evil and had no wish to know her name.

On the way to the stables, she heard Niall's aunt's voice and Niall himself headed in her direction. She rushed as fast as her shaking legs could take her down the opposite hall. 'Twas not the fear of being caught, but the fever and chills that consumed her. Och, it was the fear of being caught also. Who was she trying to fool?

Continuing past another large chamber, she discovered backstairs most likely used by the servants. She hurried down them and found her way to servants' quarters, a large room with rushes strewn across the floor and sleeping pallets stacked against one wall. Everyone seemed to be at the meal except for Niall, his mother, Tavia, and another man who spoke angrily to them. The laird of the castle? James?

'Twould be her luck that they had hidden the fact she was being harbored here against the laird's will.

Two brawny, bearded Highlanders stood near the main entrance of the keep, blocking her escape. Luckily, they didn't see her before she slipped outside toward the kitchen where the aroma of boar and baked brown bread wafted. Most likely the kitchen doorway led to a garden, and, from there, she could reach the stables. The kitchen staff would be busy serving the meal. Mayhap if she ran fast enough, no one would pay her any mind.

Fraught with indecision, she stood frozen to the cold stone floor, her bare feet growing icier by the second. Men's voices headed in her direction decided her fate. She darted for the kitchen and ran through it, where women stirred broth in iron pots over fire and others carried food into the great hall. Most didn't seem to see her. But when Marsali nearly ran down a young girl carrying a platter of cheese, the girl cried out.

"What...?" the cook said, but Marsali bolted outside into the garden of herbs and flowers and for the second time in so many hours felt a sudden rush of freedom.

Having no time to tarry and ponder why she felt such a thing, she ran straight across the inner bailey. She thanked God the men on the wall walk looked out toward the hills, paying no heed to the small panicked woman who would steal a horse under their noses if she could and ride away from here as far as possible. Everyone else was inside the great hall, eating their meal. She prayed.

Dashing into the stables, she found a horse to borrow. He whinnied at her, poking his head over the stall as soon as she entered the stable. She didn't think a horse oft chose her. But she did think she could ride.

She hadn't time to saddle him before men shouted from the way of the kitchen. Her heart skittered. The cook must have raised the alarm.

After scrambling atop a stack of hay, she slid her legs over the horse's back. She prodded him with her feet until he exited the stable. With her heart hammering hard against her ribs and her feverish head pounding, she gasped when several men ran toward her.

Half the laird's staff she guessed. She was only one wee lass to cause such an uproar. If they hadn't wished to kill her before, she had surely changed their minds now. The hardened looks on their faces, bearded, smooth faced, young and old, their mouths in grim lines and their eyes narrowed and fierce, like every one of them was ready to do battle, put the fear of God in her.

Kicking the horse, she raced for the open gate, praying if He had any mercy, she would escape.

Someone whistled, the horse halted, and she flew forward on the bony ridge of his back. After nearly throwing her, the horse turned toward the keep to her horror. She quickly grabbed his neck and held on tight, trying to direct him toward the gate, kicking his flanks again, without result this time. Doomed, she waited, shivers shaking her body with vengeance.

"Who are you?" a man asked, stalking toward her with a purposeful stride, his looks similar to Niall, the same stubborn chin wearing a light sheen of whiskers, but a scar marred his cheek. The same auburn hair, except streaked in places by the sun. His intense look and the deep, angry timbre of his voice left her slightly dazed. Or mayhap it was the fever. His eyes the color of burnt umber narrowed when he reached up to grab her. His lips pressed together in a thin, straight line.

His huge hands grasped her arms and pulled her from the horse, nearly causing her heart to stop. His fingers pressing against the brat still covering her sent a scorching flame through the woolen cloth and touched her skin. *'Twas the fever, naught more.*

"Stealing my horse, Lady?"

He…he seemed familiar somehow. Like Niall, and yet she couldn't remember.

Niall smiled, seeming to take the man's actions in stride. "No one but you can ride the ornery creature, James. Think you that you have met your match?"

Her heart fluttered. She should have known by the arrogant tilt of his stubborn chin and the way he carried himself with a rugged elegance that he was the laird of the castle.

James grunted and cradled Marsalis in his brawny arms. "If she is a Dunbarton, you have brought the devil down on our heads."

He stalked back toward the keep, holding her tightly against his hard chest, not allowing her the freedom to struggle or to keep a modest distance. Although she relished his touch and didn't wish to get away, or mayhap she did but she was too weak and her mind with fever too muddled to know it.

The men all cleared out of his way.

His mother ran after him, her small footsteps pounding the pavement. "She is ill, my laird. Keep that in mind."

"I should lock her in the tower for..." He glanced down at Marsali. His heated gaze locked with hers. Heavens, he was a powerfully handsome man.

For an instant, emotions warred in those pools of umber—concern, anger, a hint of fascination—and if she didn't know better, recognition. 'Twas truly the fever making her so confused. For 'twas a gift she normally had to know other's feelings before even they did oft times. But her mind was playing tricks with her now.

His gaze shifted to the plaid blanketing her, and his dark brows rose. "She has even stolen my brat!"

Though he sounded just as angry as before, a trace

of humor reflected in his voice. Mayhap he was not as brutish as he appeared.

Niall laughed. "Mayhap that is why your horse accepted her, cousin. He thought she was you."

James made a half grunt and lunged up the stairs, taking two at a time as if he had to get rid of his charge before she scalded him. "She should not be in the chamber reserved for Catriona who is—"

His mother interrupted. "Catriona is not coming for a fortnight, and I make the bedding arrangements. The young mistress will stay in the quarters she has been assigned."

His head whipped around to face his mother. "What say you of Catriona? You mentioned it before, but I did not believe—"

"I will speak to you later concerning the matter, James."

He gave his mother a stern look. "I should have been apprised of the situation at once." He gave Marsali a cursory glance, refusing to look into her eyes again.

She should have looked demurely away when he had chanced to catch her eye before. But she would not cower before His Lairdship. 'Twas like staring down a mean-hearted dog. If she gave in, he would win. Well, not that this Highlander looked like any sort of dog, but—

"What if this woman is the lowest of servants? She should not be staying in the chamber reserved for Catriona." James scowled at Marsali, and this time, he dared her to look at him with the same kind of fierce determination. She obliged, although her eyes blurred slightly from the fever. She thought his lips turned up just a hair, but she could not be sure.

"She wore the finest of woolen garments, my son. This one is not a servant."

Somehow, Marsali knew that. At least she was gladdened to hear the news.

Although James seemed to hold only contempt for her, he carried her close to his heart, which beat against her ear with a thunderous roar. His touch was gentle, but firm, his actions and his words not the same. Did he put on a show for his clansmen? What did he intend to do with her?

What if she could make this man care for her? What if she could get his clan and hers, if she were a Dunbarton, to cease their hostilities? She felt no animosity toward these people, and she could very well understand his being angered with her, first, because his people didn't tell him she was staying in his castle. Second, because she had tried to steal his horse. And third, because she had stolen his brat.

Closing her eyes, she snuggled tighter against the powerfully built warrior and thought she heard him groan and curse simultaneously under his breath. Mayhap she could steal his heart as well?

Nay, she knew now the fever had thoroughly addled her mind.

***

James glanced down again at the petite woman cradled in his grasp as he carried her to the chamber adjoining his own. Her temple was swollen and purple, her eyes blackened, and the rest of her skin flushed with fever. Yet despite the discoloration, she seemed oddly familiar—the way her sea green eyes boldly challenged him, the way her tongue licked her dry lips—he shook his head. He'd never met the lass before.

Although she was fair whereas his beloved sister, Seana, had been dark-haired, she was much the same way, spirited, ill with fever, and could die like his sister had done in the blink of an eye. And for what? Because he had forbidden Seana to run off with the Dunbarton's great nephew? For over a century there had been bad blood between their clans. There wasn't any way he would have permitted his dear sister to marry the enemy. Now she was dead. As was the lad she had wished to marry.

James scoffed at himself. Had he allowed Seana to wed, mayhap she would be alive today.

Whatever animosity he felt for the Dunbartons had naught to do with this young woman, he reminded himself. If his mother and the healer could make her well, he gave his blessing.

Her hair draped over his arms in silky red-gold masses, and he imagined the ladies must have washed the seawater from the strands. A faint aroma of lilacs drifted to him, and he tried not to breathe in her subtle fragrance. Although her eyes were clouded with fever, they taunted him, defied him, capturing his gaze more than once.

'Twas ludicrous that he should feel anything for the lass. Yet just the way she held his gaze and would not look modestly away and the way she snuggled closer to him like some wanton woman, turned his body into a raging fire. 'Twas because he had left the lasses alone for the past several weeks in anticipation of wedding and bedding the fair Catriona that this lass was setting him ablaze.

When the lass should have been afraid of him, what did she do? Stared him down like a Highlander readied for a sword fight. Would her tongue be as sharp as the looks with which she speared him?

She barely weighed anything more than an empty sack as her body burned with fever. 'Twas the reason she had made him so hot, naught more. Although he could not account for the stiffening of his shaft. She was soft and feminine, smelled like a wee bit o' heaven, and...well, no wonder she had made him as hard as the steel of his sword.

But the business with Catriona was another matter. "What did Catriona say about not arriving on time? Was there some difficulty? Is she ill?"

His mother clucked. "'Tis all the lass's doing, James. She is not ill and gave no reason for delaying the journey. Mayhap she is shy."

"Not Catriona." Not the way she came willingly to his bed or beseeched him to join her in hers. Which bothered James overmuch. What was the reason she had delayed seeing him? He had made her well aware he had turned down the other ladies and wished to see her promptly. Shouldn't that have endeared her to him?

Niall cleared his throat, and James glanced back, not realizing his cousin was still following him. "James, if the lady is not betrothed or from a clan we do not get along with, would you mind if I...well..." He shrugged and nodded at the feverish woman.

His younger cousin could not be meaning he was interested in her.

"Nay," James said sharply.

"Why not? You are not interested in her."

James blew out his breath and stalked into the chamber adjoining his. "The lady is near death."

Niall snorted. "She has too much spirit to die on

us."

"We have no idea which clan she is from, let alone if her da would be willing for you to court her. Or what status she holds, even though she wore the finest of gowns." James gave his mother a searing look.

"My da is dead," the feverish woman said when James laid her in the bed.

"Died in the shipwreck?" James asked, his brows furrowed while his mother hastily covered the lass. He hovered over the bed, wanting to know now who the woman belonged to even more than he wished to know Catriona's reasons for not coming to see him. After all, if the lass were from an enemy clan, it could put them in a bad way. "Who are you, lass?"

Tenderly touching the side of her head where the bruise spread across the raised area the size of a hen's egg, she squinted and stared at the bed. "I...I cannot remember."

James settled his fists on his hips. "You remembered you have no da!"

"I...I do not know why I remember that."

He looked at his mother whose wrinkled brow showed concern. She patted the woman's arm reassuringly. "Leave her be, James. I will speak with her without your badgering her."

"I want to know by evening meal who she is." He gave the lass one last look, as harsh as he could manage. He wished the truth from the lass's lips, and if he put the fear of a battle-enraged Highlander in her, he was certain she would speak honestly. Although the way the lass looked, her cheeks crimson, the bruise and swelling on her temple, her soggy eyes, he couldn't help feeling a wee bit like a brigand. But he had his people to think about. If she was from an enemy clan—

"By evening meal," he reiterated then stalked across the room and out the door. Glancing back when his cousin didn't quit the bedchamber, he hollered, "Niall!"

Niall smiled and winked at the injured lass then followed James out of the room.

"I want you seeing no more of the lass until we know who she is. Leave her to Tavia and Mother's care."

"You do not truly believe the lass is holding out on us, do you, James?"

"Mayhap. What if Tavia frightened the lass about being a Dunbarton?"

"The lass does not appear to be easily frightened. I believe she cannot remember because of the bump on her head or mayhap the fever also."

James scoffed, "You think she is the one for you no matter who she is, just because she is a bonny lass." He had to agree the lass didn't seem to be frightened of him, despite the way he had acted. Being the laird of Craigly Castle was not an easy task. 'Twas important his people respected and obeyed him, and he could not give in to the unbidden feelings he was having over the wee lass.

"Does she remind you of Seana just a wee bit?"

"She is too fair." Although he got his cousin's meaning well enough.

"Aye, but 'tis the fever and the way she tried to steal away that reminded me of Seana, just as willful. I feared your mother was about to faint from upset, seeing the young woman so flushed."

Not wanting to think anything more about his dear

sister, James changed the subject. "I have clan business to attend to, and I will ask you to see to the villagers' claims that the butcher has been overcharging them. But take some men with you."

Niall frowned.

He knew that look. Niall didn't wish to be coddled, but James would be damned if he would let his cousin go anywhere without adequate protection in these dangerous times. "God's knees, you have run into trouble with the enemy once this day. Take a tail to ensure everyone's safety."

"Aye." Niall glanced back at the chamber.

"And stay away from her, Niall. I mean it."

"'Tis not because you are interested in the wee lass, cousin?" Niall cast a smug smile then strode off before James could comment.

Of course, James wasn't interested in some lass he knew naught about. The Dunbarton's raids on his borders had to stop. And the lass, should she be a Dunbarton, had to be returned forthwith before new trouble erupted, particularly if she was a lady of import. Although he could use her as a bargaining tool. He shook his head. He would not use an injured woman to obtain peace with Dunbarton. Stringing up their scrawny necks was the only way to deal with the raiders.

Yet he couldn't dismiss the feelings that stirred deep inside him when he had held the feverish woman close. 'Twas like naught he had ever felt before for a woman he had only just met. Except—he shook his head. The lass he'd saved from the incoming tide had been but a girl, and he had never found her in all his searches.

He glanced back in the direction of the stairs. The younger lass's hair was darker red, less golden.

This one had barely worn enough to be decent, and she had snuggled against his chest like a child under his protection. But her feminine curves and the sweet fragrance the ladies had bathed her in countered the notion she was a child. No, she was a voluptuous woman full grown—mayhap a wee bit frightened, bold, pleasing to the eye, despite the discolored knot on her forehead and blackened eyes.

He should not have held her so close. He should have had one of his other men carry her to the chamber. Yet, how would any that he put to the task have felt if they had carried the near naked woman tight against their chests?

His groin stirred with renewed interest in her. Shaking the image from his mind, he reminded himself any woman he would touch in such a manner would raise his shaft. So why did it happen again now, with just the thought of her in his grasp?

'Twas time to get Catriona to agree to marriage, he decided.

When James spied Eanruig, he narrowed his eyes, irritated that his seneschal had not told him about the lady. 'Twas understandable why Niall hadn't. He was already smitten with the lass. There was no excuse for Eanruig to have hidden the truth.

He strode across the hall and joined Eanruig, his countenance stern. He would tolerate no insubordination from his people.

"I will have a word with you about the lass, Eanruig, now."

\*\*\*

45

"You must not worry about James's brusque ways, lass." Lady Akira offered a goblet to Marsali. "Even if you are a Dunbarton."

A harried woman screamed outside the chamber, and the sound of small scampering feet ran closer to the guest chambers. "Eilis! Eilis! You come right back here, you scamp!"

*Eilis.* Marsali barely breathed.

"*Eilis!* I shall have your hide, you willful lass."

Lady Akira smiled. "Eilis keeps her mother running."

*Eilis.* Now she remembered. Her name was Eilis. The name was fine, and she didn't feel any shame in it. So why fear the Dunbarton's name?

"I am not a Dunbarton," Eilis said softly, picking at the blue wool coverlet resting at her chest. At least she hoped she was not.

"Then why were you afraid?"

"I...I could not remember who I was. When your healer seemed upset I might be a Dunbarton, I feared I was. But I am not."

"You remember your name, dear?"

"Eilis."

Lady Akira's brows perked up.

"I...I guess 'twas the mother calling for her daughter that helped me to remember it." She was Eilis and not Agnes, her cousin. But why did she even think such a thought? *Think, think.* The harder she tried to remember, the more her head splintered with pain. She still couldn't remember her clan, only that she had a cousin named Agnes, and for whatever dark reason, she did not want to be her.

"Eilis of...?" Lady Akira asked.

46

Eilis shook her head, but the pounding renewed, and she lay back still against the bedding. "I know not the name of my clan, only that it is not Dunbarton."

Lady Akira observed her for some time, not speaking a word. Tavia continued to wipe Eilis's brow with a wet cloth, although she cast glances at the older woman.

Finally, Lady Akira raised her dark brows heavenward, gave an almost imperceptible smile, then nodded. "Mayhap your memory will improve before evening meal."

# CHAPTER 4

James barely had time to question his seneschal further about the lass when his mother approached. Thinking she had some word about the shipwrecked lass, he waited for his mother to speak. Her brown eyes sparkled, and her lips curved slightly upward, making him think his mother had good news. Yet her cheerfulness seemed subdued.

When she did not speak but wrung her hands, he frowned. Her actions were not what he wished to see. "She is a Dunbarton?" he fairly roared.

Several servants carrying fresh rushes into the hall stopped and watched him.

His mother shook her head. "She says no. Her name is Eilis, which I believe."

James thought about her name. Eilis. A good Irish name and since the MacNeill clan originally came from Niall of the Nine Hostages, High King of Ireland in 379, the name suited the lass.

"And the clan she hails from?"

"She remembers it not."

James didn't believe it for a minute. How could a woman know some things and not others? "And you believe her?"

"Aye. I have an idea, my son." The glitter in her eyes told him she was up to some match-making mischief.

"What is it that you have in mind, my mother?"

"Until the lady has recovered and we can return her to her people, why not have her 'serve' as an enticement to Catriona to see you? Eilis is a lovely lass. Mayhap Catriona needs a nudge to encourage her to come forthwith?"

James considered his mother's devious smile. "Aye, she might be jealous to learn I am considering another lass to wed."

"Aye, you get my meaning. Send a messenger to inquire as to Catriona's health and have him remark, perchance, about lovely Eilis, who is brazenly attempting to catch your eye. I would think Catriona would mount her swiftest horse and find out who the lady is. Although to ensure Catriona does not know her, have the messenger describe Eilis's beauty, but he must not reveal her name or clan's name."

"Which we know not anyway."

"Aye."

"I like this idea of yours."

His mother again smiled, and he wondered why his father sought mistresses to pleasure him up until the time of his death instead of loving James's charming mother.

"I fathom fair Catriona will be here without delay," she said.

James leaned over and kissed his mother's cheek. "Here I thought you were trying to get me to commit to Eilis."

"Eilis indeed." His mother laughed. "She is too much for you to handle."

James frowned. He did not think the lass too much for him to handle one whit. "Niall has not put you up to this, has he?"

"Think you he is interested in the lass?" The unbridled amusement on his mother's face indicated she already knew it was so.

"Aye, I know he is."

"Nay, he did not put me up to this as you say, James. I believe Catriona is delaying the marriage because she thinks you have no other choice but her. 'Tis a game she plays. See if you become desperate enough to force the issue. Eilis is bonny enough that she should make Catriona think twice about the way she is treating my son."

"What if the ruse angers Catriona, and she refuses me?"

"Then she is not the one for you."

"I am not interested in my distant cousin." He glanced in the direction of the stairs that led to the chamber. "What about Eilis? Will she go along with this?"

"I will speak to her and ask if she will play the game. 'Tis the least she can do for us for providing her shelter for a few more days."

Not one to play games, James wasn't overmuch interested in the prospect. But if it would force Catriona to see him, it was worth a try. "Aye. I shall send a messenger at once."

The business concerning his brothers also still troubled him. He motioned to Eanruig. "What news have we of my brothers?"

"Nary a word, my laird. Mayhap they are already enroute from Brecken Castle. Or possibly they are still trying to solve the mysteries there."

"Send a messenger to Brecken. I wish to know if I can rely on my brothers' help or not." James knew his brothers would help him anytime he needed their assistance, which meant something must have gone wrong.

*** 

Early that evening while melting tallow scented the bedchambers and the flicker of candlelight cast shadows against the bare stone walls, Eilis stared at Lady Akira, not believing she understood the lady correctly. She had never heard anything so absurd in all her life, although in truth she still couldn't recall her past. The very idea she would have to pretend to care for James in an attempt to make his real intended envious seemed ludicrous.

She looked at the healer, Tavia, who gave her a slight smile. Turning to Lady Akira, Eilis folded her arms. "I thank you for your kindness and generosity in taking care of me after I nearly drowned, but I do not see how acting smitten with His Lairdship will aid him in obtaining Catriona's hand. 'Tis folly I wager to believe this. I would more than likely anger her instead and ruin His Lairdship's chance with her."

"Worry not your bonny head, dear," Lady Akira responded. "You just play your part well. Act the adoring lass, besotted with the laird of the manor. Should be easy to do as handsome as James is, and the fact he is chief should help also. The better you play your part, the sooner James will marry. The clan will forever be in your debt."

"His Lairdship can barely abide me. How can I act infatuated with him when he only returns scowls?"

"He will be well-studied in returning your simple gestures of affection. Never fear. As soon as Catriona arrives, the game shall be a success. In the meantime, you and James shall practice the deception." Lady Akira patted Eilis's hand. "I have to ready some of my daughter's gowns. They should fit you well. I will have a maid fetch threads and material so that you may embroider while you stay with us once you feel well enough." She touched Eilis's head. "Your fever has abated, but I worry about you taking a ride just yet. Mayhap a short stroll in the garden with His Lairdship would suffice for now."

Eilis's stomach twisted into knotted hemp. She didn't think any man had ever attempted to "woo" her, even if it wasn't really the laird's true intention. Yet, she hadn't a clue as to what to do. Had her da made sure no clansman ever approached her? What if she were betrothed to someone important? He'd want James's head.

***

Early the next morning, Dougald MacNeill glanced at Gunnolf, blond-haired and bearded, brilliant blue eyes, looking like one of the Viking warriors who had landed in Scotland some years earlier as they now made their way to his home at Craigly Castle.

Gunnolf had served as James's bodyguard until he became laird of Craigly Castle, and Dougald and his brothers sought English brides with lands to make their own. Now Gunnolf served Dougald, though he never thought of the Norseman as anything but the best of friends, in many respects like a brother.

"Has Malcolm sent word ahead, telling Laird James he has married Lady Anice?" Gunnolf asked.

Dougald shook his head.

Gunnolf grunted. "He will not be pleased that you are the only one returning to aid him against the raiding Dunbarton."

"Malcolm had to stay behind to protect his bride from the Robertson Clan who still seek her head. Angus will not be able to use his sword arm for a fortnight after the clash with Lady Anice's enemies. Besides, you make up for our fewer numbers."

'Twas oft said Gunnolf shared the berserker traits of his forefathers. He could kill four men for every one Dougald or any of his brothers put down. 'Twas good the Norseman was on their side.

"What about Lady Akira?"

Aye, his mother would have a fit to learn Malcolm had taken a wife without a word to her. Her first son finally married and to the cousin of Queen Matilda at that. He had done himself proud, despite the trouble he could have gotten himself into over the matter. Well and *had* gotten into.

Dougald smiled to himself. 'Twas he who normally got himself into a mess with the ladies, not any of the rest of his brothers.

"I will tell my mother the situation when we arrive."

Gunnolf slowed his horse. "All of it?"

Dougald shook his head. "Nay all of it, although I will give a full accounting to James. He would appreciate a good laugh."

"He will not believe the saga."

Dougald chuckled. "I still do not believe it myself."

The men had kept a wary eye out for thieves and Dunbarton's men on the way home, but when they reached the MacNeill clan border near dark, Dougald finally relaxed a bit in the saddle.

The relief he felt at reaching his clan's border instantly vanished when they spied Dunbarton clansmen rustling sheep in the distance.

Neither Gunnolf nor Dougald said a word but unsheathed their swords. They were outnumbered six to one, but they would not allow this affront to MacNeill sheepherders and to James's good name. If they went for help, the Dunbarton clansmen would already have stolen the sheep and been safely away.

With the MacNeill's mighty battle cry, Dougald shouted, *"Buaidh Na Bas!"*

"Aye, to conquer or die!" Gunnolf echoed.

They galloped toward the raiders, intending to stop the thieves anyway that they could.

***

Tavia helped dress Eilis in a pale blue gown with a girdle of dark blue fabric criss-crossing her bodice in the fashion that showed off a lady's curves. After attaching a gold belt, Tavia stood back and admired Eilis. "Aye, my lady, ye are bonny indeed. Niall will surely be taken with you." Tavia opened the door to the guest chamber, paused then crossed the room to a chest.

"Niall? I thought His Lairdship was the one whose eye I was to catch." Eilis finished plaiting her hair.

The woman choked on laughter and pulled a gold

brooch out of the chest. "His Lairdship is too hard to please. 'Tis Niall who speaks of you every hour of the day."

"Then this shall be an interesting game. I have no interest in His Lairdship, and he has none in me."

"Is that so, Eilis?" James stood in the entryway, filling it as he leaned against the doorframe, his arms folded across his broad chest, one dark brow raised in question.

His dark eyes studied her reaction as much as she tried to slow down her hastily beating heart. She wanted to melt into the rushes. Her face felt so hot, she was sure the fever had returned.

Tavia quickly curtsied to His Lairdship, then smiled.

"Can you manage a walk in the gardens, Eilis, or are you feverish again? Your cheeks are positively crimson."

Her mouth dropped. She didn't believe she had ever been so overwhelmed by a man's beauty, the way he carried himself so regally, or observed her like she was his for the taking. 'Twas only a ruse they were to play, yet the way he looked at her, well, Lady Akira did say he would be well conversed in how he was to handle her to make it seem as though they were smitten with each other. The look of pure lust that filled his expression made her heart flutter wildly like a caged bird.

Now she really didn't believe she could do this.

"I can manage a *brief* walk, my laird."

James eyes sparkled with mirth. He held out his arm, and after she rested her hand on his sleeve, he walked her down the stairs. She tried to ignore the way touching him heated her thoroughly. They were fully clothed, for heaven's sakes. The long looks he gave her, like he was ready to devour every inch of her, sent a ripple of tension down her spine.

How could she pretend to care for someone she didn't know, who had earlier scowled and spoken to her angrily? She was certain she would have a devil of a time attempting to play this game.

Yet, the way her body reacted to his professed interest in her unnerved her. 'Twas a sign no one had ever courted her, or she wouldn't feel so...so lightheaded with the way he watched her. She would have to keep her wits about her if she was to pull this off.

***

James couldn't believe how beautiful the lass was dressed in the elegant gowns befitting the queen herself. 'Twas his duty to look at her like a besotted dolt, yet the pleasure he felt in observing the lass, made it all the more easy to feign interest. She moved like an angel, gliding down the steps, her narrow hips swaying slightly, the movement of her skirt rustling, her hand feather light on his arm. She had the bearing of a fine lady and would give Catriona a good deal of competition. Except that he had no knowledge of who Eilis truly was, and he would exercise no true interest in her, except to attempt this pretense.

He recalled the look on her face, flushed with embarrassment when he had overheard her comment in the guest chamber.

*Then this shall be an interesting game. I have no interest in His Lairdship, and he has none in me.*

Yet, he did not believe she was uninterested in him.

Not the way she had challenged him earlier with her entrancing eyes. Although for now, she avoided looking at him and seemed much more demure. Had the fever, mayhap being delirious, emboldened her? And now that the fever had passed, she was like so many of the other women he had considered in marriage, afraid of him, unable to measure up?

He sighed deeply. 'Twould not be soon enough before Catriona arrived.

His mother and Eanruig watched from the first floor of the keep, as if he was leading his bride to the feast after the celebration. He was only taking a walk with the lass, naught more. He wished his people wouldn't insinuate further than that.

They walked outside into the inner bailey where the blacksmith pounded a sword on an anvil, sending sparks flying and stone masons worked on the south wall, heaving the heavy stones in place. Everyone stopped what they were doing to watch His Lairdship walking with the lady, an unusual sight for him to be sure, but they need not be so obvious about it.

Eilis seemed mortified, staring straight ahead, looking at no one, as if terrified to see what they thought. Was it so bad to be seen with him?

Aye, she said she had no interest in him, yet, he had observed the way she looked at him with her sea green eyes. He intrigued her, even if she tried to deny it. Unless, she was truly a Dunbarton and was afraid he would discover the truth.

He took a deep breath. If she did not quit acting so afraid of him, the ruse would not be a success when Catriona arrived. "Have you regained any of your memories, Eilis?"

"Nay."

Her answer was not what he wished to hear. Walking her into the herb gardens, he asked, "Have you found everything to your liking here?"

"Aye."

Och, if she did not help with the conversation at all, he could not suffer another moment with her.

"Does it truly distress you to be putting on this charade, lass?"

"I..." She looked up at him, her eyes misty with tears. "I...I have never been courted before...I do not think."

For a moment, he stared at her in surprise, then he couldn't help smiling. "Ah, that is the only difficulty." He had to remind himself she might still be wed, or that men might have courted her, but that she couldn't remember. Still, the notion he might be the first filled him with a sense of intrigue.

Her innocence was refreshing—since ladies oft made their interest in him known, although for many he had no intention of dallying with the likes of them—but she did not push herself on him like the others did. She neither batted her eyelashes nor gave him winsome smiles designed to solicit his interest. That was what intrigued him most about her, he thought.

"Mayhap I can help your memories return." He motioned to the variety of flowers blooming in the garden. "Which, if any of these, is your favorite?"

She pulled away from him, knelt beside creeping ladies tresses, and touched the creamy white petals. Her golden red hair swept the flowers, and she looked as pretty as any of the varieties blooming there. "The sweet scent of the blossoms and the way the flowers

58

look like ladies' braided hair is why I like these the best." She waved at purple heather planted nearby. "And the flowers of the heather also." Looking up, she smiled like the sun sparkled on a clear blue loch, refreshing and inviting. "I think I like all flowers, my laird."

He couldn't help but smile back, which made him realize it had been many months since he had felt so lighthearted. "Call me James, lass."

She rose to her feet and clutched her hands. "I fear our plan will cause trouble with your Catriona. I have already told your mother this, but she would not listen."

He shrugged and tried to sound as nonchalant as he could. "Then I shall seek another lady's hand in marriage." But it was his most fervent desire Catriona would quit this foolishness and agree to marry him.

Reaching out to Eilis, he pulled her hands apart. Her eyes widened, but she did not step back. He leaned over and brushed his lips against hers, not sure why. Mayhap to see her reaction, to judge whether their ruse with Catriona would succeed.

'Twas the most chaste of kisses, although even so, he feared her refusal or quick rebuke. Neither occurred, and when he pulled away from her velvet mouth, she leaned forward as if expecting more.

'Twas not at all what he anticipated, and his lips curved up.

Was she more well-versed in dalliances than he had at first presumed? Yet, there was something innocent and naïve about her reaction. Mayhap a ruse as well? He had known women to act one way and feel another.

Did she truly fear for her life if he should learn she

was a Dunbarton?

Taking a deep, settling breath, he put space between them. She didn't look shyly away but studied him with widened eyes. Even with such an unpresuming kiss, she had started a slow burn deep inside him. He reminded himself 'twas only the fact he had left the lassies alone for a fortnight, readying himself to take a wife to the marriage bed that sparked his desire for the lass.

His lips curved up at the sight of her, the silky strands of hair fluttering against her cheek, her skin flushed like a blushing bride, and her eyes darkened. Whatever clan she was from, she was remarkably attractive.

He reached up and touched her hair, remembering the way it looked splayed upon the pillow in the chamber adjoining his. She tilted her chin up, her eyes challenging him to go further, yet her hands clung together again in a death grip. She didn't reach out in an attempt to force his hand, to get him to partake in more. No, this one was innocent all right.

He should have left off where he had begun until he knew which clan the lass belonged to, but what harm would it do to kiss her once more?

Cupping her face, he leaned down and kissed her again, only meaning to press his mouth against hers more firmly, naught more. When her fingers tentatively touched his waist, the notion concerning which clan she belonged to and the fact she was probably an untried maiden were tossed asunder. Instantly, he deepened the kiss, wishing to plunder the lady from the sea, his treasure, his find. He expected her to swoon, or step back, or slap his face, but she parted her lips and gave a soft mew.

'Twas his undoing as his trewes tightened uncomfortably. Again, he had the incredible feeling he knew her. He moved his hands to her shoulders in case she became faint while he pressed his advantage.

'Twas he who was shocked when she gave into his probing tongue and mated tentatively with his. Her lashes brushed her cheeks, hiding her eyes while her fingers clung to his waist. Aye, she was ready to swoon, the beat of her heart rapid and wine-sweetened breath shallow.

If she had been one of his usual conquests, a lass who wished a quick romp and no attachments, they would have been naked and buried in the fragrant flowers already. Seemed strange to be with a lass, plying her with kisses, wanting to take his actions further, but knowing he could not, even if she wished it so.

She did not know who she was, whether she was betrothed or widowed, or in love with another man, who her family's clan was, naught much at all. He would not take advantage of the lass.

Separating from the kiss that left him agonizing for much more, he again stepped away from her, his own breathing just as ragged.

Her cheeks flushed anew, and after looking at him with a mixture of fascination and surprise, she finally had the good grace to look demurely away. 'Twas more than disturbing to feel so hot and bothered for a lass he had no intention of bedding. Catriona's arrival and getting this charade over with would not be accomplished soon enough.

He took the lady's arm and walked her farther

along the garden path, waiting for her to say something, expecting small talk but having only silence.

"What think you, lass?" he finally asked, to break up the insufferable silence stretching between them.

"You are well versed in kissing lassies."

This bit of witticism brought a smile to his lips. Her cheeks again blossomed with color. Was she thinking he had gone farther with the others? She would think right. With an eager lass, he would have made sure they were somewhere private before the kissing began. 'Twas only natural what would follow.

"May I ask you a personal question?" Her voice was very small, mayhap a little reluctant.

He couldn't wait to hear her query. "Aye, ask away."

"Do you kiss Catriona the same way?" Her gaze snagged his.

What could he say to that? Catriona had buried her first husband at the age of six and ten. She had not given up men for the last four years of her life, pretending to be the sweet, grieving widow languishing for her dead husband. 'Twas an arranged marriage.

That's why James presumed Catriona would do sufficiently as his wife. She was well-versed in pleasuring a man. Taking an eager woman to bed was much more satisfying than bedding a lassie who was not, he assumed.

"I see by the smile on your face 'tis so," Eilis said.

Emotions fluttered across her face, but he couldn't tell what they were exactly—condemnation, fascination, envy?

She didn't know him and wished to escape from her captivity here. Why would she feel anything about his relations with Catriona at all? He had never understood the female mind. Even with Catriona he thought as good in bed together as they were and because of being the chief of his clan, she would jump at the chance to be his betrothed.

'Twas his duty, though to consider other Highlander's daughters. No, more than duty. 'Twas necessary to keep the clans from taking offense should he have not considered other leaders' daughters. Now he had done so, and Catriona was the one to receive the prize. She should have been more than pleased.

"I...I do not think I have ever been kissed before."

James brought her to an abrupt halt. "Your memories are returning?"

She touched the tip of a slender finger to her full lip and stroked it like he wished to do with his tongue. "I think I would have remembered."

"Did my kiss give you pleasure then?" He had no need to know the answer to his question. He wasn't sure why he even asked. Mayhap because he might have been her first and wished to know if he met with her expectations or exceeded them. And why it should have mattered was another point he didn't wish to consider too closely.

Footsteps approached, and they both turned to see one of his men hurry into the garden. Ian bowed quickly. "I beg your pardon, my laird for, ahem, interrupting you, but Niall wished me to bring this to you at once."

"Aye, what is the matter, Ian?"

"My laird, the lady of Castle Craven sends a missive."

His heart pounding, James ripped open the

parchment and took a relieved breath. "Catriona is coming this way in just two day's time. Splendid." He took Eilis's small hand in his. "We have much work to do, lass, if we are to pull this off. But first, we must decide on a clan name for you. The situation would be odd not to have one in mind when Catriona comes to call. But we can think on the matter later. 'Tis time to break our fast. You shall sit by me and tell me all the foods that you favor."

*Two days.* In so much time, he hoped the lass and he could learn enough about each other to play the game. *Two days.* The time left would have to suffice then Catriona would no doubt give up her procrastination and accept his hand in marriage.

Ian waved another missive. "And this came also, my laird. The missive is from Eanruig."

James read the message, his blood boiling. More sheep had been stolen near the MacNeill border. Blood littered the heather, and the plants trampled mightily as if a mighty battle had been waged. None of the MacNeill living nearby had seen or heard anything because they had been attending a wedding feast in one of the villages too far away. And none of the clansmen were missing. Eanruig surmised it would not have been the sheep's blood because the raiders liked to keep the meat on the hoof until they needed it.

The situation was more than strange. Particularly since no bodies were left behind. Although if the Dunbartons had lost a man or two, they would have taken their wounded or dead with them. Still, who had fought them if none of his own people had died, been injured, were missing, or owned up to fighting the Dunbartons?

Intending to discover more about the situation, he kissed Eilis's hand and led her back to her chamber. He had meant to stay with her longer and learn more about her, but Dunbarton was wreaking havoc on his lands once more, and James would stand for none of it. The time had come to discover what had happened at the Macneill lands bordering Dunbarton's again.

***

Like before, James and his men could find no sign of anyone along his boundary with Dunbarton's. Although he questioned his people again, they all offered the same story. None were in the area when the thieving occurred. Unsure as to what to think of the situation, James and the party returned to Craigly Castle to partake of the supper.

By the time James and Eilis sat at the high table overlooking the rest of the tables set up in long rows stretching outward from the dais that eve, the sconces were lighted, and the smell of tallow filled the hall.

Lady Akira gave Eilis a gracious smile and took her seat next to her while James sat on the other side of her. "We have good news, aye? That Catriona will soon be here?" Lady Akira asked.

Eilis didn't think it was good news, rather, that she could not pull this off. What was more, she kept feeling it was the second time she'd had to live such a lie. As much as she tried to recall the circumstances of her past life, she came up empty.

"My son says we must come up with a clan name to make your own."

"MacNeill," Eilis said quickly. She thought she had heard the MacNeill were an affable lot, though she remembered hearing they were thought of as being prideful. She didn't think her clan had ever had any trouble with them.

"MacNeill," she repeated, hoping God wouldn't strike her down for lying. Mayhap MacNeill was her clan name after all. She just could not remember.

Lady Akira's mouth dropped slightly, and she glanced at James. James's mouth hung agape as well.

The situation was not good.

"You have remembered your clan's name, then?" Lady Akira asked, frowning.

"Aye, my lady." Although Eilis was certain the name did not bode well with James and his mother, she couldn't think of a way to get herself out of the quandary she was now in.

Lady Akira seemed to ponder the notion then asked, "Where from?"

"Glen Affric." Eilis knew the area well enough, having spent many a summer with a cousin there. And why she knew that, but not the name of the cousin? The gaps in her memories bewildered her, yet as hard as she tried, she could not fill in the details of her past life. Why did she remember Glen Affric so well?

If she visited a cousin there in the summers, it must not have been her home. Why could she not remember her home?

"Glen Affric. Hmmm, that is very interesting, my dear. My other sons are there, helping the Lady Anice of Brecken Castle. Know you her?" Lady Akira lifted a piece of brown bread and buttered it.

Eilis gulped. James had family there. 'Twas not good. "Aye, everyone in the area knows of the lady. She is known to be kind to those who serve her." And again, she couldn't fathom why she could recall Lady

Anice of Brecken Castle, but not her family's name.

"Have you served her?" Lady Akira asked, her brows lifted. "Do you have word of my sons?"

"I…I have not been back there for some time, I do not think. And I do not know anything much about her except…" She frowned, trying to dredge up the elusive memory. "Her uncle died, and she became King Henry's ward."

"Aye, 'tis true. Know you, Eilis," Lady Akira said, her words said deliberately slow, "we are of the Clan MacNeill?"

# CHAPTER 5

Eilis could scarcely breathe, the part of her meal that she had managed to eat now sitting like a solid rock in the pit of her stomach. Why had she not thought to ask someone, anyone, which clan James was the chief of?

*MacNeill.* Mayhap in her semi-unconscious state someone had mentioned the name and that's where she had gotten it from.

"You have a clan name now, Eilis," James said, dryly, his jaw taut.

He didn't seem at all pleased, and Eilis had a hard time choking down her fowl, but she didn't feel she could change her name so easily now. What if she picked the name of an enemy clan? She thought of many clan names, but had no idea which the MacNeill might not like, except for the Dunbarton.

"Aye, MacNeill is my clan's name." She lifted her chin and dared him to disagree.

"From the Glen Affric branch?"

"Aye."

"Tell me what you know of the area, Eilis *MacNeill* of Glen Affric."

She buttered a piece of bread, trying to calm herself, attempting to quell the trembling in her fingers. "I love picking berries from the rowan trees beside the Allt na Imrich stream in Glen Affric. My da, when he was alive, made drink from it. I collected blaeberry also to dye my cloth blue or to give to our healer who used them to aid the digestion. South of Loch Beinn a'Mheadhoin, I gathered berries from the juniper to add to the meal and hazel nuts from the trees at the falls. I have watched the beavers build damns on the river and the crossbills courting one another in early spring, singing to each other, then fighting for ownership. I have seen the red deer stag with velvet-covered antlers in summer grazing on the grasses and heather against the backdrop of the Five Sisters of Kintail. I have found the home of the red squirrel, its drey of twigs and leaves in the fork of a pine overlooking Glen Affric lach."

She looked at him finally, her eyes challenging him to dispute her recollections.

His look devilishly sinister, James nodded. He motioned for a servant and spoke to him in a hushed voice.

Eilis tried not to attach any importance to his actions, but a trickle of unease snaked up her spine.

The servant spoke to Eanruig sitting beyond Niall. He glanced at James, who nodded. When the seneschal looked at Eilis, she noted the surprise in Eanruig's expression, and she quickly shifted her gaze to the table.

Somehow, she believed she had sunk deeper into a

quagmire of quicksand like the kind she had accidentally gotten into along the banks of the river Nith.

Eanruig joined James. "Aye, my laird?"

"The lady says she is one of your kin."

Eilis shrank in her seat.

Eanruig leaned closer and looked at her, then smiled. "Aye, I do remember a bonny lass who looked like the lady. She was with a woman in the village whose family married into mine…a distant relation, as I recall. I thought she resembled someone I knew when first I pulled the lady from the sea."

*Och*, this could not be.

"Do you wish for me to take her home to her kin?" Eanruig asked James.

James's hard gaze remained fixed on her. "Eilis?"

"I…I thought you wanted me to assist you with Catriona." Eilis hated the way she sounded so desperate.

In an arrogant way, James tilted his head to the side. "Would you wish me to send word to your kin you are here?"

"I…I think if you tell them I am here, they will wish me returned home at once." Eilis felt as hot as when she was burning up with the fever, but a vague worry nagged at her that 'twould not be in her best interest to return to Glen Affric and meet her kin.

"I would not wish them to think you are dead, Eilis." His tone of voice had softened, but she did not think he was as concerned about her family's worry than he was about finding out who she truly belonged to.

"Nay." She set her bread down, her hands shaking.

If they located her cousin and the word reached her family she was still alive, she feared she was doomed. Though she could not remember the reason she was so afraid to return home. And she could not even recall the name of her cousin. What horrible thing had she done? Had she stolen away on the ship and run away? Had she…she killed someone?

"Why do not you want your family to know?" Lady Akira asked, her voice concerned.

"I…I do not feel verra well. May I be excused?" She wasn't lying. Her head felt too light, and her stomach swirled with upset.

Nobody uttered a word at the high table, and the hall grew quiet while most everyone watched the intrigue.

Finally, James signaled to the healer. "Tavia will accompany you to the guest chamber." He turned to the servant. "Have Fergus guard the lady's chamber."

Annoyed James would have a man watch over her, Eilis shakily walked with Tavia to the guest chamber without a backward glance at James or his mother. She had really gotten herself into a mess this time, and she didn't even know what it was she was afraid of.

Fergus, a massive Scotsman, broad shoulders, red-bearded, piercing green eyes, gave her the impression he was not one to disobey. He walked behind her, his heavy step reminding her she was going to the chamber and nowhere else. The stables seemed a good place for her right about now, stealing a horse, although not James's this time that could so easily be stopped with a whistle, and escaping.

Knowing James would have Eanruig try to locate her cousin, Eilis pondered a means of gaining her freedom. *Think, Eilis, think.*

"Mayhap I could have something to drink," she said to Tavia, hoping the woman would fetch it, and Eilis could figure a way to get around the bear-like hulk that followed on their heels.

Tavia gave her a sly, knowing look. "Once you are settled in your chamber, I will fetch a servant to bring you something."

Was Eilis as transparent as the veils she sometimes wore over her hair? With every passing second, the urge to flee grew.

When they reached the chamber, Tavia closed the door behind them then crossed the floor to the bed and pulled the linens back. "I do not think you are so verra ill. Why did you say you were one of our clansmen?"

Eilis walked over to the closest window and stared out. In the distance, she could see the Five Sisters of Kintail. How far were they from Glen Affric? Eanruig could learn the truth about her soon. Mayhap she would remember who she was then. Even so, the constant nagging voice at the back of her throbbing head told her it was wiser not to know.

"Eanruig will soon enough discover who you truly are then what will you do?" Tavia asked. Her words were spoken without malice, softly, with a hint of concern.

"Can you not understand a fate worse than death awaits me if my family learns I am still alive?" At least that's what Eilis truly believed, although she could not conjure up the reason for the fear she had that her family would discover her whereabouts.

Her brown eyes rounded, Tavia stared at her. "Surely you exaggerate your circumstances."

"Nay." Eilis brushed a wayward curl behind her ear. "I am better off dead to my family."

"I cannot believe anyone would feel that way. You have no scars on your body. No one has beaten you. Why would you think so ill of your family?"

Feeling desperate, Eilis pleaded, "Help me to leave here before Laird James sends word to them, Tavia. I beg of you."

The oddest thing was she felt as though she had pleaded her heart out with her family, to no good end. That she could not fathom the reason was maddening. Except it was not a good situation, and she had to leave this place before her family discovered her.

"Nay, Lady. If I were to help you leave, His Lairdship would have my head." Tavia patted the bed. "Come, lie down, and I will have a servant fetch you something to drink."

Eilis considered the long drop to the courtyard. Without a rope… She glanced at the bed linens. Tied together, would they be sturdy enough and long enough to—

The door creaked open, and Lady Akira walked into the room, her gaze worried.

"She wishes something to drink, my lady," Tavia said.

"Tell a servant."

"Aye." Tavia hurried out of the chamber.

"What is this all about, Eilis?"

Eilis wrung her hands, considering the door left wide open. But she was certain the hulking Highlander was standing just beyond the door out of sight. "I must leave at once, Lady Akira."

"After agreeing to help my son with Catriona, most

73

certainly not." Lady Akira's brows furrowed. "Why are you afraid your family will learn of your whereabouts?"

"I beg of you, do not let them know I am here."

"My son has already dispatched Eanruig to locate the woman he saw you with last summer."

Eilis could have screamed. She turned her attention back to the window. Torches glowed in the dark, and she envisioned guards walking along the wall walk, watching for intruders. Mayhap she could slip over the south wall, which was in ill repair.

"Why not tell me what is wrong, dear?"

"My…my family must not know I am alive." Eilis began to unplait her hair. "They must not. That is all."

Lady Akira let out her breath. "This sounds to me like a betrothal you are unhappy about. If your da has died, some other male member of your family must be your guardian, and you will have no say in the matter."

Was she betrothed to some disagreeable Highlander? "I am *not* betrothed to anyone." She hoped. Pulling off the borrowed belt, Eilis laid it on the chest. "What happens to me is no one's concern. I died when the ship went down. That is all."

"Except everyone here at Castle Craigly knows better. Tell me what ails you, Eilis. James is very clever at working out matters that benefit most concerned."

"Forgive me if I feel he would fail in this venture. I fear my family will not be dissuaded. If Eanruig finds my—the lady he saw me with last summer—she will tell my family that I am still alive. It will not go well for me, my lady. Believe me. There is naught His Lairdship can do about it."

Lady Akira frowned. "Then you *are* displeased about a disagreeable betrothal."

"I am not betrothed…" Eilis stopped, nearly saying she didn't remember, but then how could she know she was a MacNeill if she didn't recall why she feared returning to her family? If she didn't remember anything, her family name, the reason for her concern, they would discount her fears and attempt to locate her family. She worried then, her life would be forfeit.

"Why not tell me what it is all about?"

Lady Akira waited patiently for Eilis to finish what she was saying, but when Eilis shook her head, Lady Akira asked, "You are going to bed now?"

"Aye, my lady, if it pleases you."

Tavia returned with a goblet. "If you are ill, you need to be abed." She strode across the floor and set the goblet on a small bedside table. "I will help you with your kirtle."

"I will see you in the morning, Eilis," Lady Akira said.

"Thank you for your kindness, my lady."

James's mother's expression revealed not a clue as to what she was feeling. She said naught, bowed her head slightly, and left the room. Fergus closed the door, and Eilis took a ragged breath. As soon as Tavia left her alone again, Eilis would make a rope out of linens and pray they held her weight when she made the perilous climb out the window.

Getting beyond the wall, that was another matter.

\*\*\*

"Eanruig, since there is still no word from my brothers, make a trip to Brecken Castle also as you seek answers concerning Eilis, and see what is keeping them. Do you have spies inquiring into the recent sheep theft?" James asked, as his seneschal prepared to leave at his request.

"Aye, Laird. Two of our men are attempting to determine what has occurred." Eanruig took the pouch of rations the cook offered him.

"It seems the Dunbartons must have known a wedding was taking place. I wish to know if someone in the village had leaked this information to our enemy."

"Aye. I will return as soon as I am able with all the news." Eanruig gave a nod then hurried out of the hall.

James stretched his legs in front of the stone hearth, the sweet-smelling peat burning blue. "Ah, my lady mother," he said, spying her coming his way, hoping at least his mother had more success at clearing up yet another mystery. "You look like you did when da passed away. What is the trouble with the lass?"

"I think Eilis is betrothed, although she denies it."

The news shouldn't have mattered to him, except to be concerned her suitor would be anxious to secure his bride, but the thought irritated James that she would not be free to wed another. Feeling such a way was more than foolish. He combed his fingers through his breeze-tangled hair. He told himself it was just his concern the man she was betrothed to would take her away before Catriona arrived, and his plans would be tossed asunder.

When he did not speak, his mother continued. "She is afraid of her family, but something else is the matter, although she would not say what."

"Och, why would she deny she is betrothed to marry someone? The truth will come out soon enough. When her family learns she is still alive, they will take her home, and that will be the end of our ruse with

Catriona." There, he said it. The real reason for his concern that Eilis might be betrothed.

Lady Akira sat down on a bench next to James and stretched her hands out to the fire. "Ah, but Catriona will be here, whether Eilis is or not."

Niall stormed across the room, his cheeks red and a frown digging into his temple. "The lady cannot be forced against her will."

"We can say naught about the matter if her guardian has already decided this for her," Lady Akira said.

"You say guardian?" James asked, his curiosity piqued. "Why not her brother, or an uncle, or mayhap a cousin?"

"She did not say, just spoke of her family."

In a gesture of irritation, Niall threw up his hands. "Why would she say she is not betrothed? Should we not take her word for it? What if some other matter frightens her?"

James faced his mother. "Well?"

"She did not say."

James let out a disgruntled sound.

Niall paced, then stopped abruptly. "What if the lady is in danger? You should not have sent Eanruig on this errand."

At hearing his cousin distrust his decision, James quashed his growing temper. "He will keep the questioning to a minimum. Several of his family members live in Glen Affric. They will speak not a word of the matter."

"And if their tongues wag?" Niall asked, his voice at a fevered pitch. "If word reaches her family, and they demand her return at once?"

James took a settling breath. "We will deal with that when we come to it. No sense in worrying about what might or might not happen."

"Know you she will attempt escape," his mother said, her eyes shifting from the fire to him. "She will not stay here if she can help it. She is like a frightened, cornered animal, and she will make every attempt to flee her cage."

"Tavia knows to stay with her tonight? And Fergus will stay on guard until he is relieved by another?" James asked, although he could not imagine the wee lass would try to leave the castle grounds again.

"Aye."

"I liked it better when she did not know who she was," James mused.

"I believe she did as well," his mother agreed.

"I like her just the same. Eanruig will put her life in danger, of that I am certain." Niall stalked out of the keep.

James jumped up from the bench, but his mother grabbed his arm. "Let him go, James. He only wants to help."

Shaking his head, James stared in the direction his cousin had gone. "He cannot have the lady, although I know it is his most fervent desire. I need to speak to Fergus, to remind him not to give the lass an inch, if she thinks she is leaving here without my say. The woman will be her family's concern when we discover who they truly are. I do not want to lose her before then and have to explain what has happened."

Although James couldn't help wonder if the lass was truly in danger or if his cousin's usual flights of fancy were getting the better of him. Worse, he couldn't help wondering if the lass did know the clan she was from, and she was attempting to hide it from him. He took off for the stairs and a word with Fergus, mayhap a word with the lass as well because he was certain his mother used too soft an approach to get the truth from Eilis.

***

Dougald MacNeill touched his forehead where his temple pounded something fierce. He found his wrist, no, both wrists in chains that rattled with his movement. The horrific odor that filled the cold air was no doubt from the dank, dark confines of a cell in Dunbarton's dungeon. Every inch of his body ached, and one eye seemed to be swollen shut. He tested his teeth. They all seemed to be in place and no bones broken. Thank God for small miracles. The lassies loved his handsome face. 'Twould be a shame if the Dunbartons had ruined his charming looks, he thought facetiously.

The way his naked skin burned, he was sure he had suffered a few lacerations as well.

Easing himself up on one elbow on the foul-smelling straw he reclined on, he winced as his head nearly shattered with the pain. Mayhap a couple of ribs were broken after all.

"Dougald?" a harsh voice whispered nearby but not near enough.

"Gunnolf?" Dougald called out, meaning to announce in a warlike voice and ready to take on every last Dunbarton, but he sounded weak and in pain, which frustrated him all the more.

"Across the hall from you. How fare you?"

"Methinks I have been beat about a bit like the time we fought the last battle in the Crusade. And you?"

"Ja. Have you come up with a plan to escape, yet, mon?"

Dougald chuckled under his breath, although even that hurt every part of his body. He wasn't used to being the one in charge. James, being the eldest, had always made their decisions. Then when Dougald and his other brothers had sought their fortune, Malcolm, the next older brother had led them. Now 'twas his turn, though he wished the circumstances less dire.

"I have only just come around. Give me some more time, and I will come up with a plan, Gunnolf."

"Dunbarton's men said they would have rather hung us from a pike, but they realized you were James's brother and I, his close companion. They plan to ransom us after we have rotted down here a while, figuring they would like James to wonder what had become of us first. They hoped, mayhap, he would come begging for us afore long."

Dougald snorted. "James, no doubt, is unaware we were on our way to aid him. So how many of their kin will no longer wield a sword?"

"Six."

"Six too few."

"Aye. If our horses had not been so tired, we would have finished the rest off in good order." Chains rattled across the hall then Gunnolf said, "They stripped us naked in the inner bailey, although you were out cold. The intent was to treat us like filthy prisoners, but 'twas more than one lassie's eye that looked on with admiration."

Dougald smiled. "Then if a lassie should come to feed us or take another peek, mayhap we shall have our escape plan."

# CHAPTER 6

Eilis climbed onto the straw-filled mattress in the guest chamber but watched in the shimmering candle light while Tavia prepared herself for bed also. "You are not sleeping in here also, are you?" She failed to conceal the surprise in her voice.

"Aye. His Lairdship was concerned you may become unwell during the night." Tavia gave a furtive smile. "'Tis best if I am close by to assist you."

"'Tis unnecessary." But Eilis's words did not sway the healer.

Tavia combed out her long dark tresses then snuffed out the candles. Joining Eilis, Tavia sent the mattress to swaying slightly on the ropes holding it in place. "His Lairdship decides what is best for you."

How was Eilis to strip the linens to tie together and make a rope? How could she light candles to see what she was doing without waking Tavia? She ground her teeth and stared upward at the ceiling she couldn't see for the darkness. Mayhap, she could leave the bed and dress without waking Tavia. Then she might be able to slip past the guard if he grew sleepy.

She rolled onto her side. Served James right if his supper didn't agree with him, and the healer wasn't readily at his disposal.

For hours, Eilis lay still, waiting for some sign Tavia was asleep. When she heard her softly snoring, Eilis thanked the Lord. As carefully as she could without rocking the mattress too verra much, she slipped out of bed, although the ropes creaked a wee bit.

Her feet crunched on rushes that she normally wouldn't have noticed, but every sound seemed to echo off the stone walls tenfold. She fumbled for her kirtle and, after several excruciating minutes, finally located it in the cave-like darkness and yanked it over her head. Then for several more minutes, she crawled around on the floor, patting it, searching for her shoes. She would have to forgo her hose and garters because she feared she would take overlong to locate them. When her fingers finally gripped the soft leather shoes, Tavia stirred.

Eilis froze in place. Och, if she caught her now…

Tavia shifted on the mattress. Her snoring stopped, but she didn't raise the alarm that Eilis was not in bed.

Praying Tavia was still asleep, Eilis slipped her shoes on then made her way to the door. Beneath the massive oak, the light of a candle outside the chamber shone, the only reason she knew where the door was in the dark.

Would Fergus still be standing guard? Mayhap he had retired for the night because Tavia was sleeping with her. Or if he had not retired, mayhap he would be half asleep or sleeping fully and not notice a wee lass slip out.

With her ear to the door, she listened for any sounds, conversation, snoring, but there was none. Taking a deep breath, she glanced at the door leading to James's chamber. If she slipped out through his chamber, would the guard at hers see her? But what about James? Was he sleeping, or away from his chamber still?

She stared at the bottom edge of the door. No candlelight shown. Yet, she couldn't bolster her courage to go to the laird's door.

She opened the one leading out of her chamber. It creaked, shattering her resolve. No one came to the opening or said a word. Her spine stiffer than a taut bow, she gambled that the laird had removed the guard. Tavia was with her after all. Why make a man serve extra guard duty for naught?

She opened the door further. It squeaked again. She hadn't remembered it was so noisy before. The space was still not wide enough for her to see out. Her skin chilled. No response on the other side of the door though.

Swallowing hard, she pulled the door open enough that she could squeeze out.

Fergus watched her, his eyes and stance as hard as steel.

Her heart shriveled. What now? Pretend she needed something? Shut the door and return to bed?

"Could you fetch me something to drink?"

He gave his head a shake.

"I cannot sleep as I am parched."

"Wake Tavia and have her fetch something for

you."

Eilis frowned. "She is sound asleep."

"Shut the door then and return to bed."

Lifting her chin, Eilis motioned to the stairs. "Fine, I will get it myself." With that, she stormed out of the chamber.

Seizing her wrist, Fergus glowered at her, the fire burning in his eyes. "His Lairdship says you shall remain here at Craigly Castle. Until he says otherwise, you willna go anywhere, lass."

She tried to wriggle free. "Let me go!"

"What is wrong?" Tavia asked from inside the chamber near the bed, her voice groggy with sleep.

Eilis heard Tavia moving around in the room, probably trying to locate her kirtle in the dark.

"The lady is thirsty, so she says," Fergus growled.

Her hair tangled about her shoulders and her kirtle rumpled, Tavia joined her and glowered. "I will fetch her something to drink."

Fergus released Eilis's wrist as she seethed at him.

Tavia rushed past her while Eilis returned to the chamber and shut the door.

Having no other choice, Eilis headed straight for James's bedchamber. Again, she listened at the door for any sounds. Silence.

Pushing James's door open cautiously, she was relieved it made no creaking noise.

Inside, she could see naught except the faint illumination beneath the door leading outside. Like a beacon of light on a cold black night, she headed straight for it and ran into the sharp and flat edge of a table. And bruised her thighs.

Instantly, something crashed on the floor. Shaken,

she darted for the door, her shoes crunching on what she thought were bits of clay. The mattress creaked, feet hit the floor, and most likely James pursued her. Her heart couldn't have beat any harder as she tried to keep the panic from overwhelming her. Halfway to the door, a hand grabbed at her arm, then seized her wrist. She screamed.

The outer door flew open, spilling light into the chamber while four men rushed in with swords drawn.

James tsked, still confining her wrist in his iron grip, heating her blood. "You look like you just fell out of bed, lass. Have you lost your way?" He motioned to one of his men. "Naught is the matter that I cannot handle. Light a candle for me, Fergus, will you? The wee lass has made a shambles of my chamber."

"Aye, my laird."

Chuckling and shaking their heads, the other men sauntered out of the room with backward glances at Eilis and their laird while Fergus lighted a couple of candles.

The word would be all over the castle by morn as to what she'd done. Her whole body flushed anew.

"Do we need to post a guard in my room also, lass?" James asked, touching her hair with a gentle sweep of his free hand, his other still holding firm. "You did not wish to share my bed with me, did you?"

Her cheeks grew even more feverish, and she tried to twist her wrist free.

A slight smile curved Fergus's lips. "Wish you anything else, my laird?"

James's expression mirrored Fergus's. "Nay. Just a good night's sleep, which the lass seems intent on disturbing."

"I was thirsty," Eilis snapped.

"Aye, and Tavia has already gone to fetch her something to quench her thirst," Fergus said, his words verging on a growl. "She had no reason to come in here, my laird." He bowed his head slightly.

Eilis flashed him a derisive look. Anyone but a fool would see the obvious reason behind her intentions, and she need not explain the matter further.

James raised his brows, his eyes twinkling with amusement. "You did not intend to traverse my chamber to tell Tavia you were hungry as well, did you?" He turned to Fergus. "You may go."

Fergus bowed his head again, gave Eilis a look of displeasure, then closed the door on his departure.

Eilis fought feeling vulnerable alone in James's presence, but his capturing her wrist and holding her tight and way too close made it difficult to think otherwise.

"You can let go of me," she said between clenched teeth, her whole body heating despite the coolness of the chamber. The smell of his heady masculine scent overwhelmed her, and if he did not release her soon, she didn't think she'd remain standing for long.

"Can I now?" His vexation was evident in the tone of his voice, and his eyes blazed with fire as he assessed her. "How far do you think you would have gotten?" He motioned to the window. "The castle is locked tight at night. You would not have gotten beyond the walls. 'Tis not safe for a wee lass to be roaming the castle by herself in any event. Some of my men might have thought you were seeking male companionship."

She narrowed her eyes. "I was thirsty. The salted meat made me thus."

James gave her a look like he knew better than that.

She had not managed to eat a bite, only drank some of her mead. If she truly drank anything more this eve, she would float away.

"Aye, well, Tavia will remedy that. The next time you wish something, wake Tavia and have her get it for you. Fergus is under strict orders to ensure you do not leave the chamber. He will not disobey me in this matter. So do not try him." Instantly, the darkness faded from James's face, and a small smile appeared. "Shall I tuck you back in bed?"

When he was angry with her, she felt less wary of his intentions. 'Twas much better than when he put on his seductive air. Besides, they were alone in his chamber and…

She frowned at him. "I am not a child."

His face hardened again. "Nay, you are not. That is why you will not roam the castle alone at night."

Before surprise could even register, he leaned down to kiss her. She should have turned her head, discouraged his attentions, but she couldn't. Breathless, she waited with great expectation and watched as his lips touched hers. At first, 'twas naught more than a brush of warm velvet against her mouth. She trembled, not from fear, but from the sheer pleasure of his touch.

Her bones turned to soggy oats, and if James had not tightened his grasp on her wrist, she was sure she would be kneeling before him. His lips turned up slightly, mayhap because she did not object to his kiss. 'Twas highly inappropriate, and she should step away. But she lifted her mouth to his and solicited more.

To her frustration, he did not oblige. Instead, he touched her cheek with his fingertips and caressed the skin with a gentle sweep, his smoldering gaze fixed to hers. Mesmerized, she could not look away.

"'Tis not safe for you to be in here, lass." His words were huskier than she'd ever heard them. "You need to return to bed."

But he did not release her, nor did he move her from the spot of floor she was affixed to. Worse, she did not try to pull away either.

She licked her lips and dropped her gaze, studying his chest, well muscled and bronzed, the dark hair trailing lower toward his trewes. 'Twas then she saw the bulge between his legs beneath the fabric, straining against the seams. Her cheeks heated, and her eyes shifted up, away from his tantalizing treasures. He gave her a wicked smile.

*** 

Pulling her against his body, James let her feel the way she had aroused him. He knew he should have returned her to her bed, but he wanted to join her in it, despite his conscience telling him otherwise. Her lips were honey-flavored from the mead, sweet and tender, her body soft and warm as he pressed himself against her. The slight intake of her breath tantalized him all the more. Again, he bent his head and kissed her.

Lips like silk caressed him back. Demurely at first. He released her wrist and wrapped his arms around her as her breasts rose with her quickened breaths. Her fingers skimmed across his naked back, sending ribbons of desire coursing through him. Never had he felt in such a way, tortured to the outer edges of the world, filled with ragged desire that he knew he could not fulfill. 'Twas more than foolish to press his advantage with the lady.

Yet when she tentatively kissed him back, she ignited the flame deep within, and he tossed aside all convention. He wanted her more than he had ever wanted a woman. She was his gift from the sea, his to keep and hold.

He deepened the kiss, and she opened herself to him. His knees weakened. 'Twas more than daft. No woman had ever made his head spin. He would kiss her and be done with the infatuation. 'Twas Catriona whom he would wed and bed soon.

Caressing Eilis's tongue with his, he forgot all about Catriona and concentrated on the sea nymph in his arms. He stroked her breast and felt the nub peak, begging for his attention. He closed his eyes, desiring to bare her to his touch. Why did the lass not push him away? Instead, she leaned into his embrace, her breath nearly inaudible, her heartbeat racing.

"Tavia," Eilis managed to get out, and he cursed himself inwardly as he finally heard the woman's light footfalls nearing the lady's chamber.

Taking a deep breath, he moved away from the lass, his painful arousal reminding him of where he'd nearly gone with her. It could not happen again. 'Twas only a ruse he was bound to play with Eilis, naught more, and he could not be with her in his bedchamber, alone, without witnesses again.

Tavia greeted Fergus at the door to Eilis's room. "All is quiet, Fergus?"

"She is still in His Lairdship's chamber," Fergus replied or warned.

James couldn't tell which. He should have sent Eilis back to her chamber, but instead, he waited with her until Tavia came to his, not willing to give Eilis up just yet.

After crossing the lady's chamber, Tavia peeked into James's chamber, her face flushing as she observed Eilis with him. Tavia lowered her eyes. "My laird, I am sorry if the lady disturbed your sleep." Her words expressed profuse apology.

"Nay, 'tis not a problem." He motioned to the goblet. "Drink up, Eilis, so I will be assured you can sleep."

Annoyed James would watch her, Eilis drank the mead. Even Fergus and Tavia kept an eye on her progress. She tried to leave some of it, but James motioned for her to finish it all then bowed his head to her slightly when she was done.

"Now, may we all get some sleep?" James turned to Fergus. "You may retake your post."

When Fergus closed the door, James said to Eilis, "I would tuck you in if it meant you would go where you need to be. But I will let Tavia take care of it."

Eilis scowled at him, whirled around, and returned to the bedchamber. Instantly, her head swirled. By the time she reached the bed, she felt verra woozy.

From a great distance, she heard James and Tavia whispering to each other. How discourteous. Yet she greatly wished to know what secrets they shared with one another.

She barely made it into bed, dressed and all. Tavia hurried across the chamber and pushed Eilis against the bed before she collapsed on the floor.

The low light in the room faded to pitch.

"Sleep well, my lady," James said, his lips curved up slightly as Tavia removed Eilis's shoes and covered her with the blanket. The lass would not disturb his sleep any longer this eve.

'Twas only a short while later after returning to bed, that rough pounding on the door wakened James. Now what was the lass up to? "Aye," he called out from the bed.

"My laird, Daran MacLeod has come seeking your help. Dunbarton's men raided his farm near our border and took his young daughter, Anna."

# CHAPTER 7

"I want five men ready to go now," James told Fergus as he jerked his tunic on, ready to end this business with Dunbarton and his men once and for all. Never had they done anything so low as to steal a child. "Five volunteers. But not Niall."

"Aye, my laird." Fergus hurried out of the chamber.

James had barely made it down the stairs when Niall waylaid him. "You cannot mean to take on Dunbarton's men with only five our own."

"We are slipping in and out with the girl, naught more at present."

"But Fergus said I cannot go."

James grabbed his cousin's shoulders and gave him a firm squeeze. "While my brothers, Eanruig, and I are away, you have to be in charge, Niall. The clan is counting on you. 'Tis your place."

Niall's eyes widened. "Let me go in your stead then."

James rushed down the stairs. "Nay. Not this time. Stay and make sure Eilis does not run away again."

"She tried again?" Niall asked, keeping up with his quickened pace.

"Aye." James headed outside the keep. "Fergus was guarding her chamber, but he will come with me. Have someone else take his post."

"Aye." Niall slammed his fist into the palm of his hand, itching for a fight.

James knew Niall would do right by them if he was needed to govern the MacNeill clan in his absence.

"She is sneaky, Niall," James cast over his shoulder as his cousin followed him to his saddled horse.

In all seriousness, Niall nodded. "You have my word I will keep the lass here. You can see for yourself upon your return."

James and his men mounted their horses and, with well wishes from the men on guard, the party slipped beyond the curtain wall into the pitch-black night. James and his men knew the land, whether it was night or day, and made their way to where Dunbarton's men had fled across the MacNeill border.

No one spoke a word, the only sounds the horses clopping on the ground and a cool breeze stirring the heather. In the distance, peat smoke burned in a dwelling. When they grew closer, James recognized it as the croft where the girl had been taken.

The men separated from one another, making bird sounds to keep in touch. 'Twas not too far into Dunbarton's land that James heard the raucous peal of laughter from a bunch of drunken men. Had they believed themselves invincible from the MacNeill at this late hour? That James and his men would not track them down and thwart their evil deed?

Fergus cawed to James, and he signaled him back as they drew closer to the peat smell of a campfire. The light danced in the dark from the crackling flames. Six men sat drinking while a seventh struggled with the girl, no more than twelve summers old.

'Twas the redheaded girl James and his companions sought.

With his men in place, James galloped into camp, signaling the beginning of the battle. *"Buaidh Na Bas!"* he and his men cried out.

The startled Dunbarton men scrambled to gain their feet before they could unsheathe swords.

Instantly, James's men clashed with the brigands while James targeted the one holding the girl. His black eyes hard, the man held his sword to the girl's throat, threatening to cut her.

"Do and all your kin are dead men," James warned, drawing closer, as the steel of swords striking one another rang out in the woods.

The girl sobbed and shrieked.

"I will let you go, if you release the lass unharmed," James conceded, although he didn't wish to make any such concession with the brigand.

"And the others."

The woods had grown still, deathly quiet. James glanced back, but his men had already dispensed with the others. "They have met their Maker. What of you?"

The man peered around James and, seeing his claim true, shifted his gaze back to James. "You will let me go?"

*Aye, you coward.*

"I said I would and know you I always give a man my word and keep it."

The man threw the girl at James and ran off into the dark.

"You cannot let him go, Laird James," Ian said, stalking in the direction of the swine.

"Aye, lad. Stand down. I gave my promise. Anna's life was more important." James pulled her onto his horse. "There now, lass. We shall return you to your da's croft and give you and your family safe passage to the keep in case Dunbarton's men plan further mischief this eve."

The young girl clung to him, her body trembling, but the tears had finally ceased. Anna's fear made James reconsider how worried Eilis was about her family knowing her whereabouts. If 'twas a betrothal she didn't wish, he could do little about it, he feared.

Before long he was certain someone would make mention of the lass they'd plucked from the sea. Surely, someone would have been looking into the matter. And the way tales spread, no telling how far the stories would have traveled.

\*\*\*

Much later that eve, James and his party had escorted Anna and her family and all their sheep to Castle Craigly. Niall hurried to greet them, his face brightening to see James return whole.

"Who is the guard for Eilis?" James asked, as he made his way to her chamber door.

"I was keeping vigil."

His heart skipping a beat, James glanced at his cousin.

Niall gave him a shrug. "She did not escape."

"But you came and greeted me upon our arrival and left the door unguarded."

"For only a wee bit."

Clenching his teeth, James shook his head. "The lass would only need a wee bit o' time. Fetch a guard for what's left of the eve."

Neill hurried off down the hall. James grabbed a lighted candle and peeked into the chamber. Not being able to see the ladies in bed for the dark, he walked into the room.

"Tavia," he whispered.

Silence.

He couldn't help but feel the lass had managed to slip away.

"Tavia," he said a little louder, to no avail. He drew closer to the bed, until he was able to see Eilis, her covers down at her waist, her arms bared in the sleeveless chemise, the fabric so sheer he could make out her enticing breasts. He stared at the rounded soft mounds and the rose-colored nipples standing out against the fabric, knowing he should look away but could not.

Tavia stirred, and the ropes holding the mattress creaked.

He glanced in her direction.

"My laird," she whispered, her eyes rounded. "What is the matter?"

"The door was left unguarded. I called out to you, but you did not wake. I had to ensure Eilis was still here."

Tavia looked over at Eilis then raised her brows. "All of her appears to be here, my laird."

The tips of James's ears grew hot.

Tavia smiled. "The herbs I plied her mead with will not wear off 'til late in the morn."

"Aye." He meant to keep his eyes averted and return to his chamber, but he couldn't help himself and glanced down at the lass's angelic look. And a little lower, at the treasures she possessed.

"Good night, my laird," Tavia said, yawning then she rolled onto her side with her back to James.

"Night, Tavia," James muttered, and to ensure a guard was posted, he returned to the hall instead of going through his chamber door.

Ian greeted him with a boyish smile. "Niall gave me guard duty for the lady, my laird."

The lad was excellent at horsemanship, keen with the blade, and a tremendous spy, but when it came to women, they easily got their own way.

James gave him a warning look. "You will not let her pass."

"Aye, my laird. Niall warned me she is as slippery as a pearl."

James shook his head and made his way for his bedchamber. "That the lass is."

After this despicable business with his neighboring clan, another raw concern came to mind. What if the Dunbartons waylaid Catriona's escort?

She and her escort would know the troubles he was having in the land. He rubbed his whiskered chin. He would send some of his men to meet and escort her safely to Castle Craigly. 'Twas the only way he'd be assured of her safe journey.

***

Late the next morning, James found Eilis getting a piece of brown bread from the cook in the kitchen to break her fast, although the rest of his people had done so much earlier in the day. He smiled at her, glad the herbs had worked. "Did you have a good sleep this morn?"

She gave him a scalding look like he'd better not say another word.

He hadn't given the order for Tavia to drug Eilis so she'd sleep the rest of the morning, although if he'd thought of it, he might have done so to keep her from attempting another escape.

As annoyed as she acted, he assumed practicing their charade that she was interested in his hand in marriage would not work this day. Although the way he had mishandled her the night before made him realize he needed to ensure he was never left alone with the lass again.

The swollen knot on her temple had faded considerably, and the skin around her eyes was more of a yellow-greenish color now. Again, he was reminded of the girl he had rescued a couple of years earlier from the incoming tide before she'd been swept into the cave and drowned.

Eilis looked up from the table, and her face blanched. Turning to see what concerned her, James found one of his mother's ladies-in-waiting staring at Eilis. Lady Allison quickly looked at James, curtseyed then headed for the kitchen garden.

"Hold," James said. "You look as if you have seen my father's ghost, Lady Allison. What ails you?"

The woman cast a glance in Eilis's direction, looked at James, turned her gaze to the floor, and quickly shook her head. "Naught, my laird."

"You seem to recognize the lady. Do you know

her?"

"Nay, my laird. 'Twas just that I had not expected anyone to be in the kitchen since the meal has been eaten sometime past. Forgive me, my laird."

If it were not for the fact that Eilis seemed just as distraught to witness Allison as the maid was to see her, he would have assumed the woman was just flighty the way so many of them were when they were in his presence of late.

Even now, Eilis wrung her hands and seemed ready to take wing.

He nodded. Mayhap his mother could speak with the woman when she seemed unwilling to speak with him.

"Verra well, Lady Allison. Continue with whatever you were about." He turned his attention to Eilis. "Come, you and I have work to do as well."

Eilis looked faint, and James smiled. Teach her to keep secrets from him. Before long, he would know all about the lovely lass.

"A moment of your time, lass." James offered his hand to Eilis.

She looked cross but took his hand and rose from the bench. "Tavia had no need to drug my mead last eve."

James cast her a sardonic smile. "Tavia needed her sleep. If you had sent her to fetch for you all night long…" He tsked. "Surely, wherever you are from, you did not mistreat servants thusly."

She scowled further at him.

"I want to know the truth about you, lass. You seem to be recalling some memories. Know you your clan's name now?"

"Nay."

Her eyes challenged him to disagree with her. She appeared to be telling the truth. He led her out of the kitchen and into the garden and took a deep breath of the lavender scenting the air. "But you recognized Allison."

Eilis looked at the ground.

"How do you know Allison?"

"I do not."

"Eilis…," he said, unable to curb the exasperation in his voice.

"I do not," Eilis said sharply, her green eyes spitting fire. "She seemed somewhat familiar, but I do not remember her. I think 'twas the way she looked at me that startled me most. As if she knew me and yet, although I sensed the same about her, I could not capture the reason. How would you feel if you have some memories and some of them are missing? The situation is more than frustrating, my laird."

"Call me James. If we are to pretend you are smitten with me and are boldly pursuing me, we must dispense with proper protocol."

Her eyes rounded.

Aye, he wouldn't mind in Eilis's case if she initiated a kiss or two. "Do you object?"

"In calling you…James, nay. I must learn to get used to it is all."

"Aye, that is the right of it, lass. Do you have a favorite color?"

She glanced down at the green dress she was wearing then looked at James's tunic. Reaching out, she touched it. "Blue like the cloudless sky." She ran her hand over her gown. "And green like the pine needles in the forest."

"Who did you stay with in Glen Affric? You know the area too well not to have been there on frequent occasions. Eanruig believed you did not live permanently in the area, or he would have remembered you better."

She shook her head and observed the flowers, but if he could read her mind, he imagined her thoughts were elsewhere.

"You know your da is dead. What about your mother?"

"Aye," she said softly. "I do not recall how or why I remember they are both dead, but only that they are."

"Who is your guardian?"

"I do not know."

"An uncle?"

She shook her head.

"What about brothers or sisters? Have you any? Mayhap an older brother who is your guardian? A cousin?"

"I do not remember." Then she turned her chin up and asked, "What about yours? I should know more about you also."

"Aye. Malcolm is a year younger than me, then Dougald, and lastly Angus. My brothers are helping Lady Anice with the troubles she has had at Brecken Castle."

"Some of her staff disappeared."

Surprised, he stared at her. "You know of this?"

"I do not remember who, but just that an urgent missive was sent to King Henry since she had become his ward when her uncle died."

"How do you remember some things and not

others?"

She shook her head.

"Tavia said you were tossing and turning overmuch in your sleep." The vision of Eilis's near naked breasts came to mind, and James reluctantly forced the memory from his thoughts. "Do you recall any nightmares?"

"I was drowning. 'Tis easy to know why I would have a nightmare like that."

"Who were you with on the ship? Family? Servants?"

"My laird…"

"James."

"James. I do not know. All I remember was clinging to…" Her words hung in the air, and she quickly looked away.

"What Eilis? You were clinging to…?"

"Bits of the ship's wreckage. Then Eanruig and Niall rescued me, although I do not remember how."

He was certain she'd remembered something else. She was clinging to what? Someone on the ship? Someone she loved?

The ship was being tossed about in a turbulent sea. Wouldn't she have been below deck or in the captain's quarters if her family had paid enough for her voyage?

Most likely the turmoil would have upset her stomach.

"Were you ill? When the ship was being tossed about in the storm?"

"Aye."

So she remembered more than clinging to the ship's remnants after it went down. "Who was with you?"

"I do not recall."

Didn't she? This time he didn't believe her.

He took her arm and started back to the keep when she pulled him to a stop.

Tears glistened in her eyes, and she swallowed hard. "I do not know who the woman was, but she…she said I would bring shame to our clan if I jumped from the ship."

James stared at her then touched her pale cheek. "What did you fear, lass, that you would consider ending your life?"

She broke eye contact and looked at her shoes. "I truly do not remember."

A betrothal, he was certain.

He lifted her chin and met her gaze. "You are too much of a woman to let whatever ails you get the best of you. I promise, I will aid you in anyway I can in dealing with your family."

He leaned down and kissed her full lips. This time she wrapped her arms around his neck and pressed her mouth against his. In gratitude? He groaned at the feelings she stirred in him. With the way she leaned her body against his, his shaft grew rigid, and his skin heated. He'd been so intent on kissing the lass in return, he'd forgotten they'd quit the garden and stood now in the middle of the inner bailey where many of his staff were carrying on their chores for the day.Until he separated from the lass and found nearly every servants' eye upon him and the lady. He cleared his throat while she avoided looking at anyone as he walked her the rest of the way to the keep.

Eilis's cheeks were beautifully colored as she watched her feet all the way back.

He cast her a small smile. "You are getting into the

spirit of our ruse, Eilis. I warrant even my own people believe I might have changed my mind about Catriona."

"But you cannot." She quickened her step into the keep.

"Why not? I can make my own choice."

She turned and looked at him as though he'd lost his mind. "My laird, you do not know me, where I am truly from, or anything. Thinking that you would consider me as a bride choice would be foolishness."

"You are calling me foolish?" He quirked a brow and watched her cheeks blossom with color anew. "I thought not."

She touched his chest and traced the embroidery stitches on his tunic. "Aye, you are foolish if you think you have a chance with me."

Loving the challenge in her words, he smiled. But the way she touched him sent a signal straight to his groin. "Be sure to press your fingers against me like that in front of Catriona, and you will no doubt get her attention." At least, she certainly had his, and he didn't want her to stop.

Horses entering the inner bailey distracted him, and turning, he saw his Aunt Beatrice and her daughter, Nighinn—the cousin he thought to inspect in a month if Catriona would not agree to marry him. Whoever told the lass he wished to see her now?

He would wring whoever's neck was responsible for the difficulties this could cause. With Eilis, the problem did not exist because she had no real plans to wed him. Nighinn could cause a scene with Catriona. If this was Niall's doing, he'd thrash him soundly.

Releasing Eilis to his mother's care, he turned and headed out to deal with Nighinn and his Aunt Beatrice, hopefully to send them back home at once where they belonged.

\*\*\*

The look on James's face when he saw the matronly woman in blue, and a younger woman, just as plump in tow, reminded Eilis of…

For a fleeting instant, she nearly had it. Then the elusive memory was gone but not James's glum expression. Although once he released her to his mother's care, he had put on a false smile and joined the women in the inner bailey.

Lady Akira motioned to Tavia. "Accompany Eilis to her chamber. I will have Fergus sent right up."

She headed outside, and Eilis got the distinct impression the lady was not too entirely pleased to see the arrival of the other women either.

"Who are they?" Eilis asked Tavia, not caring whether she breeched protocol. She still had no intention of staying, especially when James's rakish charm made her whole person burn with desire. 'Twas good he didn't intend to bed her or she no doubt would offer herself as a wanton without a care.

Mayhap Eilis had already thoroughly disgraced her family and was being sent away to wed the man who compromised her. Yet, she couldn't summon any recollection that she'd ever been kissed so…thoroughly.

Tavia followed Eilis into the bedchamber, then shut the door. "The older woman is Laird MacNeill's aunt, Beatrice. A verra shrewd woman and determined that her daughter marry James now that he is earl. She waited until he had turned down the other lassies, but seeing as how James was unable to draw Lady Catriona here, the word must have reached his aunt. I cannot imagine he would have invited her here when Lady Catriona is on her way. I am sure His Lairdship is not pleased about it."

"Mayhap his cousin will force Catriona's hand, and she will agree to marry His Lairdship. Then I will not truly be needed."

Which relieved her to think if she could leave, James could still encourage Catriona's concession. On the other hand, the thought of not being needed weighed heavily on her, like the ship's anchor tossed into the Irish Sea. The notion she didn't belong anywhere was beginning to bother her as much as not knowing why she was afraid her family would discover her.

"Not Nighinn. I dare say Lady Catriona will find it a mockery," Tavia said.

"Why?" Eilis sat on a cushioned bench and pulled her embroidery work from a table. 'Twas generous of Lady Akira to have had a maid fetch Eilis strands of blue, green, and yellow silk and wool threads to use in designing a lion to embroider a cloth that she could hang on the wall. Although, she had not had much time to work on it.

Tavia said, "I…"

A knocking at the door made Eilis jump.

Tavia answered it, and after listening to a servant, she said to Eilis, "I must see to a lady in childbirth. Fergus is here so if you need anything, let him know."

Eilis nodded, although she assumed if she needed anything, Fergus would not oblige her if it meant leaving her alone for even an instant. When Tavia shut the door, Eilis jumped from the bench and rushed to the window. Although clouds covered the sky, making for a gray day, she didn't think she could slip out of the keep unnoticed.

Then again, if everyone was busy with James's kin and they thought someone was with Eilis in her bedchamber...

She glanced at James's chamber. And smiled. Aye, she could slip out that way and make her way through the keep, mayhap.

Without wasting another moment, she hurried to his chamber, yanked the door open, and froze.

Standing in the center of the chamber, James was utterly naked from his broad shoulders and dark-haired chest trailing all the way to his shaft. She blinked, never having had seen a naked man before or at least not that she could recall.

Then like a flash of a dream, like one of her strange memories that was there then was not, James's glorious body vanished along with the chamber and everything else as if the flame of the lighted candle of her mind suddenly was snuffed out.

# CHAPTER 8

"God's wounds, Eilis," James's growled close to her face as she lay on her mattress, his voice sounding far away, only his warm breath fanned across her hair as she attempted to recall what had just happened.

Her lashes fluttered, and in a dense fog, she saw James's furrowed brow and the angry set of his mouth.

"Were you looking for me again?" he asked, his voice gruff.

Her mind clearing, she shifted her attention from his brooding face to his bronzed chest, every muscle in his torso straining with tension. She looked further down, but his plaid brat now hung low on his hips. She imagined he must have carried her into her chamber after she fainted dead away, then returned to his own room to throw on his brat before he came back to scold her. She licked her dry lips and swallowed hard, unable to lift her gaze and face his condemning expression.

Why did he have to be in his chamber? Naked?

"Eilis?"

"Aye," she said, her voice catching in her throat. He would know she was again attempting escape.

"If you wish to take the charade further..."

He let his words hang ominously in the tension strung out between them.

Her gaze shot up, her cheeks burning. "Nay."

He cast her the most deliciously sexy, but decidedly wicked smile. "'Tis up to you, lass. Only give the word." Taking her hand, he lifted the palm to his lips. He pressed his mouth against her hand, his gaze never leaving hers. "If you continue to venture into my chamber while I am in various states of undress, I will assume you wish to join me in my bed."

The message was clear. Quit trying to escape through his chamber or else...

He traced her jaw with his fingers in a tender way, forcing a thrill through her. "Did you like what you saw?"

Before she could find her tongue, the door opened, and a female servant gasped. "Pray pardon, my laird. Tavia sent me to..." She lowered her eyes. "...to watch over the lady."

"She was momentarily indisposed. But I believe the color is returning to her pale cheeks. You may help her get ready for the meal, however, Nesta."

"Aye, my laird." Nesta bobbed a curtsey, then James disappeared into his chamber and shut the door.

Eilis still couldn't catch her breath, her heart racing like the sea's swift tide.

"You look flushed," Nesta said, tucking a wayward red curl back into her braid. "But then seeing His Lairdship..." The girl quit fussing with her kirtle, and her green eyes widened. "Oh, pray pardon. I meant no disrespect, my lady. Only I, well, seeing his Lairdship in only his plaid and naught else…"

Now Nesta's face blossomed with color. "Let me dress you in a fresh gown, afore I say more than I ought to. Not than I have not already."

Eilis gave a small smile, glad the woman could fill the silence, because she couldn't summon her tongue to speak a word.

While the woman rebraided Eilis's hair, Eilis sat quietly on the bench, her gaze fixed on James's door, only she envisioned *him*, not the door, as she remembered the look of his unclothed body. If she were betrothed, she hoped the man would look like James. Powerful shoulders and muscular arms strong enough to wield a sword against his enemies and carry a damsel in peril to safety, a bronzed chest furred lightly in dark hair trailing to the apex of his thighs. She thought he had large feet that suited the rest of his form, but she couldn't be sure because of the staff he carried between his legs. 'Twas as beautiful as the rest of him.

"…but Lady Beatrice is Laird MacNeill's da's sister, and she and his da never got along. His father was a rake, left his mother all on her own to raise the four boys and her nephew, Niall, when his parents died," Nesta continued, and Eilis realized the lady had been talking the whole while, but she'd missed quite a bit of the conversation. The lady didn't seem to notice.

"I have to say, Lady Akira is anxious to get His Lairdship married off so he will provide an heir, but I do not believe Lady Beatrice's arrival was planned and even Lady Akira, who is always very gracious, seems not at all pleased. I can see…"

Footsteps sounded down the hall, drawing closer

and closer, then stopped before the door. A muffled voice spoke to someone, most likely James speaking with Fergus. Would he tell him Eilis was not to be trusted as she continued to attempt to escape through his chamber?

"We all know His Lairdship is interested in Lady Catriona, but she will surely be upset when she sees you have her room," Nesta said.

"She has stayed here before?" Eilis asked, unable to hide her surprise. The rake! He had already been with Catriona? What need had he of Eilis then? If he was as good a lover as she assumed he was the way he charmed her without even trying, the woman would join him in his bed or he in hers, and Eilis had no need to be here.

The realization that Catriona had been here before in the chamber adjoining the laird's could mean only one thing. James had access to Eilis just as easily as he had to Catriona. Not that there was any cause for concern since Eilis was being chaperoned nearly all of the time, and the only times she had intruded on His Lairdship's chamber was with the mission of escaping. But Catriona would not know it and would be incensed.

Someone knocked on the door.

Eilis jumped.

"Aye, Lady Catriona has been here several times," Nesta said, then hurried to get the door. "My laird." She bobbed a curtsy.

"Is Eilis ready?" James asked, his tone abrupt.

"Aye, my laird," Nesta said.

She opened the door wider, and Eilis rose from the bench. She raised her chin and challenged his smug smile and saw his eyes bright with humor. He must not have been angered with her then. Although the look in his eyes indicated his thoughts were still on their bedchamber encounter. Discomfited anew, she felt her skin heat.

Joining him, she rested her hand on his arm with a feather-light touch, then walked with him to the great hall, but she feared the meal would not digest properly. Not only because of the realization James had a more than distant relationship with Catriona, although why it should have mattered she couldn't fathom. But once his cousin saw the way James treated Eilis with fondness, she feared the lady would not take it well.

When they entered the hall, everyone grew quiet and greeted Laird MacNeill and cast speculating glances at Eilis.'Twas the icy stares Eilis received from James's aunt and cousin that caused her the most discomfort.

Now that she could see a little more of the women, she noted Nighinn's expression from the downturn of her lips to the narrowed blue eyes as frozen as the loch on a winter's day. Dark hair was pulled back tight against her head, emphasizing full ruddy cheeks and the woman's nose three sizes too small for her face. Her saving grace was her startling blue eyes, if they weren't so condemning.

Her mother looked similar—except she was taller and broader. Both wore gowns befitting royalty. Mayhap to impress James and his people?

When Eilis discretely looked away from James's aunt and cousin, she saw Nesta speaking with three women, which garnered her immediate attention. She couldn't be telling them what she'd seen transpire between Eilis and James. Could she?

The ladies turned to observe James and her, their eyes wide, brows raised. Eilis felt as if she'd been slaving over a cauldron of boiling beef all day. The women turned to talk to others and surprised expressions filled faces all along the table, then small smiles accompanied the news. Before long, the word began spreading from table to table. Eilis was certain the news would cover the farthest reaches of the MacNeill's land before everyone retired for the eve, that James was found half-naked with Eilis in the guest chamber, and he had undoubtedly bedded the lass.

If she could have enjoyed the experience, at least that would be something, but to be innocent and presumed wanton... She glanced at James and found him enjoying his new notoriety. She quickly pulled her hand from his arm and sat at the head table beside him. Which thankfully blocked her view of Nighinn whose very glare threatened to slice Eilis in two.

"Who is she?" Nighinn spat.

The woman's shrewish words were not the way to a man's heart, Eilis thought.

"She is Eilis McLennan of Glen Affric."

So James did not wish to let his cousin know she was a MacNeill also, although she was not truly one of his distant kin, she didn't think.

"What is she doing here?"

"Visiting much the same as you are, Nighinn." He buttered a slice of bread and smiled at Eilis.

She couldn't shake loose the notion that the days would progress badly if his cousin stayed here for very long.

"She looks pale and thin. She is not ill, is she?" Nighinn asked, her voice haughty.

James glanced at Eilis and quirked a brow, his mouth turning up at the same time. "Nay, her cheeks are quite rosy."

"A fever?" Nighinn quickly responded, implying Eilis should be whisked away from the table at once.

He smiled at Eilis, and aye, the feverish way her body felt grew even hotter. Then her embarrassment turned to anger that the ruddy-cheeked cousin would attempt to intimidate her. Eilis would leave before long, but she could play His Lairdship's game just fine.

James reached for his goblet, and Eilis touched his hand with a tender caress. "'Twas kind of you to take care of me when I became indisposed."

His brows shot up at her forwardness in front of his people. Then a sinister glint appeared in his dark eyes. He leaned over, and his honey mead breath caressed her ear. "You will not leave here until I command it, lass. I am verra well aware of your maneuvers."

Not expecting that kind of a response, she scowled back at him.

He took her hand and pressed his lips to the tender skin at her wrist, making her breath hitch. He would be just like his father, she imagined, taking a wife, leaving her with a castle full of heirs, but finding his pleasure in other women's arms at night.

"Your thoughts, Eilis?" he asked for her ears only.

She took a deep breath. "Nesta will have told all your people what she saw."

"Nay," he said, with a devilish smirk.

"Aye. She has already told the ladies closest to her, and the word is spreading."

Nesta was again speaking at the lower table to one of the women while two others leaned in to hear what she had to say. Eilis imagined 'twas not good. The women sitting close to Nesta had wide-eyed expressions as they shot looks James's and Eilis's way. What more could Nesta be saying? 'Twas Eilis's misfortune that Nesta had come to serve her at such an inopportune time.

James patted Eilis's hand, which did not go unnoticed by many of James's people. "Nesta is a great weaver of tales. I assure you, she will elaborate much more, and the story will grow into an epic tale."

Groaning, Eilis drank several gulps of her mead. "You are trying to shame me."

"I am not the one who barged into your chamber whilst you were naked, lass. When you fainted, what choice had I but to catch you and carry you back to your bed? Of course, I donned my plaid before I woke you, worried that had I not worn it, you might faint again." He smiled as the heat returned to her face. "Did you like what you saw?"

She tried to gather her composure to appear unaffected, although the way her cheeks burned, her efforts were in vain. "I have naught to compare you with. I imagine every man is the same as any other."

James laughed out loud.

Nighinn leaned over to James and said something Eilis didn't hear, but it was Eanruig's arrival that caused her heart to stand still. He looked at James, nodded, then smiled at Eilis with smug satisfaction.

In that instant, she knew he had found out who she was, and although she wanted to bolt, James must have surmised as much and clamped his hand around her wrist.

"Appears we may have some news, lass. Mayhap

even good."

She knew deep in her heart the news could not be good. She felt it with the tightening of her muscles, with the skittering of her heart, and the way her mind sorted through options. Escape remained the only alternative to her way of thinking.

For now, she stiffened her back, waiting to hear who she was and dreaded learning the truth.

\*\*\*

Dougald MacNeill drank some more of the wormy gruel, knowing he needed any sustenance he could get if he was to keep his strength in the Dunbarton's dungeon and ultimately make his escape. He had no intention of being bartered for ransom.

The dark, dank place smelled of human waste, although Dougald thought he was becoming accustomed to the stench because it didn't seem quite so odorous. Now that his eye was less swollen and his head pained him a wee bit less, he considered his surroundings.

Groundwater seeped through the stone walls covered in green moss, and the air was cold and damp. Chill bumps covered his bare skin. A sliver of light from a barred window high above and the torches flickering in the hall outside the cell kept the tiny room shadowed in gloom. He devoured the rest of his gruel, angered that a battle-hardened warrior and not a sweet lassie had delivered the putrid tasting stuff.

"Have you come up with a plan yet?" Gunnolf grumbled from his cell across the hall. "I will be laid to waste if I have to endure another bowl of this slop."

"I am still attempting to remove the chains from my—"

The door creaked open down the hall, and Dougald waited, the tension building in his muscles as he prepared himself to spring on anyone who might get near him. If he didn't attempt escape soon, he feared he'd be too weak.

The telltale light footfalls of a lassie taking one step, then another, made him smile. He knew Gunnolf would be smiling his fool head off.

When the small lass finally appeared before Dougald's cell, he swore a golden halo radiated above her dark curls. Wearing a brown woolen kirtle, she looked like she served on Dunbarton's staff. Doe-like eyes betrayed fear and intrigue.

"Lass," he whispered, hoping his voice would shake her from the way her dark eyes devoured his nakedness.

Her eyes shot up, caught his, then her hands shook as she fumbled with a key in the lock. She trembled so hard, he feared she'd never get the lock open before she was caught. Then, as if deciding it was now or never, she managed, yanked the lock free, and rushed across the floor to join him. She attempted to unlock the manacles around his wrists and ankles, her hands shaking just as hard as before while her silky hair tickled his chest.

Slightly built, pretty of face, and smelling of sweet waters, the maid was truly a heavenly apparition.

Once she freed him, he tossed the chains aside and took her wrist, then led her to Gunnolf's cell in a rush. She shook her head. "Not him."

"Aye. He will come with me. I will not leave him behind." Dougald took the keys from her and freed his friend. "What is the plan, lass?" At least he hoped she had a plan if she'd made it this far without being stopped.

"I will lead you out of the castle while Laird Dunbarton is having a grand feast in celebrating your capture. But I can do no more for you. You will have a long way to travel on foot."

"Without clothes or weapons?" Dougald asked.

She looked up from his nudity and pointed to a bundle on the floor. "Some of the servants' clothes. They are not much but will have to do."

They grabbed the bundle of the mended and tattered woolen garments and shoved them on while the lass watched for signs of trouble.

"What about the guards?"

"Sleeping. I know a potion or two."

"Your name, lass?"

"Allison," she said. "Speak not from here on out. We must be silent."

Dougald kept feeling it was some kind of trick, and the shared look Gunnolf gave him assured him he felt as uneasy. But no one gave them a second glance while busily imbibing ale, laughing and joking about capturing the MacNeill and Viking as Dougald, Gunnolf, and the lass hastened out of the keep into the inner bailey. They quickly made their way to the outer bailey, and once they were beyond the curtain wall, he and Gunnolf were free men. He glanced over his shoulder, but before he could thank the lass, Allison had disappeared back inside.

Not wanting to alert anyone, they stalked through the grass, wanting to run, but quelling the urge as they made their way west toward Castle Craigly. In the distance, the ancient forest loomed and would provide them relative safety if they could reach it in time. With a lot of luck, they would arrive on the MacNeill land by midday tomorrow.

Shouts from the wall walk made Dougald's heart race even harder. Forced to sprint for the forest, he prayed they had not been sighted so soon and that the agitated yelling was for some other reason having naught to do with Dougald and Gunnolf's escape.

# CHAPTER 9

Had Eanruig located the woman in Glen Affric acquainted with Eilis or not? James assumed he had by the satisfied smile he had cast Eilisa while they were seated at the table, eating their meal.

Eanruig crossed the hall to stand beside James and glanced in Eilis's direction, then said to James, "My laird, may I have a word with you in private? I have some information, but..."

'Twas not good, he surmised from the disturbed tone of Eanruig's voice. James rose from his chair. "Continue with your meal," he said to his people.

His muscles rippling with tension, James stalked out of the hall with Eanruig by his side.

"What did you find?" James asked, barely able to suppress his anxiousness.

"I believe I have found a young woman who knows the lass."

James narrowed his eyes. "You *believe*?"

"Aye. A woman named Fia denied she knew her. Fia is the niece of a woman who married one of my cousins. She is around Eilis's age but dark haired and eyed and doesn't look at all like Eilis. I had hoped they were related, but I was afraid to ask too many questions just as you had warned."

James raised his brows. "And?"

Eanruig cleared his throat. "Fia grew flustered, as if she were lying. She was clearly distraught, and I am sure she is the one I saw with Eilis last summer. When I first questioned Fia, she seemed reluctant to speak of her. When I mentioned the shipwreck and how we had rescued the lady, the lass seemed overjoyed. Her expression quickly changed, and again she denied knowing her."

"I want her brought here. We will see if she can continue this mockery when the two women are reunited."

"How will I be able to convince her da the woman should be allowed to come here, my laird?"

"Is the lass married?"

"Nay, and not betrothed either."

"Tell Fia's da I wish to consider her as a bride choice. Not that I want to give the lady false hope or that I would be interested, but I must know who Eilis truly is."

"Aye, my laird. I will send an escort for her at once."

James motioned to a servant. "Bring a meal for both Eanruig and me to my solar."

"Aye, my lord." The man rushed off to the kitchen.

"What news have you of my brothers?" James asked, unable to wait to hear the news in the privacy of his solar, although there was no one about as most were at the meal.

He and Eanruig headed up the stairs.

"Angus was injured in a fight with some of Robert Curthose's men, but his injuries will heal, and he will have use of his sword arm before long."

James sat down at his desk in the small room and motioned to another chair. "And the others?" Although the news about Angus was not the best, he gathered from Eanruig's furrowed brow it was not the worst.

"Malcolm married Lady Anice."

James closed his gaping mouth. "My brother has a death wish? I release my brothers from my service to find English brides and what does Malcolm do? He marries a Scottish lady, ward of King Henry I, who wishes her wed to one of his Norman barons? Here I have my own battles to fight, and now I will have to take up arms against the English king to save my brother's neck? Whatever possessed him to do such a foolhardy thing?"

"He would not give me the details, but he did receive King Henry's permission, after the fact."

Unable to believe it, James stared at his seneschal. In all the years he'd protected Malcolm and his brother

123

had done the same for him, not once had Malcolm acted in any manner, well, rash, when it came to dealing with a woman. He'd had his share of lovely lasses, aye, but to lose his head over King Henry's ward and then claim her before getting the sovereign's permission?

"God's teeth, I did not think Malcolm had it in him! This calls for a celebration, although my mother will be furious to learn of this when she was not invited to the wedding. And why is Malcolm not here to assist me? Lady Anice has already shackled him to her wedding bed?" He smiled at the thought. Not such a bad reason at that if he had Catriona in his own.

"She has had some trouble with a Laird Robertson, and Malcolm did not wish to leave her alone until he dealt with the matter."

Servants carried in trays of food, and James seized the mug of mead and took a swig. After dismissing the servants, James turned his attention to Eanruig. "You have not told me about Dougald."

"Nay, my laird. Both he and Gunnolf should have arrived here already."

A sickening feeling swamped him, yet, James couldn't believe his brother and Gunnolf could be dead. He would not believe it. He slammed down his mug. "Get as many men together as we can. We search for my brother and Gunnolf at once."

***

Eilis couldn't eat a bite of her food when James and Eanruig returned to the great hall. Everyone watched their laird as concerned as she was.

James leaned over to whisper something in his mother's ear then kissed her cheek. He glanced at Eilis, but he hid his feelings well, and she couldn't tell what the matter was. Then he stalked out of the hall while Eanruig spread the word about the trouble. All the men began rising from their benches and followed James out of the hall, like sheep following their sheepherder, only they looked ready to do battle with some unseen force.

Dunbarton's men again?

Lady Beatrice was speaking to Lady Akira about the matter, Eilis was certain, but she couldn't hear their words. At first, Nighinn listened to her mother and Lady Akira's conversation but then she turned to Eilis and gave her an icy glower.

"Ye are not from a clan James is considering to tie with his own through marriage."

Eilis didn't intend to respond, but Lady Akira was closely watching Nighinn. As if she feared Eilis might say the wrong thing and ruin the charade, Lady Akira abruptly rose from her chair and ended the meal.

Which, considering most of the men had left and the women were in a tither over the matter, was just as well. Besides, Eilis was grateful she didn't have to contend with James's cousin for a moment longer.

The best news was Tavia was nowhere in sight, and Eilis assumed the healer was still with the lady who needed her help in delivering her bairn. Even Fergus had left with James, and it appeared Eilis finally had a means of escape.

But Lady Akira motioned to Nesta, and when the maid joined her, she said, "Stay with Eilis."

"Aye, my lady."

Och, of all the women to serve Eilis, why the woman who wove the greatest tales? Still, there were no men sent to guard Eilis and...

His expression concerned, Niall reappeared and crossed the hall to join them. Before he even spoke a word, Eilis's heart sank.

He said to his aunt, "James asked me to stay and take charge here in his absence." He glanced at Eilis, and she knew he meant to foil her plot.

"Aye. See that Eilis is taken to her chamber. I hear she became indisposed earlier, and she must rest further." Lady Akira's dark eyes studied Eilis.

She couldn't discern how his mother felt about Nesta's accusations.

As kind as she'd been in taking Eilis in, she hoped the lady was not too perturbed with her. Lady Akira, Lady Beatrice, and Nighinn hurried off, while Niall, his mouth turned up slightly, his dark eyes even darker, escorted Eilis back to her chamber. Nesta trailed behind them.

"I believe," Niall said, his words lowered for Eilis's hearing only, "Lady Catriona is already too late in coming." A devilish lift to his lips and a glint in his eyes indicated his amusement.

She was much relieved he made the comment only

for her, because she knew if Nesta had caught his words, the tale would be all over the castle by morn. Eilis worried about the way Niall spoke low to her, his mouth a hair's breadth away from her ear. What if Nesta would make something more of their relationship also?

"You think Nighinn has caught His Lairdship's eye?" Eilis asked demurely.

Niall gave a short laugh. "Playing the innocent does not become you, dear lass."

Och, she could slug the rogue if it were not that Nesta would tell everyone and it would get back to James. Then he'd want to know why she had struck his cousin. She was certain James would not appreciate his cousin's teasing her. She wanted to ask Niall what he meant, but she didn't truly want to hear what she feared everyone was saying.

"Nesta, straighten the chamber." Niall motioned to the guest chamber.

"Aye, my laird." Furrowing her brow, Nesta didn't look happy to be dismissed.

After he shut the chamber door, he led Eilis to James's chamber, and her heart beat wildly. Surely, he did not think she had succumbed to James's charms and now would Niall's? In James's own chamber, for heaven's sakes?

Niall shut James's door. "Who is Fia?" He leaned against the solid wood, his arms folded.

She couldn't have been more surprised when he

asked about Fia and apparently had no notion of attempting to seduce her. Her heart slowed with the realization.

He was handsome and arrogant, just like James, but she would not be forced to say a thing. How could she? She didn't have a clue who Fia was.

"The lady in Glen Affric?" Niall persisted. "She has kin who married into Eanruig's line. I did not get the whole story because James and Eanruig had to rush off—"

"Why?"

"His brother, Dougald, is long overdue in arriving here."

Her mouth dropped, and the notion that his brother might be in trouble made her forget her own woes for the moment. "His brother? What of the others?"

"They were still at Castle Brecken. Dougald traveled with Gunnolf, a friend, and both are missing."

"I...I am sorry."

"Aye, so about this Fia..."

"I do not know any Fia."

Niall cast her a small smile. "Somehow, lass, I knew you would say that." He gave her a nonchalant shrug. "Then I will have to wait until Eanruig returns to hear the whole story."

"Do you not worry about Dougald and the other?"

"Nay. I fear more for whoever tangles with the two of them." Niall escorted her to her chamber and bowed his head. "Until later, lass. Although without James around, I imagine you will not become indisposed again." He smiled. "Lady Catriona will be a terror when she sees you."

He shut the door on his departure, and as soon as he did, Nesta began talking. "'Tis a shame about Dougald and Gunnolf. I hope His Lairdship finds them in one piece, or there will be another battle waged like the one twenty summers ago when I was but a wee lass. 'Twas a horrible thing with heavy losses on both..."

Someone knocked on the door.

"...sides. We have been fortunate not to have another one so terrible as that." Nesta opened the door and curtsied.

Her face flushed, Nighinn walked into the chamber without invitation. Her blue eyes still glittered with menace. Since she was James's cousin, Eilis didn't feel she had any right in telling the woman to go away. Yet that's what she would have done had the circumstances been different.

"Fetch us some mead," Nighinn ordered Nesta.

Nesta glanced at Eilis, her dark eyes worried, but then she hurriedly obeyed.

When the door closed, Nighinn remained standing, her hands clenched tightly together. "I have learned from the servants that James is keeping you under guard in this chamber. Why, if you are seeking James's hand, would that be so?"

"Mayhap His Lairdship is concerned I will have unwelcome visitors to my chamber."

The woman's lips lifted slightly, but her eyes remained flat. "Mayhap 'tis because you are his prisoner. 'Twould be in my best interest to help you leave here. He should not be keeping you against your will."

Hope skittered through Eilis that she might have a chance to leave this place far behind. But she really didn't trust James's cousin. On the other hand, she might not have any better means of escape. Rashly, she said, "I accept." And prayed she wouldn't regret her hasty decision.

For the first time since Eilis had met her, Nighinn gave her a full-fledged smile. It wasn't a pleasant smile, rather one borne of contempt, with a hint of greedy design. "Excellent. Niall is looking for someone to serve as your guard. Come with me to my chamber before Nesta returns. You can change into my riding gown and cloak, and I will have one of my men escort you in whichever direction you wish to take. As long as 'tis far away from here. Let us no' tarry any longer."

Eilis should have been elated to be able to leave without James's knowledge so why was she having a sliver of a doubt? Then she reminded herself he wanted Catriona. Nighinn could ensure Catriona wanted James in return. Or not. It was his problem, not Eilis's.

She had far worse considerations, finding a safe haven before James and his people learned who she truly was and turned her over to her kin.

\*\*\*

In Nighinn's guest chamber, Eilis quickly changed out of Jame's sister's gown and into the brown woolen traveling kirtle Nighinn had worn. The fabric gaped at her bodice, and the hem of the skirt puddled in folds at her feet. Worse, it smelled of sweat and horse.

Nighinn's frown deepened. "Ye will have to use the belt to tighten the garment around ye." She tsked. "I can see James would no' wish such a bony bride. Do hurry or Niall will discover our...ploy."

Eilis touched the belt since it belonged to James's sister. She didn't wish to take anything with her, just as she didn't want to take the lady's clothes. But Nighinn's gown would fall off if she didn't secure it with the belt.

Nighinn fingered a brown woolen cloak. "It pains me to have to give away my favorite traveling clothes. Although I...have no choice." She shoved it at Eilis. "Hurry, put it on." She motioned to her maid. "Tell Cyn to gather two more men and ready four horses. Have him speak with me at once."

"Aye, my lady." The maid rushed out of the chamber.

Nighinn wrung her hands.

Her own stomach fluttering with anxiety, Eilis went to the window and peered out at the inner bailey below. Niall would surely stop her before she even left the keep.

"Come on." Nighinn strode for the door. "We will meet my men at the stable." She jerked her head around. "Wear the cloak and hide your face, for heaven's sake."

After they left the chamber, she led Eilis down a set of back stairs. Despite her rounded figure, Nighinn stalked through the keep at a rapid pace, her focus straight ahead.

Servants glanced in their direction, and Eilis feared someone would warn Niall she was about to escape. No one made a move to stop them, apparently not recognizing her, thank the heavens. Before long, Nighinn and Eilis were beyond the keep.

Dark clouds covered the sky, and the air was laden with moisture. Wind whipped about linens hanging to dry.

"You might get a rain," Nighinn warned, her words pleased. "Cyn, you will take the lady to..." Nighinn paused, when a couple of stable boys milled about within earshot. The rest of the conversation she spoke low so that even Eilis could not hear her words.

What if James's cousin wished her men to murder Eilis, not just remove her from the castle? She was about to change her mind when Cyn glanced at her, then looked back at Nighinn and gave a sharp nod.

Before Eilis could react, Cyn whipped around, grasped her by the waist, and lifted her onto a saddle. Nighinn turned and scurried back into the keep without a backward glance.

"Come," Cyn gruffly ordered. "Away with us at once."

Mounted, they trotted out of the bailey. The hood of Nighinn's cloak sufficiently hid Eilis's face as she rode between the other two men in the escort while Cyn led the way. Were the men posted on the wall walk watching their progress? Would someone stop them?

"Hold, mon!" a gruff male voice snapped, motioning to Cyn.

A tremble slivered down Eilis's spine.

"Lady Nighinn wishes a ride," Cyn said. "Let us pass."

Eilis kept her lashes lowered and avoided looking at the men who had stopped them.

"Ride not far from here as Dunbarton's men are wreaking havoc at the MacNeill borders."

"Aye, only a short ride." Cyn again drove his horse forth, the rest of her escort and Eilis cantering to catch up. Eilis wasn't sure if she should be relieved she'd made it this far or more concerned.

As soon as they left the outer bailey, she rode up to join Cyn. "Where did Nighinn tell you to escort me?"

"The nearest village. From there, ye will have to make your own way." Sour faced, scraggly like a horny toad, his lips thinned and his eyes ice blue with contempt, Cyn stared straight ahead and said not another word.

The cold forced another shiver through her as she huddled closer to her horse. A crack of thunder broke overhead, and Eilis stifled a gasp. Then the deluge of rain began. Her head bowed, she tried to keep the rain from dripping over the hood into her eyes, but the winds whipped this way and that and, after several minutes, it ran down her throat into Nighinn's gaping gown.

"Will you show me the way to Glen Affric?" Mayhap she could find Fia, her memories, and a way out of this mess.

"Aye, I will point out the way from the village."

And then he spoke no more. She was too cold to care and concentrated on clutching the cloak to her throat, trying to keep the rainwater from running down the gown any further.

But a couple of hours into their journey, riding through soggy heather in the glen with the rain pounding relentlessly, she glanced about to see where Cyn was. Gone. She looked back over her shoulder. All of the men had slipped away.

# CHAPTER 10

A twinge of panic attacked Eilis as she halted her horse in the middle of nowhere, wondering where she was as the rain continued to soak her through and through. Now she realized how vulnerable she could be alone without an escort, unprotected. She suppressed the impulse to turn around and seek the shelter of Craigly Castle.

Had Nighinn hoped something untoward would happen to her, unescorted as she was? She didn't doubt it.

With another ripple of shivers cascading down her spine, she pulled the cloak tighter and hoped when she finally dismounted, Nighinn's gown wouldn't fall off her it was so big. But she was glad to leave James's sister's gowns behind. They were not given to her to keep and mayhap Catriona could wear them some day.

Eilis bit back the fit of jealousy that swamped her. She had no right to feel any way concerning James and Catriona's relationship. He wanted her for his wife, and

Eilis was unimportant in the scheme of things except as a means to an end.

With that dismal thought and the cold rainwater running down her face and gown, she reflected how terrible it was to have nobody to care for and no one to care for her in return.

The cold wind whipped the hood off her head, and the rain doused her hair. With numbed fingers, she struggled to pull the hood back in place.

A horse whinnied some distance off. Cyn and his men? Mayhap they were looking for her? Heart racing, she jerked her head around, but saw no one, just sheets of gray water so heavy, she couldn't make out the lay of the land. What if it was James or one of his men searching for his brother? Och, she hadn't considered that. She turned her mount away from the sound of the horse. What if she ran into the search party? Mayhap they wouldn't recognize her.

Nay, they wouldn't. She imagined she looked as drowned as when Eanruig and Niall pulled her from the sea. *Eanruig.* Aye, he would recognize her.

More horses whinnied, and men shouted over the wailing wind. She couldn't make out their words though, and because she couldn't see them, she presumed they couldn't see her, which gave her a shred of relief.

Heading farther away from the men, she hoped she wasn't riding in a circle and looping back in the direction of Craigly Castle. She nudged her horse into a grove of trees and prayed the branches and needle-like leaves of the larch would deflect some of the drenching rain. When she dipped her head to keep the rain off her face, she saw a cave half hidden by underbrush. Did wild animals live there?

To get out of the wind and rain, she'd take her chances as cold and wet as she was. After slipping off the horse, she tied him to a branch, then ducked inside the cave. 'Twas so dark, she could see naught but groped along the rugged walls until she was well away from the entrance and out of the wind. But still, she was chilled to the bone, and inside the cave it was even colder.

What she wouldn't have given for a fire and dry...

She tilted her head up and sniffed. The smell of smoke drifted in the chilly, damp air. She froze. Then faint light deeper in the cave caught her eye. Before she could flee, a giant of a man rounded the crag, rushed her, and covered her mouth, stifling her scream. He lifted her into his arms as if she were naught but a cloth doll and stalked deeper into the cavern.

Although she craved telling the man to let her go, she feared he'd harm her so she bit her tongue and said naught. Mayhap she could talk her way out of this, after she dried her clothes by his fire.

The way his blue eyes speared her with intrigue, she thought mayhap not. His blond hair hung loosely about his broad shoulders, and his sturdy build and blue eyes reminded her of a Norseman. She briefly wondered what he'd be doing in these parts. Although the worry about what he intended to do with her soon made her think of naught else.

His footfalls echoed off the rock, and the fire crackled and popped in the distance. She shivered from the cold and fear.

When the roof of the cave reached downward, the man stooped low, holding her closer to his body. His heat slightly warmed her, his actions reminding her of James when he carried her into the keep after she attempted her first escape. She shivered again in a man's warm embrace but wished she was in James's protective arms instead. Even though the Norseman didn't scowl at her like James had.

In a darkened corner of the cave, a man's abrupt laughter erupted. She jerked her head around to see who it was.

Long dark hair and eyes the color of a mink watched her. His bemused expression and build reminded her of James. His brother? Dougald?

"I am usually the one to catch the lasses so quickly, but do you not think in our current predicament this is neither the time nor the place for such frivolities, Gunnolf?" His smile broadened, and his eyes sparkled with mischief.

Gunnolf? Wasn't he the man traveling with James's brother? Praise be to God they were safe.

"Ja, but I thought she was one of them," the Norseman said, his mouth curving upward as he set her on her feet next to the fire.

She rubbed her arms and moved even closer to the flames.

"Aye, she looks very much like a hardened warrior, minus a sword. Unless you already disarmed the lass and dropped the sword yonder." The man's dark eyes caught and held her attention as he strode across the cavern and joined them. Just as beautiful as James, the same way he walked, with purpose and nobility…and charm.

The Highlander pulled off her cloak, and she squeaked, the sound bouncing off the limestone walls.

"You will catch your death, lass." He shook her cloak out, sending water droplets flying, some sparking the fire. He set the garment next to the flames.

"You are Dougald?" Eilis asked, her breath in her throat.

He raised his brows. "Do not tell me my brother has sent you to rescue me?" He cocked his head to the side and considered her gown, the fabric voluminous enough to attire two women, clinging now to her shivering form.

"You need to remove your gown, lass, or you will become ill."

"Nay." She vigorously shook her head.

Dougald shrugged out of his worn tunic, revealing his naked torso, as bronzed as James was, and now wearing only a pair of trewes. "You will learn I am not easily dissuaded when a lass's health is at risk." He handed his tunic to her. "We will turn our backs."

Her skin flushed with heat, she hurriedly yanked the wet gown down to her feet then pulled off the skin-clinging shift. After slipping Dougald's tunic over her head, his own body heat still warming the wool, she laid her garments beside the fire.

"I...I am dressed." Although in a man's short tunic she felt nearly as naked as when she had no clothes on at all and still felt chilled to the very depths of her person.

Dressed only in the pair of ragged, checkered trewes, Dougald retook his seat by the fire. The light of the flames glistened off his skin and the moist walls. The wind howled eerily at the entrance to the cave, muffled by the thick rugged stone. Droplets of water dripped off daggers of rock clinging to the ceiling into shallow pools. The fire spit and crackled as she stretched her fingers over the scant warmth.

"Now, explain why you are out in this weather all alone," Dougald commanded, as authoritative as James would be. Did all his brothers sound the same?

Gunnolf considered her nearly sheer shift lying beside the fire, a small smile tugging at his lips. She had heard men oft had the most wicked thoughts about women even when they were fully clothed, but God's knees she wasn't even *half* dressed.

"Sit." Dougald motioned to a natural stone bench situated next to the fire.

She took a seat. "James and his men are searching for you. They might be quite close."

His eyes dark, Dougald frowned. "You have not explained what you are doing out here all by your wee self, lass."

"I have business that is none of your concern," she snapped.

Gunnolf smiled. "'Tis not that James has upset another wee lassie who belongs to some clan chief who wishes James to marry, eh?"

"Of course not!" She glowered at Gunnolf. "He is marrying Lady Catriona who should be here…soon. His cousin, Nighinn is trying to win his hand, if the marriage fails to occur with Catriona."

"Nighinn?" Dougald groaned. "Not her."

"Aye and Lady Beatrice is there."

"James would not allow a bonny lass such as yourself to travel alone across his lands." Dougald leaned closer to the fire, and the flames danced off his eyes, entrancing her.

Yet there was something about James that had

Dougald beat. She couldn't decide what it was. Mayhap that James was angry with her more oft than not which inspired her own temper to flare, making her feel full of life. And he did not use his rakish charms on her *overmuch*. Dougald did not even know her, yet he was trying to exploit his handsome features to seduce her.

"I had an escort, but I lost the three men."

"Three men? Not enough to protect a lovely lass," Dougald said, his gaze so intense, she felt he wished to force the truth from her with just a look.

She again took note of the rags they wore, well, and now that she wore also. She couldn't imagine James's brother would be so attired. "Where are your weapons?"

"Taken. Dunbarton's men captured us, and one of his lasses freed us. They are now in search of us. Mayhap that is who you heard calling out yonder way."

Her heart sank. She'd thought it was James and his kin, although she had worried the men might have been thieves. She considered the rocky cave floor and wondered what she'd do now. If she ventured forth alone when the rain let up, she'd surely run into someone—either James and his men or the Dunbartons. After some of the tales she'd heard about the evil the Dunbartons had done recently, she didn't wish to meet up with any of those men.

"Who are you, lass? I am Dougald MacNeill, James's second eldest brother. And this is Gunnolf, friend and bodyguard."

"I would change my loyalties in the blink of an eye to guard the lady's body." Gunnolf cast a rakish smile, but she thought him only teasing, to a degree.

"The lass is a genteel woman. Mayhap a lady even.

Although a wee big, her garments are of the finest wool, her shift the kind of chemise only ladies of higher standing wear. So who are you?"

"Allison," she lied.

Dougald's eyes widened, and he glanced at Gunnolf.

Every time she made up a name, it seemed to be the wrong one.

"She is not the same Allison who freed us from the dungeon," Gunnolf said.

Allison? No. It could not be the same lady-in-waiting in Lady Akira's employ who seemed to recognize Eilis. But if it was, then did it mean Eilis was a Dunbarton and so was Allison? But then why would she free Dougald and Gunnolf if she worked for the Dunbartons? Did she work as a spy for James or against him?

She could not mention her suspicions for fear of giving herself away. Or getting the lady in trouble who might not be the same one who had freed Dougald and his friend.

"You look a bit pale." Dougald leaned back. "Why?"

She shook her head.

"She is running away." Gunnolf poked a stick in the fire. "'Tis the only reason she is out here all alone."

"I had an escort," she reminded them.

"Three men who all vanished." Dougald quirked a brow in the same way James did. She could just imagine what James would say if he saw her here with his brother in a cave and she half dressed and Dougald in a state of undress as well.

"You were not running away with a scoundrel and

became separated, were you?" Dougald asked, his countenance darkening even further.

Aye, he looked very much like James now that he was angry with her. Would he let her go when the weather improved? She doubted it. They would take her back to Castle Craigly and let James deal with her.

Gunnolf laughed. "She is trying to think up a good tale."

"Save it, lass. You can share it at Craigly when we return you there on the morrow."

She would leave before then. As soon as her kirtle, *Nighinn's* gown rather, was dry and the men asleep, she would slip away.

*** 

Eilis opened her eyes, vaguely aware she lay against a warm body, a heartbeat lulling her into a sense of security. Until she realized she was wrapped in Dougald's arms. The rogue!

"Shh," Gunnolf said to her and quickly extinguished the fire.

She heard what had awakened her then, the sound of men clomping through the cave, torchlight growing closer.

Dougald moved Eilis into a tiny dark alcove and whispered into her ear, "Stay here, lass. If 'tis Dunbarton's men, we will attempt to hide you. If 'tis James, you will be fine."

She clutched Nighinn's cloak tighter, remembering she'd changed sometime in the night when her clothes had dried and Dougald again wore the tunic. Uncontrollable shivers had wracked her body, and Dougald had finally pulled her into his arms and shared his body heat, although she had soundly protested. But he was as obstinate as James. She'd fallen asleep before the men had, and she'd never chanced her escape as she'd planned.

Dougald kissed the top of her head, then left her alone.

If it was James and his men, he'd want her head, she was sure. Not to mention Nighinn's. If they were Dunbarton's men, she didn't even want to consider that scenario.

As soon as Dougald and Gunnolf vanished in the darkness, their footsteps echoing farther away, she felt an overwhelming sense of abandonment. Worse, sheer terror that it might be Dunbarton's men and they would find her also swamped her.

From her hiding place in the dark and the distance the men had gone, she couldn't see what happened next, but her heart was torn asunder when she heard the men's words.

"'Tis the dogs, my lord! Dougald and the Viking! We have them again."

"James will not be pleased," Dougald said, his voice stern and proud, as he and Gunnolf moved farther away from her toward the cave's entrance.

Thank heavens it appeared they believed Dougald or Gunnolf were alone.

God's wounds where were James and his men?

Desperation coursed through Eilis. She couldn't return to Craigly. Not when she finally had a chance to escape. She couldn't!

As soon as the men's voices faded and the horses galloped off, Eilis stumbled in the dark toward the cave's entrance. Outside, the rain had stopped; Nighinn's horse was gone. Eilis closed her eyes, fighting the tears gathering in the corners. Had Nighinn's horse given Dougald and Gunnolf's location away?

She had to warn James that the Dunbartons had taken his brother hostage. As much as she wanted to avoid her family, she couldn't let Dougald and Gunnolf suffer further if she could help in any way.

\*\*\*

Now that the rain had stopped, a cold fog filled the area, cloaking the early morning in a gray blanket as James and his men searched for his brother and Gunnolf.

"They could have been waylaid way before they reached our lands," Eanruig reminded James as they looked across the glen.

"I lay odds Dunbarton's men have them. What about the blood we found when the sheep were stolen?" James ran his hand through his damp hair. None of his people had been missing. But what if Dougald and Gunnolf had fought Dunbarton's men? What if it was their blood they had found?

James ground his teeth.

"You think they saw Dunbarton's men raiding the sheep and attempted to stop them?"

"Aye. If Dougald and Gunnolf had witnessed the thievery, they would have ridden into battle and not bothered to gather men."

"My laird!" Ian shouted, his eyes wide, his red hair wild, his horse glistening with sweat and breathing hard. Ian looked as though his father's ghost was in pursuit as he galloped toward James. "My laird, word from Niall." Ian pulled up short and dismounted.

God's wounds, it couldn't be bad news about his

brother and Gunnolf.

Ian continued, "I have searched for ye through half the night. Niall...he said Eilis escaped."

James clenched his teeth. How in God's name could she have managed?

"He is certain Nighinn aided her."

If Nighinn hadn't been his cousin, a woman to boot, James would feel justified in hanging her. If any harm came to Eilis...

"A lady wearing one of Nighinn's gowns and riding one of her horses left yestereve. Three men escorted her, but neither Nighinn nor any of her men will admit to it. She has soundly accused Eilis of stealing her clothes and horse."

"And an escort?" James's head pounded with renewed anger. 'Twas enough he had to deal with trying to locate his brother and Gunnolf. The wee lass was more than trouble. But Nighinn...

He gripped his reins tighter.

"Aye. And Nesta said Nighinn sent her from the chamber."

"Why was there no guard?" James fairly roared. Had he not warned Niall of the lass's deceptions? That given any breathing space, she would make her escape?

"Niall told me to guard her, but I thought the women were still in the chamber. Not until Nesta returned and said Eilis was no longer there, nor was Nighinn, did I become concerned. Even so, we searched until we located Nighinn to ensure Eilis was not spending time with her."

"We have rested the horses long enough. We search not only for Dougald and Gunnolf but also for Eilis." Damn the woman for not minding him.

He didn't want to imagine what might have become of the lass, who still didn't have all her memories back. 'Twas dangerous enough for armed men to travel through the region. A lady as comely and refined as she wouldn't last a night on her own.

"Did she pilfer a weapon when she stole Nighinn's gown and horse?" James asked Ian.

He shook his head. "She is unarmed."

"With three men as escort." James doubted they would have stayed with her for verra long. He wanted to wring Nighinn's neck, but it would not bode well with his clan. However, she would not stay any longer at Craigly. If he lost Eilis for good, his cousin would regret having put the lass in harm's way.

\*\*\*

Praying she'd find her way back to Craigly Castle, Eilis ran from the cave and hoped she might come across James or his men. She cursed Nighinn's gown as the hem tripped her up, and she took a tumble on the hard earth. The sky remained dark and ominous, threatening to rain more. Her clothes were cold and damp. Chilled in the breezy weather, Eilis rose to her feet, gathered the gown and continued to race over the uneven terrain, until her side ached, and she was short of breath.

Before long, after treading over the rocky ground in thin-soled shoes, her feet were sore and burning. But she had to reach Craigly. Had to warn Niall and get the word to James that Dunbarton had taken his brother and Gunnolf hostage.

Her stomach grumbled for food, and her mouth was parched for want of mead. The day wore on, and for as long as she'd been walking, she assumed mid-day was upon her. Despite her weariness, she kept on, forcing herself to stretch out her stride, although she felt it shortening despite her best efforts. Her feet pained her with every step. If she didn't reach the castle soon, she'd have to resort to crawling.

After a long while, she saw the castle spires in the distance. Movement to her right caught her eye next.

"How now?" a man said, his face wrinkled with age, his gray eyes kindly as he herded goats. "What ye doing out here by your wee self, lassie? The wild beasties, either four legged or two wouldst do ye harm."

"Do you serve Laird James?"

"Aye."

"I..." Her breath faltered, and Eilis felt ready to collapse as she held her waist. "Word must be sent to his cousin, Niall, at once. Dunbarton's men have taken Dougald and Gunnolf hostage."

"God's knees. Beg pardon, lass." He seemed at a loss as to what to do as he scratched his bearded chin and looked from his goats to the castle to Eilis. "Are ye all right?"

"My feet hurt. If I could, I would run all the way to Craigly."

"Can you watch my goats? I will fetch help and give word to Niall about James's brother and Gunnolf."

"Aye, hurry."

Despite his aged appearance, the herder tore off toward the castle as if he'd suddenly turned into a young man again. His slight form grew smaller and smaller the closer he got to the castle until he disappeared.

Then the goats bleated in distress, and Eilis glanced at them. The goats lowered their tails and moved restlessly about, their gazes focused on the woods. Eilis turned her attention to the shadowed darkness of the forest hiding any sign of danger.

Wolves? Wild boar? Lynx? Two-legged beasties?

If only Eilis had a big stick or a rock or...

She searched the ground and found a cairn of various sizes. Digging at the stones, she pulled one free and again observed the woods. She prayed whatever it was hidden in the needled forest stayed there.

When she looked back at the woods, the stone tight in her clenched hands, she saw the glint of a pair of amber eyes staring back at her from the dark forest.

Then another appeared next to the first.

Two gray wolves sized her up, the only perceived danger to them, she assumed. The goats continued to bleat, readying to run. "Stay together," she said to them, trying to calm them with her voice, motioning to them to remain in a group.

One of the wolves continued to watch her while the other looked over the goats for the weakest link, the oldest, the youngest. She readied the rock. If she threw it at the wolves and hit one of them, mayhap if she could get one of them in the nose, he would run off. And the other would follow.

If they charged the goats or her, would she have time to arm herself again?

The one wolf crouched, warning he was getting ready to leap. She aimed the rock, heard horses leaving the castle in the much too far distance, and threw the rock as far as she could.

It fell with a thud just beyond the goats, not anywhere near the wolves, and the goats panicked. The crouching wolf leapt several feet in the air, nearly making her heart stop. Eilis gasped and dove for another rock, grabbed it up, and turned.

Both wolves targeted an older goat as the rest scattered in every direction.

"Nay!" she screamed and lobbed the rock at the wolf nearer her, this time hitting him in the flank.

He yelped and darted away from the goat. She grabbed another rock.

But it was enough of a distraction that the wolves missed the goat.

Then the horse's hooves pounded the earth, and the vibration sent the wolves fleeing back into the forest. Eilis clung to the rock, waiting for the wolves to return, but they melted into the darkness. The goats! She dropped the rock and waved her arms, calling to them like they were her wee bairns, trying to regather them.

"Eilis!" Niall shouted.

# CHAPTER 11

A mixture of relief and worry consumed Eilis. They'd want to hang her for attempting escape. But at least word about James's brother would reach him. Ahead of the group of men, Niall rode, his face scowling.

"Lady," Niall said through clenched teeth, but he didn't say anything more. He leaned down and scooped into his lap. "James has his hands full with you. Are you injured?"

"You must tell him about his brother."

"He will be told, but he will wish that you are taken care of first." He nodded to the goat herder as he dismounted from one of the men's horses. "Thanks be to you, Everett. James will reward you well."

"'Tis reward enough to find his missus and give news of his brother and the Viking."

"Aye," Niall agreed.

"Wolves tried to kill one of the goats," Eilis warned.

"Aye, and you beat them off with rocks. You would make a laird proud if you defended his castle half as well when he was away on business." Niall turned to his men. "Take care of the wolves." Then he tightened his hold around Eilis's waist and galloped to Craigly as four of the men tore off for the woods and the rest escorted Eilis back. "Have you injuries, my lady?"

"My feet hurt something fierce."

"Then I will leave you with our healer and Lady Akira."

"But what about Dougald and Gunnolf?"

"How is it that you came to know about them?"

"I came upon them in a cave. But Dunbarton's men found them and took them hostage again."

"'Tis fortunate they did not discover the real treasure."

"Och, James will not think me a treasure but his worst nightmare."

Niall smiled.

***

Dougald clasped his hands behind his head as he reclined on the filthy straw again, his chains clinking. He stared at the gray stone ceiling, praying the lass reached a safe place, that James found her and returned her to Craigly soon.

"Another plan, Dougald?" Gunnolf asked from the cell across from his.

"I am considering other options."

"Think you the lass is safely with James by now?"

"I pray that it is so."

Gunnolf grunted. "I did not believe you were thinking about how we would get out of our current predicament."

"Do not tell me you were thinking of means of escape, either."

"Think you James has interest in the lass?" Gunnolf asked, his voice amused.

"If he has not…" Dougald let Gunnolf come to his own conclusions.

"Aye. Mayhap the lass would be interested in a strong Viking."

Dougald laughed. "We know not whether James has made her his charge and if he wishes more of a relationship than that."

"Aye. So let me know as soon as you quit thinking about the bonny lass and come up with a plan."

\*\*\*

'Twas early eve when Niall rode out to see James. His cousin's expression was hard, his jaw taut.

James feared the worst. Yet, not only had Niall lost Eilis when he should have guarded her like his treasury, but he was supposed to be in charge of the castle should anything untoward happen to James. "You are expected to be—"

"'Tis Eilis, my laird. Rather rumpled but well when she returned on foot to Craigly."

A torrent of emotions washed over James—relief, anger, joy, irritation—and he could not segregate them to deal with any. He clenched his teeth. "What happened?" Rumpled could mean a lot of things, and his imagination was already running away with him.

"She told us Dunbarton's men have Dougald and Gunnolf. They were bruised and cut but well otherwise when she discovered them in a cave. She was beside herself with self-loathing, claiming if she had not tethered Nighinn's horse outside the cave, the Dunbartons would not have found your brother."

"Nay, they would have searched every cave in the area before long."

"I told her thus, but she feared she had delayed them overmuch because they worried about her well-being."

James turned to Fergus. "Have our men return home. Now that we know Dunbarton has taken our men hostage, I will have to negotiate for their safe return. Naught more we can do now."

For now, he had other extremely pressing matters as well. A word with Eilis, and he hoped like the devil Niall wasn't hiding her true condition from him. And he'd have several words with Nighinn and his aunt before he sent them on their way.

***

As soon as James and his party returned to Craigly, women raced out to greet their husbands or sons. Notably absent was his mother, Aunt Beatrice, Nighinn, and Eilis. He glanced up at Eilis's chamber window, but there was no sign of anyone. More than concerned, James dismounted while the stable boy grabbed the reins.

In a rush, James headed for the keep.

"She is in Lady Akira's chamber as it has only one door and no other means of escape," Niall explained, hurrying to join James.

Ian wasn't far behind.

"The only place safe for the lady to reside is a locked room." James stalked inside. "I want a bath prepared."

"Aye, I will tell the servants," Ian said and hurried

off.

As much as James had wanted Niall to obey his command to remain at Craigly at all costs, he understood Niall's actions. And approved.

Although James needed a bath, a meal, and a few hours sleep, he had to see Eilis for himself, to know she was safe. He sighed. She would most likely have never made it to wherever she intended; however, he couldn't help admire her for giving up her freedom to return and give him news of his brother's whereabouts. "I need to speak with Eanruig about ransoming Dougald and Gunnolf."

"Aye," Niall agreed.

James stalked in the direction of Lady Akira's chamber while Niall kept up the pace beside him. James glanced at him. "You need not accompany me."

"Is that an order, cousin?"

James snorted. "I thought I gave you an order to stay here. Why did you not send a messenger in your place?"

"I had to tell you the lass was safe, and your brother was being held prisoner. No messenger would do."

"Aye, and I am glad for it."

Niall gave him a worried look. "You will not be too hard on the lass?"

James lifted a brow and considered his cousin's serious face. "Mean you Eilis or our cousin?"

"Not Nighinn—the devil with her. Eilis I am meaning."

"The lass gave up her freedom to warn me of Dougald's imprisonment. Why should I be angry with her?"

"She escaped."

James clenched his fists. Aye, he was angered with her for her actions. Couldn't she see how dangerous her efforts had been? 'Twould not do to show great relief when he saw her, or she might misconstrue his meaning. He was damned angry with her.

"She is not ill from the weather yesterday?"

"Nay, not this time. She has the heart of a lion, though."

James glanced at his cousin to see his meaning when he didn't readily offer an explanation.

Niall smiled broadly. "She single-handedly fought off a pair of wolves that tried to take down a goat under her watchful eye."

"With her bare hands?"

"Rocks, actually."

"A goat?"

"Aye. Everett's goats. He came to warn me about your brother and get help for the lady while she watched his goats. She will make a fine battle maid should a laird wish to wed her and have need of her when he must leave the castle in her hands."

"With rocks." James shook his head. He couldn't think of any lass who would be brave enough to fend off wolves for the sake of a goat. But his stomach clenched when he thought of how the wolves might have killed her.

Reaching the door to his mother's chamber, James knocked, and the ladies' voices within grew silent. Footsteps approached; the door opened. Nesta curtsied, but avoided James's look. She was not at fault. Nighinn had dismissed her, but he could see Nesta felt she had done wrong just the same.

"A word with you, Eilis, if you please," James said, unable to keep his eyes off her. Despite what Niall had said, her cheeks were colorless, her green eyes avoided his, she wrung her hands in her lap, and looked like she was about to be led to the hangman's noose.

"Eilis," he said again, displeased he had to speak more firmly than he had intended.

She rose stiffly from the bench and only then did he realize she probably ached from being out in the inhospitable weather and all the walking and running on foot she must have endured. He noticed then her feet were bandaged, and she wore no shoes.

He cursed to himself then strode across the floor and lifted her off her feet. She gasped, but so did the rest of the ladies. His mother gave him a look to mind his temper. The other ladies' mouths gaped.

Niall smiled at him.

With the lass secure in his tight embrace and glad she appeared well otherwise, James stalked to the guest chamber with Niall at his side. "I want a guard posted." Although he did not believe the lass was physically capable of any further escape attempts at the moment. "When I am through speaking with the lady, have Nesta join her."

"And our cousin?"

"I will speak to her and my aunt after my bath. I will pen a missive also concerning the ransom for my brother and Gunnolf as well."

"Aye. Did…you want me to remain here?"

"Shut the door on your way out."

Niall shook his head. "I surmise even if she is not from the enemy clan you do not want me to have her for myself."

James smiled to himself. His cousin surmised right. The door clunked shut, and James sat Eilis on one of the benches.

She said, "I am sorry—"

James raised his hand to silence her. "None of us could locate my brother and Gunnolf. But you managed when we all failed. I am grateful—"

"Because of me, he was caught," she insisted.

The woman was a contradiction—sweet and innocent, yet protective— and...och, the lass would be his undoing. James leaned down and kissed her cheek. "Because of you, I know my brother is alive and well. Tell me what happened. And spare no details."

He was certain when Eilis spoke of what had happened she left out a few details. She said her brother and Gunnolf wore rags and were unarmed which accounted for them not fighting Dunbarton's men. But also they had kept her safe. However, he knew his brother would not have allowed her to wear wet clothes all eve. The thought soured the mead in his belly. Although he was dying to know every detail, he'd get it out of Dougald once he'd paid his ransom rather than embarrass the lass any further.

"I knew he was your brother as soon as I saw him. Younger, his hair and eyes not quite as dark, but he had the same smile, the same sparkle in his eyes."

She was describing Dougald when he attempted to seduce a lass. Mayhap himself as well. James fought the possessiveness he invariably suffered when it came to Eilis.

He intended to wed Catriona! He had no business feeling anything for the lass he knew so little about.

"Nighinn apologized to me several times already,"

she continued.

"She lied to Niall."

"She was afraid you would be angry."

"She would be right."

Eilis reached out and took James's hand. "She only wanted to be your wife."

Her touch stirred feelings of want and desire. Between the two women, James wanted Eilis. Not just in the way she heated his blood, but he knew his feelings bordered on something much deeper. A need for commitment, to cherish her always, to…love her?

He shook his head of the dangerous thought. "She lost that chance when she aided your escape and could have gotten you killed. She is my cousin so I will do naught but send her home in disgrace."

"I am sorry."

"Do not be, Eilis. I must bathe then take care of this other business. Are you hungry? I am famished. We will eat after a wee bit, lass. Rest until then." He lifted her off the bench and carried her to the bed. She couldn't have slept much after her ordeal, although she smelled springtime fresh and wore a new gown.

He smelled like his horse. "Famished," he said, thinking how wonderful she looked and how he had to get his mind off the lass and back to where it belonged, seeking a marriage agreement with Catriona and freeing his brother and Gunnolf.

\*\*\*

Although his cousin apologized to him in his solar and so did his Aunt Beatrice, James could barely stand the sight of them. Nighinn's blue eyes were red and her face blotched. Fresh tears trailed down her cheeks. Her distress would not dissuade him from sending her away, considering the seriousness of her actions.

"I am sure you know how I feel about this matter. Had Eilis died..." He couldn't say any more without revealing how truly angry he was. "You and your mother will leave with your escort without delay."

"But, my laird..." his aunt said.

"Not a word," James commanded to Aunt Beatrice. "My decision stands."

After Nighinn, who was in tears, and his aunt, her face hard as granite, left, James's mother joined him, her brow furrowed. She appeared as though she hadn't had any sleep either. "Do you think it wise to be considering two women in your pursuit of marriage when Catriona arrives?"

"Two women? Nighinn is leaving."

"I have heard you have fetched a companion of Eilis's. A maid named Fia."

Aye. He couldn't suppress the overwhelming need he had to learn who Eilis truly was. Besides, mayhap Fia would help Eilis to recall her memories faster. Wouldn't that be best for all concerned?

"Catriona may still delay her journey. I do not trust the lass until I see her here." For the first time, he found himself feeling something other than hope the lady would wish to marry him. The sooner she got here, the sooner they could get on with the business of marriage. Which was supposed to be his goal. Yet, 'twas this business of her delaying tactics that was making him wonder why he was making the effort. There were no other bride choices he was interested in, he reminded himself.

James's mother chewed on her lower lip. "I am concerned about Eilis's welfare, my son. Why would the woman in the village deny she knew her?"

The more he learned about Eilis, the more mysterious she became. "That is what we are bound to discover. Did you have any success speaking with Allison, concerning the way she reacted to Eilis?"

His mother shook her head. "She said she was startled to find you and the lady in the kitchen alone together." Her chin down, his mother gave him a pointed look like she was waiting for an explanation.

James rubbed his chin in thought, then wondered— had the woman believed he was having a dalliance with Eilis in the kitchen? Mayhap that was what had shaken Lady Allison so. She might not have wished to say a word about it to his mother.

"Aye, well, if that was all the matter." James shrugged. Although he didn't believe the scene between Eilis and him appeared anything more than a casual conversation. It still seemed to him that the lady recognized Eilis and not in a good way.

Mayhap he could solicit Niall to ply his charms on the lady and learn more from her about the matter. He smiled. Aye, that should do.

"What about the missive concerning the ransom for Dougald and Gunnolf?"

"I have already sent it, my mother. If the old Dunbarton is in the least bit reasonable, he will release them at once."

"I pray it is so. I must see to the running of the household. Please do not upset Lady Allison for naught. She has been the best of companions since she joined me a year ago. Since the happening in the kitchen, she seems ill at ease and withdrawn."

James cleared his throat. "I was only speaking with

Eilis in the kitchen, naught more."

His mother smiled, but it wasn't a pleasantly innocent look, rather one of calculation.

"Mother?"

She lifted her chin. "Aye. Lady Allison will not speak of it to anyone else. Nesta is the one you must be more concerned with." Again, his mother's lips lifted, and she had the same willful expression. It usually meant he was in trouble.

\*\*\*

Footfalls headed in the direction of Dougald's cell, and he and Gunnolf grew silent.

A gruff man opened the door to Dougald's cell. "Your brother offered a ransom, but my laird wishes to keep you both for a while longer. Mayhap forever." He gave him a surly smile, then slammed and locked the door.

Dougald groaned. It was time to come up with another plan.

\*\*\*

Late the next day, Tavia knocked at the solar door and curtseyed to James and his mother. "Fergus asked me to tell you Eilis wished to sit in the garden before the meal."

In haste, James rose from the chair, nearly knocking it over. He stormed across the hall. "She has tried to escape three times already."

Chasing after him, his mother hurried to catch up, her small leather shoes slapping the floor. "She is well-guarded, my son, if Fergus is with her. She is not going anywhere with her feet so bandaged. Although, I understand they are feeling much better. Tavia told her to keep the bandages on through the remainder of the day, though."

Tavia nodded vigorously. "Aye, and even Niall is with her."

James stopped and glowered at his healer. "Niall has other duties."

Smiling, his mother said, "Aye. He told me earlier he has done them."

Work was never done with all the rebuilding needed. James grunted and headed outside. Stalking across the grassy bailey, he spied Niall laughing, his hands on his hips, towering over Eilis seated on a bench. A fine sight it was. When everyone else had chores to do, his cousin was busy dallying with a lass?

But not any lass. James's treasure from the sea. He scowled further.

As soon as Niall spied James, his spine stiffened. James observed two men standing a short distance away, preventing the lady's attempt at another escape if she wished it. Two of his female servants were also tending the garden nearby, watching her, but now observing James's approach.

"Now that you are here," Niall said to James, "I will see to the mending of the south wall."

Attempting to slow his rapid pulse, James nodded. He turned his attention to Eilis, who quickly looked away from him. "Eanruig has found your lady companion in Glen Affric. He is sending an escort to bring her here to see you," James said, hoping to learn the truth now.

Eilis jerked her head up and looked at him. The color drained from her face, and he grabbed her arm to keep her from falling from the bench. "Are you all right, Eilis?" Not having meant to cause her so much distress, he chastised himself.

"I...I, yes, I am...all right." The color returned to her bonny cheeks.

When she recovered so quickly, he tried to conceal his dark amusement.

She glanced back at the inner bailey's castle gate, open for business during the day where his clansman entered and left at will.

Thinking of making an escape? She would go nowhere until James learned all there was about the mystifying woman who, for now, was his to protect.

He lifted her from the bench. "'Tis time to practice our ruse before Catriona arrives, lass."

She relaxed in his arms, and the softness of her body pressed against him stirred his desire. Like when he'd carried her heated body into the keep when she first attempted escape, he was as hard as the steel of his sword.

Attempting to think of anything other than his baser needs, he carried her to the south wall where the men were busily repairing the stones. "We had a landlash hit us a few weeks ago. The gale-force winds did a fair amount of damage as you can see. Do you remember anything about the storm? You must have been in the area at the time and have some memory of it. In truth, the ship you were on must have taken the brunt of it."

She shook her head. "I remember only what I have already told you." Looking up at him, she seemed like she was being perfectly honest with him, and all at once her situation struck a chord deep inside.

She truly didn't remember who she was and his badgering her could only further her frustration. If he had forgotten so many details of his life, even his own clan's name, how would he feel? Lost and aggravated.

Taking a deep breath, she glanced up at Niall, his tunic thrown aside as he helped the men move another block of stone, his muscles straining beneath bronzed skin that glistened with sweat. Niall cast a look in Eilis's direction and winked.

Eilis's cheeks colored, and James growled deep inside. His cousin had no business trying to win Eilis's favor, not while they didn't know where she was from and what her marital status truly was. But Niall had a way with the ladies, and it seemed no matter how much James tried to dissuade his cousin from making a fool of himself in front of her, James would not succeed.

He carried her away from the wall and walked toward the stables. "Would you like to ride?"

"My head pains me."

"You should have said so, lass."

She cast him a weary smile. "Nay, I am fine otherwise. I am afraid riding would jostle my head overmuch."

"Are you certain? We can sit inside and talk if you prefer."

"Nay, I am tired of sitting inside. The sun feels heavenly against my face."

And what precious skin that was, framed by red-gold curls. He wondered if all of her skin was as soft as it appeared.

Glancing at the southwest tower, he had a thought. If Eilis saw the layout of the land, would she remember anything about it?

Not knowing her past must be a terrible burden for her to bear, yet he shared her feeling. He couldn't recall any other time when he sought some knowledge more than he did now.

He carried her to the tower stairs. "If you weary too much, Eilis, you must let me know."

One of his soldiers greeted them halfway to the parapet. Others gathered nearby, openly smiling or hiding their amusement, to an extent. "You have work to do, lads."

"Aye, Laird."

The men promptly obliged, but their smiles didn't fade.

Over the stone wall, Eilis observed towering crags like pale blue mist penetrating the clear sky on the horizon. A long-tailed swallow swooped nearby. Did Eilis wish she could fly away free? He imagined so and attempted to quell the irritation that thought brought to mind.

"I do not even remember the ship I was on. How can I remember some things and not others?"

She didn't seem distraught over the missing memories, only drained.

Running the back of his hand over her silky cheek, he knew instantly he treaded dark waters. She stirred in him the desire to have a wife by choice instead of by duty to his clan, the first time any woman had encouraged the feeling. Pulling his hand away as if she had burned him, he attempted to get his feelings under control. "Do you remember Fia?"

She shook her head and again seemed to be telling the truth.

He took a heavy breath. "Mayhap the lady will help bring back your memories."

"I fear that bringing her here will alert my family,"

Eilis said in a small voice.

He could not believe she would know such a thing if she remembered not who her family was. He thought it was just her vivid imagination from her memories not returning. Yet, a small nagging at the back of his mind warned him to consider she might be right.

# CHAPTER 12

The next day, James paced across the great hall, ready to do battle with Dunbarton. He glowered at Ian. "Say again what the brigand told you."

His cheeks as red as a fiery sunset, Ian clenched his fists until they were white. "Aye, my laird. Dunbarton was well into his cups. Mayhap that was some of the trouble. He said he found a couple of wild animals in a cave, no brother of yours. If he discovers Dougald and Gunnolf, he will give them a well-appointed chamber abovestairs, the finest meats and mead, and song to please them. If he finds them. And then ye can do business with him."

James ground his teeth. "The bastard."

"Aye. If his men had not removed my sword before I had audience with Dunbarton, I would have run him through."

James slapped Ian on the shoulder. "Nay, we need you. What would I do without you fighting my battles for me?"

Ian gave a slight smile, then scowled again. "I wanted to bring Dougald and Gunnolf out of the dungeon and show Dunbarton that we knew they were there all along."

"Aye, me and you both. We will have to take care of this in another way."

"I will be happy to assist in any way, my laird."

"Aye."

Ian bowed and took his leave.

How could Dunbarton not accept James's charitable ransom offer for his brother and Gunnolf? 'Twas a travesty his brother and their friend should have to suffer so.

As much as James would like to take up arms against Dunbarton, storming the castle would only bring death to many of James's kinsmen. And they would still not be able to breach the stone walls. Laying siege and starving Dunbarton's people would take too long.

Niall hurried into the hall. "I hear Dunbarton refuses to name a suitable ransom."

"Aye, but mayhap we could play his own game."

"Take one of his people hostage? But who?"

"I have heard it rumored his bastard son, Keary, has returned. Mayhap we could give him a room at Craigly, if we could capture him."

Then James caught sight of Eilis as she entered the hall with Fergus in tow, her step steady. The woman was uncommonly bonny, and the more he saw of her, the more he...

He cursed softly. The woman was like a breath of a summer breeze, fresh and silky soft, warming him to the deepest part of his soul. Every time he saw her, he was reminded of the way she reacted to his kisses—sweet and innocent, yet a tigress lurked within. She wanted more, and he sure wanted to oblige.

He tried to imagine Catriona that way, but she... Well, what was she truly like?

Not sweet and innocent, that was for certain. As for being a tigress, she was more like a cat, prickly sometimes, friendly when she wanted to be.

He watched Eilis walking aimlessly, stretching her legs, but with no real objective. Until she spied Lady Allison and headed straight for her with purpose in her stride. He narrowed his eyes. What was it about the two women and the reaction they had to one another?

Fergus was about to stalk after Eilis but caught James's eye. James motioned for him to hold back. Let the women speak their mind. With his arms crossed over his chest, James would observe and hope to glean something from their interaction. Knowing Niall's nature, he was just as curious, although James hoped Eilis wouldn't notice them both watching her.

***

As soon as Eilis caught sight of Lady Allison alone, she hurried to speak to her, effectively leaving Fergus behind. At least she didn't hear his heavy footsteps, and she wasn't about to look back and catch his attention. She was certain her expression would appear as guilty as she felt.

Although she knew he'd soon realize his mistake and catch up to her.

She couldn't contain her enthusiasm. In the instant she'd seen Allison here, she recalled where she knew the lady from. Joining the lady, Eilis smiled broadly. "Lady Allison, I remember now where I have seen you before. You served Lady Anice of Brecken Castle, aye?"

The woman's eyes rounded, and she looked most stricken.

"'Tis true then," Eilis excitedly said. "You remember me? I cannot recall how we met, but it seems there was some trouble and..." Eilis looked down at the floor, trying to piece the memories back together, but no matter how hard she strained to remember, they eluded her. Except for one. She looked back up at the lady. "Your name was Amber. Why did you change your name?"

Allison took Eilis's hands in hers and begged, "Tell no one, Lady Eilis. 'Tis true, but..." She shook her head, tears building in her eyes.

"Why? What have you to fear?" When Allison would not reveal the reason for her distress, Eilis continued. "Did you free Dougald and Gunnolf from Dunbarton's stronghold?"

"We must not speak of this here," Allison said, her voice hushed as she glanced around the keep.

"Allison, how did you get into Dunbarton's castle?"

"My brother is—"

As he must have realized he had lost Eilis, Fergus stalked across the keep in her direction, and Allison pulled away.

"Wait! You must tell me. How can we free Dougald and his companion?"

"Nay! 'Tis no' possible. They would suspect me if I tried the same ruse again."

"Another plan? What else can we—"

Allison glanced at Fergus as he grew closer. "None

other, my lady. 'Tis the way of things. I must go." She whipped around and headed out of the hall.

Her heart in her throat, Eilis wanted to speak with Allison further, to learn of her ties to Dunbarton and to James's people, and why she knew her as Amber at Lady Anice's castle. What trouble had they encountered that Eilis…well, she could not recall. Only that there had been trouble and both she and Amber had been in the midst of it.

Fergus folded his arms and planted himself next to Eilis, his gaze focused on Allison's retreating backside. Och, would he tell James of the talk Eilis had with Allison? Of the woman's strange actions?

"Where do you wish to go now?" he asked Eilis.

She straightened her back and peered up at the veritable giant, giving her best scowl. He seemed only slightly amused. "To the village. I have need of cloth and thread." It was high time she made a gown for herself and returned James's sister's garments.

Fergus raised his brows. "I will have someone fetch them for you."

"Nay," she snapped. 'Twould be her gown and she had intended to make her own choice. "I must see the fabric myself. Ask Laird James if he will permit me to visit the village—well, with a suitable escort, of course."

"What is it you wish of me, my lady?" James asked, joining her from behind.

She turned to face him, her heart skipping beats. "I wish to make a gown of my own. If you would but permit me to go to the village and choose the fabric."

James offered a small frown, then bowed his head. "I will escort you."

She sighed. She'd hoped Allison could accompany her and she'd be able to learn more about the woman. But not if James stayed by her side.

"Naught would please me more." She hoped her smile looked genuine.

He studied her for a moment. "When would you wish to—"

"Now...if it pleases you, my laird. I wish to begin working on my gown at once."

"Aye." Without taking his eyes off her, James gave the orders. "Fergus, gather a suitable escort. Ask Lady Akira if she would care to join us."

"Aye, my laird." Fergus hurried off.

James swept his hand down Eilis's arm. "You are welcome to wear my sister's gowns."

"I...I thank you for your kindness, but I wish to have a gown to call my own."

"They are yours for as long as you wish them, Eilis." James's expression changed subtly from sympathetic to concerned. He didn't say what bothered him about her request, and she was afraid to ask.

Lady Akira hurried down the stairs to join them with three of her ladies trailing behind. Although she smiled at James, when she acknowledged Eilis, she wore the same worried expression.

"I have not been to the village in a fortnight. Tavia wishes to see a villager who has just given birth. And the rest of us will accompany Eilis to the fabric stalls," Lady Akira said.

James bowed his head to his mother. "Aye, with me as escort."

"Of course, my laird." His mother patted his arm. "As it should be."

Did they think Eilis planned to escape on the outing? She knew there was no chance of that. For once, she had no plans in that regard.

\*\*\*

After the horses were readied and the party mounted, they headed out of the bailey while Fergus and a couple of men led the force and several more followed behind. James drew his horse closer to Eilis's as the rest of the ladies rode behind them. "Do you recall anything more about your past, Eilis?"

She lowered her lashes. "Nay."

He nodded but didn't believe her. "Naught more about Lady Allison?"

Eilis glanced at him, the fear in her eyes evident. He knew she remembered more. He assumed Allison was just as worried about Eilis's recollections.

"I...I met her once at Lady Anice's Brecken Castle. I remember naught more than that." Eilis watched his response.

Did she worry he would believe her?

"I see. I did not know she had been there."

Eilis looked straight ahead. "I do not recall anything more."

"She seemed most anxious." James waited for Eilis's reaction before he spoke further.

Eilis twisted her mouth. "Did she?"

"Aye, when you spoke with her."

With her brow furrowed and her mouth turned down, Eilis looked at James. "You were spying on us?"

Not meaning to, he smiled. "An unusual choice of words. Everything about you intrigues me, Eilis. When I saw you enter the great hall, I could not take my eyes off you."

She hmpfed. "I suppose Fergus was spying on us also."

"He was guarding you from afar, allowing you, at my behest, some privacy with the lady."

"Then why did he approach and scare her off?"

"I wished him to hear what the two of you were speaking about when she became so concerned. Everything that anyone does under my rule is my business."

She glowered at him. "What did Fergus overhear?"

"I have not had the opportunity to discuss the matter with him. Mayhap you would rather enlighten me."

She lifted her chin and looked straight ahead again.

He wasn't surprised. "I can question Lady Allison instead. I will not be as gentle with her as I am with asking you, rest assured."

Eilis refused to look at him. Then she ground her teeth and pursed her lips. "I know hardly anything at all."

"Aye."

"I...well, I cannot remember how I know her from Brecken Castle. Only that I do," Eilis said, exasperated.

"All right. But she took your hands and pleaded with you about something."

"Not to tell you she had been at Brecken." Eilis let out her breath and turned to James. "There was some trouble. We were both in the midst of it. I know not how or what 'twas all about."

"Aye. When was this?"

"I do not know."

"A rumor has been circulating that the lady has a bastard brother who works for Dunbarton. I had not put much stock in the rumors since. She has served my mother well. If she has ties to Dunbarton and plans some mischief..."

"Nay, she freed your brother and Gunnolf."

James stared at Eilis. "How? When? God's wounds, woman, if she has a way inside the castle..."

"Nay, she cannot try it again. They would kill her if they discovered she had released the prisoners the first time. You cannot ask it of her. You must keep her secret." Eilis's eyes filled with tears, and her bottom lip quivered. "I have only told you thus so that you do not harm her or put her in further peril. If Dunbarton's men had not recaptured them because of my folly, your brother and Gunnolf would be with us now—and only because of Allison's courageous efforts."

James couldn't strictly see it that way. If the lass's brother worked for Dunbarton, she could cause real problems. At least for James and his brothers, blood ties meant all the difference in the world.

"She is a good woman, James. I beg of you to believe me."

"Then what trouble was she in at Brecken Castle?"

"I told you I do not recall." She pursed her lips and looked straight ahead, refusing another look in his direction.

Despite what Eilis assumed about Lady Allison, James could not base his leadership on the assumption the lady would not be forced into working against his people. As soon as they reached the village, he motioned for his mother to stay with Eilis. When the ladies rode toward the first of the stalls, James joined Ian, although he kept his eye on Eilis. His mother was talking to her, but Eilis glanced back at James to see what he was up to.

His mother turned and frowned at him. 'Twas not his doing that Eilis was distracted from the business of searching for the proper fabric to make a gown.

"Ye wish to speak to me, my laird?" Ian asked.

"Send a messenger to Malcolm and Lady Anice at Brecken Castle. I want to know what happened when Eilis and Lady Allison were there. There was some trouble. I wish to know what it was and what Lady Anice knows of Eilis. Also, have a man watching Lady Allison, where she goes, who she speaks to. She is not to leave the castle grounds unless I give her permission."

"Aye, my laird. Is there anything else?"

"Return here afterward."

"Aye. I shall return." Ian rode back to the castle as Eilis watched.

His mother dismounted and motioned to a table filled with woolen and silk fabrics, but Eilis would neither dismount nor comment on the material.

Again, his mother cast a glower James's way.

He sighed heavily. 'Twas the price he had to pay for being the earl.

Movement to the north of the village caught his eye, and he narrowed his eyes as he tried to make out the men tying up their horses in front of the tavern.

Just the man who would help him earn his brother and Gunnolf's freedom. "Fergus," James hastily said, "leave three men to watch the women. The rest come with me. Our prey is straight ahead."

"Dunbarton's bastard son, Keary?" Fergus asked. "But he will not even acknowledge him as his son."

"'Tis true, but what if he had a change of heart

since his wives died without issue? We will take the chance and see what comes of the exchange."

Fergus bowed his head. "As you wish, my laird."

James led his men toward the tavern—to where Keary undoubtedly intended to drink himself into a stupor. Mayhap to go wenching as well. The only admirable quality the man had was that he fought well in the Crusade.

Which only made his da angrier that he had abandoned him and not stood by his side in the fight against the MacNeill. Another quality that James admired.

"In there." James motioned to the Hawk and Boar Tavern where Keary's horse was tethered along with the mounts of his five companions.

James and his kin outnumbered them two to one, although he hoped the men would go quietly without any bloodshed.

He leapt from his horse, draped his horse's reins over the post, and stalked toward the entrance tavern, unsheathing his sword at the same time. His men quickly followed suit and joined him.

*** 

Eilis clenched and unclenched her hands, too upset to look at the fabrics now that she had told Allison's secrets. Although she did not reveal the name Allison had gone by at Brecken Castle. She suspected that despite telling him all she knew, he would still now interrogate the poor lady. Mayhap he had sent Ian to do the job. She groaned.

She glanced at Lady Akira who was trying her best to cheer her, smiling and waving at fabrics. All Eilis could think about was poor Allison. And what a heroic woman she'd been. For what? She'd risked her life for Dougald and Gunnolf and now would have earned both Dunbarton and James's wrath.

"Lady Eilis, what about the red wool? They dyed it with Lady's bedstraw yestereve, and the color is quite lovely, do you not think?"

"Aye," Eilis said, her response half-hearted. Until she noticed James and his men leave the women to fend for themselves with only three guards watching over them. "Where does James go?"

"He undoubtedly has business in the village. Naught we have to concern ourselves with."

Although Lady Akira attempted to appear unmoved by her son's disappearance, she threaded her fingers through her long hair and glanced back in the direction James and his men had gone. The other ladies had stopped shopping and looked about for the men.

Eilis assumed something was amiss and it didn't bode well.

# CHAPTER 13

The acrid smoke from the peat fire filled the two-story tavern as men sitting at several of the tables guffawed or talked about the battles they'd fought in the village as James and his men entered the main room.

A gray-haired woman hurried to set mugs of ale on a table, then spying James and his men, their swords in hand, her eyes widened.

James motioned with his free hand for the woman and her two serving wenches to leave. She hurried the women into a back room. Her husband came out from behind the stout counter, his brow furrowed, his expression stating, "Dinna wreck my place." But he minded his tongue since more of James's kin frequented here than the Dunbarton's. Even now, eight more of James's people sat at two of the tables. They bowed their heads or lifted their mugs of ale to James in greeting.

With all of his people sitting in the tavern, James

wondered why Keary was foolhardy enough to set foot in the place.

When one of his companions noticed James, he slugged Keary in the arm and motioned to James and his men.

The insolent whelp leaned back on the bench and tilted his chin up. "How now, MacNeill of Craigly. 'Tis a surprise seeing you here."

"I was thinking the same of you. Since we are both here, I have a proposition to make. You will come with me and be my guest for a time."

Keary raised his brows, his mouth hinting at a smile. "I see. To what do I owe such generosity?"

His companions glanced at James's men. Sizing up the competition in the advent of a battle?

"Let us not banter words. You and your companions will stay with us for a time until your father agrees he will exchange my brother Dougald and Gunnolf for you and your friends."

"Ah. I see you have it all worked out. Know you my da does not recognize me as his son. So 'tis folly to believe he would exchange your kin for me. Thank you all the same for the offer. We will continue to enjoy our meal and ale here."

"The offer was not a suggestion but an order. We wish no bloodshed this day. But you and your men, save one who will carry my missive to Dunbarton, will remain at Craigly for as long as necessary."

Keary and his men slowly rose from the benches, a bit unsteadily, their hands planted on the hilts of their swords.

"You are severely outmatched. Do not try us." To his men, James said, "If the others fight you, do not hold back. 'Tis only Dunbarton's whelp we need take alive."

Keary's men may have thought to fight rather than give up without a battle, but Keary rested his hand on his closest companion's arm and shook his head. "We will go with you. I swear my da will not give a care."

"We will see. Tie their hands, lest they change their minds on the way to Craigly."

"I promised we would not do battle with you," Keary said, indignant.

James didn't comment but waited for his men to bind Keary and his men's wrists, then herded them outside to their horses. Had his mother and Eilis not been with James, he would have allowed the men some dignity and kept their hands unbound. 'Twas not a risk he'd take with the women in the party.

As soon as the men mounted and rejoined the women at the merchant stalls, Keary smiled. "I wondered why you would have us bound when I had given my word not to fight you." He bowed his head to Eilis. "Your betrothed, I take it. She is a swan in these Highlands. Promise the lady to my da in exchange for your brother and half his earldom, and my da would most likely concede."

James's mother gave Keary a contemptuous look and took Eilis's arm, leading her to her horse as James dismounted. "'Tis Dunbarton's son," James's mother said to Eilis.

"Oh, aye. James is taking him hostage in return for his brother?" Eilis sounded most relieved.

Which created a gnawing in James's belly. Dougald hadn't managed to charm the lady into wanting him, had he?

James helped Eilis to mount her horse, his hand lingering overlong on her waist. Their gazes locked. Annoyance concerning Allison still sparked in the depths of Eilis's sea green eyes.

Keary chuckled. "My da should have taken the lady hostage instead of Dougald. It appears you would give your soul to keep the lady."

Now, James wished Keary had not seen Eilis at all. "She is merely a guest at Craigly," he said, although the words stuck in his craw. As much as he denied it, he wanted her to remain there, not as a guest, not as part of his staff. There was something about her that drew him in, made him want to keep her as his own forevermore. He had always been the most prudent of men when it came to running his castle, but with Eilis, he could think of naught else. He'd overheard his mother speaking with Niall, telling him James had fallen in love with the lass, but he couldn't consider such a thing. Not until he knew more about Eilis.

"Methinks you lie. No matter." Keary winked at Eilis. "Mayhap if she is but a guest, you could offer her to da in exchange for your brother. Seems a much better exchange than for a bastard son he refuses to acknowledge."

"Go," James commanded Fergus to lead the party while James stayed with the ladies, riding behind their hostages as they returned across the glen.

"Where is the lass from, pray tell? Why have I never had the good fortune to meet her?" Keary asked.

Fergus forced Keary and his men to increase the distance between them and James and the ladies. Soon, most of the men from the tavern had joined them, guarding from the rear.

"Will Dunbarton give up your brother and Gunnolf for his son?" Eilis asked.

James hated hearing the hope in her voice. Would Dunbarton agree to the exchange? He seriously doubted so. But he had to try any means available to them.

"We will see."

"Will you put them in the dungeon?"

"For the night for the safety of my people. During the day also, unless they wish to help rebuild the south wall. They may take their meals with us. I have no quarrel with Keary. He has been gone too long from the region to have caused us any real grief. 'Tis his da who causes all the bloodshed. But I do not want Keary or his men near you."

"The feeling is mutual."

"Did you manage to buy some fabric for a gown?"

Her expression sad, Eilis shook her head.

"We will have to return to the village for goods some other time."

Eilis no longer cared about the fabric or a new gown. All she cared about was Allison's welfare.

\*\*\*

"What did you discuss that upset Eilis so, James?" his mother asked in the great hall the moment Eilis was secure in her chamber. "She was no longer interested in any of the fabrics when she had been quite cheerful beforehand. I had a devil of a time even getting her to dismount and finally had one of our men help her down, afraid she was thinking of fleeing."

"Ian was to have a word with Lady Allison."

His mother gave James a stern look. He shrugged. "She and Eilis were at Brecken Castle and in some trouble. Eilis recalled the matter but not what about.

Worse, it seems the rumors Allison's bastard brother works for Dunbarton are true. And, she freed Dougald and Gunnolf from Dunbarton's castle. Even if she does not spy for Dunbarton, since she visits the place, what if they force her to tell them of our strengths, our plans, our weaknesses?"

His mother snapped her gaping mouth shut.

"Aye, so you see, we have a problem in our midst."

"Can the lass free Dougald again?"

"Nay, it would be too risky." James let out his breath. "We only have Keary as a pawn for now. I will send a missive to Dunbarton, stating we wish an exchange."

"But just Dunbarton's son for your brother? What about Gunnolf?"

"We have taken five men as hostages in all and will offer the whole lot of them."

Ian ran down the stairs and joined James, his face flushed. "My laird, Niall is speaking with Lady Allison, but she refuses to say nary a word."

James's mother shook her head. "You need a woman's gentle touch. I will see to the lady." She hurried off to the stairs.

James ran his hands through his hair. "My mother, as good as she is, will never get anything out of the lady."

Ian smiled. "You never know, my laird. Lady Akira can be pretty persuasive when she wishes to be."

Niall stalked into the hall, shaking his head.

"A man is watching Lady Allison?" James asked.

"Aye. Lady Akira went in to see her and dismissed me. So I left a man to guard the chamber and will make sure that Keary and his men find work to do, or they will be staying below stairs."

James slapped Ian on the shoulder. "Come, I will write a missive to send to Dunbarton, offering him an exchange for my brother and Gunnolf. Mayhap this time he will be more agreeable."

***

Eilis paced across the chamber, irritated that Fergus would not let her leave to speak to Lady Allison. Lady Akira, he had assured her, was visiting with her at the moment and wished to speak with her in private.

Eilis stalked to the window and stared out. Keary and his men worked alongside James's men on the south wall. As she watched them, she noted two of them glancing at the open gate. They spoke privately to each other, and the one nodded at a wagon filled with kegs.

Were the barrels empty? If they planned to slip away in such a manner, mayhap she could? She glanced back at the door where Fergus, the bear, guarded her entryway as usual. Tavia was still in the village, seeing to the woman and her new bairn. Lady Akira had been so busy talking to James about something in the great hall upon their return that no one seemed to have considered Eilis was alone in the chamber.

She glanced at James's chamber door. Finding him in there twice was unfathomable poor luck. Surely, he would not be in there at this time of day. She walked over to the door and placed her ear against the solid wood. She heard no one stirring in the chamber.

Steeling her back and her resolve, she pushed the door open. She saw no sign of anyone and sighed deeply. Gently, she closed the door behind her. Her legs felt heavy and her breathing so labored, the length of

James's chamber seemed to grow before her as she stared at his chamber door and mayhap her freedom.

Wringing her hands, she stalked toward the door, until voices outside the chamber made her stop abruptly. She stood frozen to the spot. If 'twas James…

Mayhap a servant had come to clean the chamber. Or mayhap no one intended to enter the room. Eilis remained indecisive, wanting to flee back to the safety of her chamber, but desperately wishing she could find the courage to stand her ground and leave as soon as whoever stood outside the chamber left.

The door began to creak open, and Eilis would never make it across the room to her door. Should she hide under the massive bed? Or behind the curtains hung around it? Which?

If 'twas a servant, she might be here to empty the chamber pot underneath the bed. Eilis dove through the curtains onto the mattress and buried herself under James's quilts and furs and a pillow she managed to snag before the door opened all the way and shut.

No one said a word. Och, had someone come to air the bedding? No. Eilis would not worry herself about it. 'Twas a servant to empty the chamber pot or mayhap change the rushes, naught more.

Footsteps stopped near the chest she'd seen against the wall. The chest creaked open. Then everything was quiet. Well, except for the noises outside—shouts of men working on the wall, someone singing in the inner bailey, the servants splashing water as they washed the linens, and a hammer striking the anvil near the stables.

In the chamber, the place was deathly quiet. Except for the pounding of her heartbeat in her ears. She lay very still, afraid to move a muscle or cause the ropes to creak under her weight, or to disturb the curtains draped around the mattress.

She barely breathed, and her thoughts grew light and fuzzy.

A bench or chair creaked. She frowned. Whatever was the servant doing in the laird's chamber? She bit her lower lip. It could not be James. She closed her eyes and prayed 'twas not him. Then she frowned. Even if the laird had come to his chamber, he would not touch the bed. Not at this time of day.

She relaxed just a wee bit, although she still barely breathed and didn't move a hair.

Boots hit the floor. Och, she clenched her teeth and held onto the quilt with a death grip. If any should find her in here while James was changing clothes and that person was as much of a gossip as Nesta...

But Eilis's saving grace was she was fully clothed. They could not make much of the situation while she was dressed, could they?

Whoever it was yanked one of the curtains aside. Her skin grew clammy, her heartbeat racing as if she'd been running through the heather all day.

As many quilts and furs and pillows covered the huge mattress and kept her properly, *she hoped*, buried, the man wouldn't discover her. Unless he or she tried to remove the bedding and planned to air the linens in that manner. But what of the sound of the boots hitting the floor?

Weight on one edge of the mattress made it rock, and she fought rolling toward the side where it tilted down. God have mercy! She was about to be caught.

The word would spread she had attempted to seduce Laird James. No, they would think she tried to escape is all.

Whoever leaned onto the mattress pulled some of the covers up. She stifled a squeak. And then the person yanked the curtain closed.

Not a servant. *James.* His heady, masculine scent. His sighs. Him. Beside her. In bed. *His* bed. She closed her eyes and groaned inwardly. What was he doing in bed at this time of day?

He was attempting to get comfortable, moving closer to her, rearranging the covers, groping for a pillow, for the one covering her face.

She cringed, wanting to back away, yet if she moved, she'd send a ripple of a wave through the ropes holding the mattress.

He moved around some more while she braced herself, fearing rolling toward him as his weight and movement threatened to dislodge her from her safe spot.

Then he seemed to find another pillow and settled back down.

After what seemed an excruciatingly long time while he resituated the furs, the quilts, another pillow, he grew quiet, sighed again, and didn't move any further.

God's teeth, what now? She couldn't move even a wee bit without rocking the mattress. She was afraid to breathe, and the pillow was limiting her air even more. If she moved and he found her here...

She closed her eyes. 'Twas all she could do and pray he would leave the bed before long, never aware she had been here.

\*\*\*

At first, James couldn't get comfortable. The scent

of lavender tickled his nose, and he assumed one of the servants had sprinkled the petals in his bed. The fragrance reminded him of Eilis, and thinking of the lass was not conducive to sleep.

He was exhausted beyond measure after all the late night excursions, searching for his brother. Although an afternoon respite served him well at times like this. When he had Catriona in his bed, he planned many of these mid-day naps to energize himself. He doubted he would get much sleep, though.

He yawned. Nor would he now if he didn't quit thinking of lovely lasses filling his bed. He pulled the covers to his chin, the chamber chilly while a cool breeze blew in through the window, his skin bared the way he always slept. He rolled over and thought the linens more bunched up than he remembered. Again, he yawned and closed his eyes, tucking a pillow beneath his cheek.

He prayed the missive the messenger carried to Dunbarton would sway the old chief to see reason this time and release his brother and Gunnolf. Although he highly suspected it wouldn't.

Attempting to think of what it would be like with Catriona naked in his arms, all he could see was Eilis's sweet face, the silky shift hiding naught of her breasts, the way her rosy nipples peaked.

He groaned and ran his hands through his hair. As soon as he saw Catriona, he would forget the lust he felt for Eilis. This time he tried to put aside all thoughts of lavender-scented lassies, calculated the money in his treasury in his head for a while, trying to secure sleep, and drifted off.

Until his hand touched a soft, silky warmth as he

stretched his fingers underneath a pillow, unaware he had even done so at first. Recognition dawned at once. A lassie was in his bed. A servant or a maid seeking his attention? He stifled a snort. Nay, 'twas a servant sneaking an afternoon nap in his bed, thinking he would not discover her.

He lifted his head and stared at the buried figure in the shadowed darkness of the curtained bed. Could not be an assassin, or the brigand would not still be lying quietly in his bed.

Nay, was the petite figure of a woman, made larger by the number of quilts and furs covering her.

One manner in which to send a woman away he didn't wish to dally with, kiss her and give her such a fright, she'd run screaming from the chamber. None other would try such a thing once the word spread.

He moved closer to the woman, but although the mattress swung slightly, the servant didn't stir. He slipped his hand underneath the quilt, sliding his fingers over her waist. She didn't respond. His eyebrows rose. The lass was more tired than he had been. With his free hand, he lifted the pillow off her face, but 'twas too dark to see her. No matter. He slid closer to reach her lips with his, her hands folded upon her chest, and kissed her mouth.

Her tongue pierced the seam and licked her lips. He kissed her mouth again, and she kissed him back! Just a gentle movement. God's teeth, the woman wasn't supposed to want him!

He touched her breast, rubbing the mound, and she moaned, the sweet, sultry sound stirring his groin. He was about to remove his hand from her breast and order her from the room, since his frightening her away wasn't working, when someone pounded on his chamber door.

God's knees, he truly didn't want the servant caught in here with him, only wishing to scare her off so she wouldn't sleep in his bed again.

"Oh," she cried out and touched his bare chest, squeaked, grabbed his pillow, and tried to scurry away from him in the bed.

He seized her arm and said in a hushed voice, "Hold, woman." To the new knocking at his door, he called out in a gruff manner, "Yes?"

The door creaked open, and footsteps hurried across the chamber. About to be discovered with a woman in his bed, James pushed her back and buried her with his pillow. "Lie still and be quiet," he whispered.

He jerked the curtain aside and scowled at Niall. "What is the matter now?"

Although James knew better than to be angry with his cousin. From the concerned expression on Niall's face, he knew it couldn't be good.

Niall looked at the bundle next to him then his expression changed from worry to surprise. "Fergus said Nesta came to stay with Eilis. She was not there when the maid arrived." He looked at the bundle next to James again.

James glanced at the maid in his bed. It could not be Eilis.

Niall waited expectantly. James let out his breath in exasperation.

Niall said, "If the lass is tucked somewhere safe, then I will need to tell everyone to cease searching for her." He again looked at the bundled figure. And waited.

James reached out and ran his hand over her blanketed thigh. "Is it you, Eilis?" She moved away from him.

Niall raised a brow. "You know not who is in your bed?"

"Niall." James gave him a sharp look.

"What do you wish me to do?" Niall asked, half serious, half amused.

As much as James didn't want to reveal the woman in his bed, especially if it was Eilis, Niall was right. They couldn't have half their people searching for her if she was safe.

'Twas the lass's folly that she got herself into this predicament. He pulled the pillow away from her face, but a quilt still hid her identity.

"'Tis a wonder you could breathe under all that." James pulled back the quilt.

Tears shimmered in Eilis's eyes as she looked from James to Niall. "We...we did not...I mean to say, he did not even know I was here until you came barging into the room."

Niall raised his hands with a shrug and turned to James. "Shall I fetch the priest?"

James frowned at him.

"I am fully dressed." Eilis jerked the covers aside, but her gown rested above her knees. She yanked the covers back up, her face flushed.

Niall smirked. "A lady does not need to remove her garments for a gentleman to have his way with her."

"I cannot wed the lass unless I know her name," James warned.

"I will then." Niall folded his arms and smiled at

her.

"You cannot either, Niall. No one can."

"Make up a name then."

James ran his hand over the hint of beard on his jaw. "She has already done so."

Fergus poked his head into the chamber. "Lady Akira is frantic to think we have lost Eilis. She wishes to see you, my laird."

"Tell her the lady has been found."

Fergus waited, undoubtedly to learn where the lady was now. James waved at him to leave. "Go to your guard post. The lady will return to the chamber shortly."

Fergus glanced at the bed, but from where he stood, he could not see Eilis. "Aye, my laird. Do you wish me to inform Lady Akira—"

"I will tell her shortly."

"No need," his mother said, stalking into his room.

His chest bare, his lap covered with a quilt, James growled inwardly. "I am not dressed."

"Of that I am well aware. What I want to know is where Eilis has slipped off to."

His mother glanced at the bed. James looked back, expecting to see Eilis in tears. But instead, he found she'd pulled the pillow and quilt over her face again.

"Who is here with you?" his mother asked. "'Tis not Eilis?" Her frown dissolved. "Is it?"

Niall smiled. James gave him a sour look.

"Fetch the priest," his mother said.

"We do not even know her name," James warned.

His mother waved her hand dismissively. "All is well. We will make one up." She sighed. "I wished to plan this more and ensure your brothers were here, but,

194

well, it cannot be helped. When a man and a woman are in love…"

Eilis groaned under the pillow.

James's mother smiled. "'Tis done." She turned her attention to Niall. "What are you still doing here? Fetch the priest!"

Enruig poked his head into the chamber. "My laird?"

James shook his head. "Everyone out. Let me get dressed!"

"I will speak to Enruig," James's mother said. She hurried to leave the chamber. "I will send another gown for Eilis. At least now we shall have an heir."

Eanruig looked to James to explain, but he just motioned for him to leave. Despite his mother's wishes, James could not take a woman to wife who still did not know her family's name.

Niall shook his head as he followed James's mother out of the chamber and shut the door.

"Think you that you can find your way to your chamber without my assistance, lass?" James said, running his hand under the covers to her hand and squeezed. "You have gotten us into a fine predicament. I fear nothing will stop my mother from having her way in this to save your honor, Eilis. Although truth be told, I am well pleased at the way things have turned out."

She pulled the pillow aside, and her eyes pleaded with him to save her from this nightmare. "Nothing happened between us," Eilis moaned.

"Aye, but that is not what will be said." God's truth, the woman had intrigued him and brightened his days from the moment he'd set eyes on her. Allowing her to return to her kin wasn't an option. As far as dealing with her family, he was sure he could come to some kind of agreement.

But he still had to know her name.

# CHAPTER 14

Below stairs in the great hall, James intercepted the priest as soon as he arrived, delaying the inevitable, while his mother searched for just the right gown to have Eilis married in. James did not know which clan Eilis truly belonged, whether she was betrothed, or even already wed. Complicating matters, Catriona was due to arrive at anytime, thinking *she* would be his betrothed.

Ian waited nearby, ready to do James's further bidding.

"Niall called you here before I have need of your services, Father," James said to the robed old man whose face was heavily wrinkled as if a river of tears had carved lines into the skin.

"Lady Akira said you have finally decided on a bride choice and that it is most urgent you proceed with the marriage."

Niall must have informed the old priest some of the reason for the urgency. James stiffened his spine. He would have a word with Niall shortly. "Aye, well, circumstances make it necessary to delay this wedding for a time."

The priest narrowed his gray eyes. "Lady Akira insisted it was most pressing."

"Later," James said, with authority in his tone.

His mother hurried into the hall, her eyes sparkling with delight and a hint of a smile played on her lips.

"You have good news, I pray." And not that she believed James would marry Eilis without knowing her family name.

His mother smiled broadly. "Aye. The young lady, Fia, just arrived. The one who knows Eilis. One of our servants hid beneath Eilis's bed while the lady was in my chamber and will eavesdrop on their private conversation."

James raised his brows, turned to the priest, and said, "Later, Father. I may need you sooner than I thought. Partake of the meal with us, and the wedding will have to take place later."

The priest nodded and left the hall. Ian said to him, "Mead and something to eat, Father, if it pleases you? Come, see how the south wall progresses in the meantime."

James leaned down and kissed his mother's cheek. "You have the devil in you, my lady mother."

"Aye, now you know where you and your brothers get it from."

"Here I always thought we got it from da."

Eanruig escorted Fia into the hall, and James considered the way the lady looked from the top of her head to the hem of her brown woolen gown. She was small like Eilis and his mother, fine-boned, but sturdy looking. Her hair and eyes were dark brown and her skin more peach. Where Eilis's face was small, Fia's was longer, more determined.

Eanruig was right. The two ladies did not favor one another, except for the small smile that lighted her lips. Well, and the doe-like eyes the two had also. Her gaze flitted to James, and she quickly curtsied, her cheeks flushed with color. In that respect, she looked like Eilis also. Mayhap they were related after all.

With a smile, Lady Akira greeted Fia and motioned for her to come with her. "You say you do not know Eilis, yet our seneschal said he saw the two of you together last summer."

The color washed out of Fia's cheeks. James was certain Eanruig had guessed right.

They climbed the stairs while James followed some distance behind.

"Your seneschal was mistaken, my lady," the woman said, her tone curt, but nervous.

"Aye, well, Eanruig is very observant when it comes to the beauty of fine lasses. He said that you and Eilis fairly shined as bright as the sun."

Fia glanced back at James, her cheeks properly blushing. James withheld a smile, hoping the lass would soon confess the truth. Once he learned Eilis's true name, the lady would be his.

A servant hurried to open the door to Eilis's chamber. He knew his mother had the matter concerning Eilis and Fia well at hand.

Time for James to get back to the business of freeing his brother and Gunnolf. He headed for the chamber where Allison and the rest of his mother's ladies-in-waiting stayed. When he reached the door, Niall greeted him outside the chamber. "I have spoken with Lady Allison. She says she has never been to Brecken. That Eilis was mistaken."

"Allison lies."

Niall let out his breath. "As for having any relation at Dunbarton's castle, Allison denies this as well. She also states that she did not release Dougald and Gunnolf."

"And you believe her?" James didn't know what to think concerning the lass's involvement with freeing his brother and Gunnolf. Mayhap that was a bit of a stretch.

Niall shook his head. "Not a word. She looked as guilty as Dougald would when your da caught him stealing a kiss from a maid a' milking the first time. What about Eilis? Will you wed the lass?"

"Fia is here now."

Niall smiled. "Then we shall soon know Eilis's clan. Then you will take her to wive?"

"What if she is betrothed?"

"Seems to me the betrothal will be for naught."

Ian hurried to join them. "Lady Akira wishes you to join her for the meal."

"And? Did she say anything…" James took a deep breath. "I shall learn the truth soon enough. Come, let us eat."

He hoped like the devil the woman was not already wed, for that would be the only situation that would thwart him in his marriage plans. For her sake, Catriona should have come when he'd asked long ago. He smiled.

Now 'twas too late.

***

Eilis attempted to embroider away her nervousness as she waited for Lady Akira to return with yet another gown she wished Eilis to consider wearing for wedding James. How could she marry him without knowing who she truly was? James and his mother could not force such a state on her. The priest could not do so without knowing her family's name. At least she didn't think so. Unless they made up a name for her. If they did, would the marriage be valid? Mayhap not.

She set aside her embroidery, stood, then stalked to the window. Keary, bastard son of Dunbarton, and his friends, though one less now, still worked on the south wall.

What if James did marry her despite her lack of name? Would he wish his rights as her husband?

Och. She wrung her hands. He could not. If they consummated the relationship, she would be spoiled for any other man.

Keary helped lift another stone in place with several others. Where was the missing man? The one who had been eyeing the wagon carrying the barrels? Now the wagon was gone. Had he escaped in one of the kegs?

The door opened to Eilis's chamber, and her heart skipped a beat. She swung around, expecting Lady Akira and a servant with yet another gown. Instead, Fia entered the room, while Lady Akira and Tavia hovered outside with Fergus.

Eilis gasped, "Fia." Thank God, she recognized her favorite cousin, her dark brown hair flowing over her shoulders in satiny curls, her chestnut eyes bright with tears.

For a moment, neither said anything because of their audience, although it took all Eilis's restraint not to rush across the room and embrace her cousin.

"Come, let us leave the ladies to visit alone," Lady Akira said to Tavia with a smile. "The meal shall be ready shortly."

Once the door shut, Eilis and Fia raced across the floor and hugged one another, both sobbing.

Fia said between choking tears, "You were…were dead. Eanruig came to our village and said so. I thought I would never see you again."

The memories flooded back at once. In horror, Eilis remembered her clan's name. MacBurness. And her uncle's mission. Marry her off to Dunbarton while she pretended to be her uncle's daughter.

Och, what if James could ransom her for Dougald and Gunnolf's release, ignoring the fact she wasn't truly betrothed to Dunbarton? Why not? She could see how important his brother was to him, and blood would come first over interest in some lassie he knew not. Besides, he still had Catriona.

"You have not heard the half of it." Disheartened, Eilis slumped onto the cushion covering the bench.

God's teeth, if Dunbarton's men had known she, who was *supposed* to be his betrothed, was in the company of James's brother unchaperoned, he probably would have killed them.

Fia lowered her gaze to the rushes on the floor.

"You *have* heard."

"Aye, Eilis. Everyone who is kin to you has been told you are Agnes and shall wed Dunbarton."

"I will not."

Wringing her hands, Fia said, "You must. You cannot think to avoid it."

Eilis slumped further on the bench. "I will not marry him."

"You are betrothed to him."

"Never I! Agnes was, and she died of a fever."

Fia let out her breath in exasperation. "Aye, but anyone who denies you are Agnes will be banished or worse."

"Does my uncle know I am still alive?"

"Rumors abound. Although when Eanruig came looking for me, he only told me he had found you. Still, I fear word may reach our uncle that inquiries were made concerning you. Once he learns you live, you will not be able to escape your marriage."

"Agnes's marriage!" Eilis jumped up from the bench, paced across the room, then stopped and faced her cousin. "Will you not tell Laird James I am Agnes's cousin?"

Her eyes wide, Fia quickly shook her head. "Nay. I cannot. You would best heed our uncle's words also."

Eilis clenched her teeth to combat the exasperation she felt. 'Twould be best if her cousin—who would not help her with her cause—knew naught about what Eilis intended.

Someone knocked on the door, shattering Eilis's composure, and she gave a small gasp. "Aye?"

The door opened, and the female servant said, "Laird James awaits your presence at the meal."

Stalwart Fergus stood beside the door, awaiting Eilis's compliance.

"Why do you have an armed guard?" Fia whispered to her.

"To protect my virtue." Which seemed was in a shambles already.

Seizing Fia's arm, she led her out of the chamber. She hated to lie to her cousin, but no one could be trusted who would do her uncle's bidding.

They walked together down the stairs and strode toward the great hall. Fia cleared her throat. "His Lairdship sent word to my da that he was considering me as a bride's choice."

"You also?" Eilis shook her head. "I thought he only wished you to reveal who I was."

Fia took a deep breath and smiled in her usual cheerful manner. "Well, he only said so to please my da, but of course the real reason was he wanted to see if we knew each other."

Eilis smiled back in return. "Aye, you were always my canny cousin. His Lairdship wishes me to make a lady jealous who is coming to see him on the morrow."

"Make a lady envious?" Fia shook her head. "I cannot see how that would make a lady want His Lairdship. You say she is arriving on the morrow?"

"This verra day," Lady Akira corrected Fia, her face beaming as she slipped in behind them. "Catriona made haste and has just arrived. I pray you and Eilis will make her work for my son's affection."

Upon hearing Lady Akira's words, Eilis's heart raced. Had Lady Akira wished to catch Eilis's private conversation with her cousin? To discover the truth of their relationship?

Then another thought occurred to her. "Where will Catriona be staying?"

"In the chamber Nighinn and her mother stayed. Yours is far nicer. That will teach Catriona to delay her journey here. Fia will stay with you." Lady Akira flashed Eilis another heart-warming smile then walked with them into the great hall.

For an instant, Eilis wondered if Lady Akira had

given up the notion Eilis would wed her son. After all, now the one he wished to marry was here, and Eilis was of no real importance. She would be gone, and no one would ever know she'd been found in such a compromising situation with James.

She still couldn't believe antagonizing Catriona would help in securing a marriage agreement with James though.

Eilis was torn over Dougald and Gunnolf also, who had ensured her safety before they were taken prisoner again. Easily, she could offer herself in exchange for their freedom, to lie and say she was truly Agnes. Yet, if Dunbarton were to find her out...och, how could she live such a lie? He might very well take her life and war with her uncle over the matter.

Then Eilis spied Catriona, and her heart nearly stopped.

Why had no one mentioned where the lady was from? She chided herself. 'Twould not have mattered as she would probably not have remembered her anyway. But seeing the woman...her bright red curls the color of a fiery sunset and blue eyes as dark as the deepest loch, a willowy figure, and ivory skin defined her, but 'twas her sharp tongue and mean-hearted spirit that kept most out of her path.

Seizing Fia's arm before Catriona caught sight of them, Eilis wished she could flee the castle more than ever. "We are in trouble now."

"Och, *she* is the one his Lairdship has his heart set on marrying?" Fia whispered to Eilis, shrinking behind Lady Akira and Tavia so they could not be seen. "Eanruig told me he wants us to pretend to desire His Lairdship's hand in marriage so that some lady will consent to be his wife. But I had no idea who the woman was."

Catriona was speaking to a maid, her mouth turned down, eyes narrowed. The maid bobbed, then hurried off.

"Catriona eats servants to break her fast. How could James wish to wed the tyrant? Although, I'm sure Catriona would be on her best behavior in front of a suitor who might care about a servant's treatment. Her servants would never complain for fear of dismissal." Eilis hmpfed under her breath. "Here I was afraid of harming their relationship. But a new dilemma presents itself. Now His Lairdship will learn who I am."

"'Twas only a matter of time before His Lairdship learned who we were." Fia offered a coy smile. "You are not concerned about wedging a boulder between them any longer, aye?"

Nay, 'twas that James might feel beholden to wed Eilis. She straightened. "His Lairdship is fair game, do you not think, dear cousin?" At least until Eilis could plan a way out of this nightmare.

Fia laughed. "Aye."

Catriona caught sight of Fia first, narrowed her eyes even further, and headed straight for her.

Eilis overheard Lady Akira say, "I believe, James, the entertainment is about to begin."

"We have not had anything but entertainment since Eilis arrived," he replied, but she couldn't tell from his shuttered expression what he was feeling.

Catriona reached Fia and asked, "What are *you* doing here?"

As if Fia were any less of a prize.

"Same as you, I suspect." Fia tilted her smiling

face up. "Wanting a chance at being Laird James's bride."

Eilis smiled at her cousin's response.

Catriona gave a short laugh. "That would be the day. You are naught but a goat herder's daughter." She glanced at Eilis, and her eyes widened. "What...when...you were dead."

Eilis held her tongue. Did Catriona recognize her to be Eilis or Agnes?

"You cannot be seeking his Lairdship's hand also. You are betrothed to Dunbarton, the old cantankerous fool. Buried two wives already, and I suspect you will be the next."

Catriona thought her to be Agnes then. Eilis's heart sank.

James's eyes darkened to nearly black, his jaw tightening. Lady Akira's eyes rounded. Eilis opened her mouth to speak, to contradict the spoiled clan chief's daughter's claim before James called one of his men to cast Eilis beyond the castle walls to seek the arms of her betrothed, who was *not* her betrothed. Although, she would have her freedom then, if he did not decide to turn her over to Dunbarton in payment of ransom for Dougald.

She caught a glimpse of Keary listening with interest as the hall was so deathly quiet. Not good. If he thought she was truly betrothed to his father, and he could somehow smuggle the news out...

Fia stole Eilis's words before she could speak them. "Agnes died of a fever before Eilis sailed from Ireland. This is Eilis. Agnes was betrothed to Dunbarton, as well you know. Alas, Eilis has nearly won Laird MacNeill's hand." She wrapped her arm around Eilis's waist and gave her a comforting hug. "You and I, dear lady, are both a wee bit too late, Catriona."

Eilis closed her gaping mouth. Hadn't her cousin refused to tell anyone Eilis was not Agnes, fearing their uncle's wrath?

Lady Akira's gaze switched from Fia to Eilis, waiting for her to respond. James looked as angry as when he pulled Eilis from his horse when she'd tried to steal away.

Glowering at Fia, Catriona's lips thinned to an angry line. "You lie."

"Nay." Fia took Eilis's hand. "You know we are like two halves of a clam shell, inseparable until she had to return to her uncle's castle. I never could abide cousin Agnes and her haughty ways, being that she was the clan chief's daughter. Reminded me of you, come to think of it. Truth be told, even when Eilis's da had been the clan chief, she never put on airs."

Catriona's face reddened.

"Come, let us sit at the head table, ladies," Lady Akira said, the color in her face returning.

When she led them to the table, Fia whispered to Eilis, "We will have to run away together when the time comes, or both have to face our uncle's harsh punishment."

"I did not want to get you in trouble, Fia," Eilis whispered back.

"Nay, we were always bound together. Come, let us take James's arms and escort him to the table. Give Catriona something to really scowl about."

Though she felt awkward in doing so, considering how intimately Nesta had already found her with James and the later incident as well when even his mother had discovered him naked in bed with Eilis… She took a deep breath, which did nothing to settle her nerves. With Fia's encouragement, Eilis looped her arm around James's right arm and Fia his left, leaving Catriona to trail behind.

Lady Akira gave Eilis a supporting smile, but Eilis didn't think His Lairdship was pleased with her the way his expression remained hard. Did he presume she was Agnes and betrothed to Dunbarton, his enemy, after all?

Or was he considering offering her for ransom to free his kin?

When they reached the table, Catriona was seated on the other side of Fia, while James sat between Eilis and her cousin.

After saying grace, James leaned over to Eilis. "Tell me the whole story, or I will send word at once to your uncle that you are here."

# CHAPTER 15

James would turn her over to her uncle? Not
Dunbarton? Eilis sat taller at the head table. Still, her
heart shriveled to think she might be returned to her
uncle and have to face his anger. "I thought Fia
explained everything, although she will be in as much
trouble as me for telling the truth."

James glowered at Eilis.

Trying to smooth the situation over between James
and her, she leaned over and kissed his cheek. The
volume of talking in the hall ceased at once. Catriona
choked on her mead. Fia smiled at Eilis.

"Think you that I will wed you?" James asked
harshly under his breath.

She drew closer and looked up at him with the
most adoring eyes she could muster, her voice lowered
for his ears only. "I am supposed to be here for
Catriona's benefit. Aye, my laird?"

Scowling at her, he steeled his back against his
chair. "Tell me what this is all about with your uncle."

She sighed. "Agnes, my cousin, was betrothed to Dunbarton, but she died the day she was to sail to meet him. My uncle said I would take her place and pretend to be her. I will not live a falsehood." Eilis snatched a piece of cheese from James's trencher and waved it at him. "How long do you think I would survive if Dunbarton discovers the truth? If he does not dispense with me at once, he might still decide to do battle with my uncle because of the deceit."

James's eyes bored into hers as if he was trying to force her to tell the truth. She refused to drop her gaze, to submit to his coercion.

"Nor did you want to marry Dunbarton," he reminded her.

"Do you blame me? Agnes did not wish to marry him, either, but she would have done so for the sake of the clan. The marriage contract was for his marriage to Agnes, never to me. Fearing Dunbarton would refuse me in Agnes's place, my uncle remains dishonest with him about what has befallen my cousin. Worse—if it could be considered worse—my uncle warned our clan that if any should reveal the truth about my identity, he would take care of them. He means in his harsh way of dealing with dissent."

The muscle in James's jaw ticked, but it was impossible to tell what he was thinking.

A girl spoke to Lady Akira seated on the other side of James, and she heard some of the conversation. Apparently, the servant had somehow overheard the talk Fia and Eilis had in the bedchamber and confirmed what was said.

Lady Akira cleared her throat to get Eilis's attention. "You are the niece of Clan Chief

MacBurness?"

"Aye, my lady."

"We have no quarrel with them, thank the heavens," Lady Akira said, sounding vastly relieved.

No, but circumstances would change if Eilis's uncle learned she lived and found her staying with MacNeill.

James rubbed his temple. "Then if that be the case, you are bound to wed no one."

"Unless you see fit to wed me." Eilis gave him a winsome smile, then cast a look Catriona's way. The woman's blue eyes had hardened. After lifting James's goblet off the table, Eilis sipped from it. "Then I would be much pleased."

She only intended to do her part as far as baiting Catriona, but she had no intention of getting James in trouble with her uncle. And no desire to have to face his furor, either. Besides, James's intention was only a ploy to get Catriona's acquiescence. The other matter, having been caught in James's bed, seemed to have gone no further than his chamber. So the notion of marrying her for her honor seemed no longer necessary.

Although Eilis would like to stop the marriage so he could find someone more suitable than the witch.

As he watched Eilis's actions, James's brooding look changed subtly from anger to fascination. The sparkle in his dark eyes returned, and his lips rose in a devilish smirk. "You are lighting a wildfire, lady, and I am certain you have not the ability to control it."

She set his goblet down, unsure as to the meaning of his words.

"We will take a walk in the gardens tonight, you and I, under the full moon and with torches lighting our way."

She leaned closer to him, hoping to push Catriona into making a move for James, or more wickedly, that she would give him up. "Aye, my laird. 'Twill be my greatest pleasure."

His mouth curved up even more, and he looked every bit the rakish rogue. For the briefest of moments, she wished she truly could be James's intended. If only circumstances were different.

Catriona squinted her eyes at Keary who was seated at one of the lower tables, James's men surrounding him and his companions while they ate. "Is that Dunbarton's son?"

"Aye." James stabbed a chunk of cheese with his knife.

"Whatever is he doing here?"

"He is a guest, Catriona."

"You would not treat him as a guest unless...has he finally turned against his father and joined you?" Catriona didn't wait for an explanation before she smiled broadly at Keary.

What was the wench's game?

Keary caught her eye and smiled back.

"The years have been kind to him."

"Do you know him well?" James asked, the ire building in his blood. Had Catriona bedded his enemy's bastard son?

Catriona coiled a strand of dark hair around her finger and smiled at James. "I know him, aye. He hunted with my late husband."

"And that is all?"

"He is an avid hunter."

Aye of four-legged beasties and of the two-legged

variety of the fairer sex. 'Twas said the man preyed on widows left well of means, while playing to their need for pretty phrases and silky seduction, no matter their age. Catriona would more than fit the role. She had to be mad, thinking she could act in thus a manner and not perturb James. 'Twas providence Eilis had been delivered to him to save him from his folly in thinking Catriona was the one for him.

He reached over and took Eilis's hand and gave it a reassuring squeeze. She would be his soon.

Eilis frowned at Catriona when the woman so blatantly showed interest in James's enemy. What was the woman's intent? To make James jealous? She was but a fool.

Eilis couldn't understand how James had ever been interested in Catriona. Then she reconsidered. She was a beautiful creature, and when around James, she probably kept her claws well hidden, only using her purrs to seduce him.

Catriona turned her attention from Dunbarton's son to Eilis. Catriona's chilly glare could have frozen all the lochs in Scotland in the middle of summer.

Eilis gave her a satisfied smile. She was not one to act unkindly toward another, but in Catriona's case, the woman deserved worse. Even as a young girl, Catriona made a play for Eilis's father who she thought would be clan chief—and he was, for the briefest of times—until he died in battle. The woman hadn't any real heart.

Eilis took a deep breath.

Did James not know what a deceitful woman Catriona was? Mayhap he liked that she shared every man's bed she could charm her way into—well, only if she thought it worthy of her time. Mayhap it made her as good a lover as James no doubt desired. Why would he be interested in an untried lass?

Fia gave Eilis a knowing nod as if telling Eilis she'd done her job well. Lady Akira chattered to another lady, more talkative than Eilis had ever seen her. The whole of James's clan seemed to watch the goings on at the head table more than usual. Even Niall and Eanruig wore perpetual silly smiles.

Eilis wished she could pretend to seduce the earl in front of Catriona and only the witch herself.

James stepped into the role way too readily. Wasn't he supposed to act a wee bit interested in Eilis but much more so in Catriona? Not once had he acted as though he desired Catriona's attentions at the meal. Several times, Eilis caught him watching her as if attempting to figure her out. Well, mayhap she was difficult to understand. One moment, shy and retiring, wishing to flee at all costs. Now, brazenly flirtatious when she had barely been that way a day in her life—she didn't think. She still could not remember all her past. She had to see someone or hear something to recall bits of it.

Except she remembered a cousin, six times removed that she had acted uncommonly silly over. Like James, dark-haired and eyed, he had the same kind of humor, a flaring temper, but a kind heart. Mayhap that's why she had a soft spot in her heart for James. Her cousin wed another, which was to be expected, but he had been the only man she'd made a fool of herself over, swaying her hips a little too much when he was around. Fluttering her lashes at him, acting coyly. What did it get her? Naught. He married another.

She hmpfed under her breath. Mayhap 'twas why she thought naught would ever come of her attempts at flirtation. Other women made men drool at the sight of them when the ladies fluttered about. Not Eilis. They ignored her as if she was too small a fish in the loch to bother with. Mayhap, though, it was because she had been the clan chief's niece after her father's untimely death, and no one wished to earn her uncle's wrath should they grow too interested in her.

She shook loose of the memory and her morose thoughts. James was marrying Catriona, and Eilis had to steal away before her uncle discovered her here. James must have known all about Catriona if she stayed in the room adjoining his chamber. Eilis was but a fool to think he wanted some other kind of woman.

James ended the meal and rose from his chair. Offering his arm to Eilis, he asked, "Are you ready for our walk, lass?"

"Aye." She reminded herself it was only for show. Eagerly accepting his arm, she nearly pulled him from the hall to escape.

James chuckled, and she looked up and found him smiling broadly. "I cannot decide which of you I like better."

She raised her brows in question.

"The sweet, retiring young lassie who wishes naught to do with me or the bold, flirtatious lass who cannot get enough of me."

As hot as her face felt, she assumed it had turned scarlet. "'Tis only a charade, my laird."

"Aye," he said without conviction. Then his smile broadened. "Which of you is a charade?"

She looked down at her feet, thinking of the way she'd acted toward her distant cousin.

James laughed. "I see I still do not know all there is

about you, but it appears you have regained more of your memories."

He led her outside where clouds now blocked the sinking sun. Clansmen returned to their tasks before it was time to retire for the night. Guards watched from the wall walk surrounding the castle, ever alert.

James's look turned more solemn. "All jesting aside, you remember who you are now, Eilis? You remember all your past? You said you have never been courted before. Is this true?"

Eilis smiled, pulled her hand free from James's, and folded her arms. "Why? You are not truly courting me, so what difference does it make to you, my laird?" Her words were hushed, meant for only James's ears in case Catriona sneaked up behind them. Knowing the way she was, Eilis would not put it past the woman.

"Call me James." He separated her locked arms and retook her hand. "I think you know I intend to wed you. After this afternoon's rendezvous in my bed…"

"Nothing happened. And as long as Nesta was not there to tell all your people and I am far away from here when you wed—"

"You have not answered me, Eilis. Do you recall all your memories? Have you ever been courted?" He led her near the stable, and a boy ran out to greet them.

"Did you and the lady wish to ride, my laird?" The boy shifted his gaze from James to Eilis.

"Would you like to ride this eve, lass?" James asked, squeezing her hand.

In truth, she'd like a ride to freedom. Glancing back at the keep, she saw Catriona watching them, her expression bitter as if she'd been drinking soured mead, which decided the matter. "I can ride."

217

"Good." James motioned to the lad. "Saddle the horses."

The lad dashed back inside the stable, and a horse softly whinnied while another snorted.

James turned to Eilis. "Well? I am still waiting to hear the answer to my question."

"Nay, no one has courted me." She looked back at the stables, vaguely remembering the day she nearly made her escape when she'd been so ill. "Are you not afraid I will run away from you?"

He studied her, his mouth curved up. "Nay. You are supposed to be feigning infatuation for me. How will you succeed in pulling this off in front of Catriona if you run away?" How could Eilis even believe he did not intend to marry her? He would make an offer MacBurness could not turn down.

"Catriona will not be going for a ride, my laird."

"Call me James, lass. The lady watches us from the keep. She cannot hear our conversation from this distance, but she looks most sour. You are creating an excellent ruse." Which, as far as James was concerned, was truly no longer needed. But if Eilis needed to play the game that would allow her to be more intimate with him, he would not deny her.

The lad led the horses to James, his own fine black steed, and a gentler roan for the lady. Rogue poked his muzzle in Eilis's face. James raised his brows in surprise.

Eilis laughed, and her voice sounded like a bit of fairy magic. "I thought he liked me because I wore your brat and he thought I was you."

"'Tis unlikely." James lifted her onto the roan. "The horse knows me with or without my brat. He would not mistake another wearing mine for me. However, he does recognize a person who has a gift with animals." He ran his hand over his horse's flank. "You see, I saved him when he was a colt from a clansman who had beaten him near death." He swung his leg over his saddle. "I have found ever since Rogue to be a good judge of character."

Eilis studied his horse. "He is a beautiful animal. I cannot imagine anyone being so cruel."

"Aye, well, I was but a wee lad but hid Rogue for some time until my da discovered his hiding place. Before my da could make his clansman pay for the crime against the colt and the violence he did against his wife and wee sons, the man drowned at sea. My da paid the family for the colt, and I raised him for my own."

"You are a remarkable man, James MacNeill. Any woman would find you a good husband, no doubt."

Aye, the Lady Eilis, first and foremost. They rode beyond the gate, and five of James's men on horseback soon followed them.

Eilis glanced back at them while James guided her to the loch. "They are for our protection, although the land is mine for many miles around. We have had problems from time to time with thieves and Dunbarton and his men, although now that the clan chief has captured my brother, I am certain he will not trouble us until I pay the ransom."

"James."

Pleased to hear the bonny lass finally speak his name, her voice as sweet as lavender, he asked, "Aye, lass?"

She took a deep breath, and he surmised what she

was going to say before she even spoke.

"You have to let me go. You know you do."

"You cannot ignore what happened between us in the chamber."

"Naught happened! Besides, my uncle—"

"He cannot force you to marry in your cousin's place."

"You do not wish to offer me for ransom to have your brother released?"

Shocked, James stared at her. "Nay, Eilis. Dunbarton is stubborn. He refuses my offer to exchange my brother and Gunnolf for whatever I have to barter. But I have sent a missive concerning his son. I would not hand you over since you are not Agnes, his betrothed. Neither Dougald nor Gunnolf would wish it, either, believe me."

She pursed her lips, and he knew she disagreed with him still. "All right. Then here is another matter. What about this business with Catriona?"

James pulled his horse to a stop before the blue loch, not getting her meaning. "What about Catriona?"

"You are marrying her, remember?"

She sounded so exasperated with him, it made him smile. "Why should I consider her, when we have been so intimately alone together, Eilis? Can we not take pleasure in our time here?" He dismounted and reached up to help her down from her horse.

"Catriona is not here to see this charade. There is no sense in—"

He pulled her down and kissed her lips, silencing her objection. Sweet heavens, the lass was like the purest silk, soft and desirable. She readily accepted his kiss, which spurred him on. With kisses that were gentle against her full lush mouth, he pressed his advantage, his body instantly becoming fully aroused.

His men looked away as Eilis leaned into the kiss, hesitant at first, then seeking his mouth, emboldened. He deepened the onslaught, licking her lips, questing an entrance, wishing again he and the lass were alone where they could take their actions further. Sweet torture was his as he kissed her mouth and desired to touch her breasts, to slip inside her willing body, to pleasure her like she'd never been pleasured before.

With the utmost restraint, he pulled away, leaving her lips swollen, her eyes rounded. Then she narrowed them, scowling. "'Tis only a ruse I am bound to play, my laird."

She could no more pretend to enjoy his attentions than he could hers. "Nay, Eilis. You sealed your fate with me when you came into my bed."

Horses headed in their direction, and James turned to see Catriona riding with her own escort to join them.

James smiled. "You see how important it is to play the game always?" Although the game was well over as far as he was concerned.

"You saw her coming?"

"Aye."

Eilis looked so crestfallen, he knew she felt the same for him as he did for her but still worried about her uncle's wrath. He would send a missive at once, offering a bride price.

\*\*\*

Eilis bit her lip, the twinge of hope that James kissed her because he truly cared for her, slipping away when he said he had seen Catriona coming and that he only wished to continue the ruse.

Nay, 'twas ludicrous to wish any kind of relationship with James. Her uncle would do battle with him. Och, so would Dunbarton. Between the two of them they would crush the MacNeill.

"My uncle will be furious if he discovers me here. I do not want bloodshed between our clans." Eilis stiffened, wishing Catriona would go back the way she'd come and leave James and her in peace to discuss matters.

James lifted Eilis's hand to his lips and kissed her so softly, 'twas like a butterfly's wing fluttering on her skin.

Catriona looked most dour, which pleased Eilis. At least the ruse was successful. As the woman closed the gap, Catriona smiled broadly at James, the look so faked Eilis wondered if James could tell.

"Why, James, you should have told me you were taking a ride to the loch." Catriona motioned to him as if she wanted help dismounting.

Eilis glanced up at the burgeoning clouds. "Think you it will rain, my lair…, uhm, James?"

"Aye," James said, his lips and eyes smiling. "'Tis time we were returning." He helped her onto her horse, then mounted his own.

"Thank you for the ride, James. It feels good to escape the confines of the castle again." Eilis figured he couldn't help but get her meaning.

\*\*\*

Catriona glowered at Eilis. "I did not know your uncle, Laird MacBurness, was interested in having ties with the MacNeill clan. I understood he was having trouble with Dunbarton's men, and I have heard it rumored he was having *both* Agnes and you married off

222

to Dunbarton and one of his chieftains.

James glanced at Eilis to see her reaction. Her lips had parted in surprise, and she looked a wee bit frightened. He couldn't believe the lass might be betrothed to one of Dunbarton's chieftains. What if she was and had kept it secret?

Or mayhap didn't remember?

# CHAPTER 16

"My uncle was too intent on making arrangements for Agnes. He had made no betrothal plans for me," Eilis said to Catriona, her back stiff as they rode back to Craigly.

Did Eilis truly remember this, James wondered.

"If he were too busy, how did he come to choose James for you?"

Eilis didn't hesitate to reply. "James had seen me visiting Fia in Glen Affric. Some of Fia's kin married into the MacNeill line—you know, his seneschal, Eanruig's. After James saw me, he wished to consider me as a bride choice."

James offered a small smile. Eilis was perfect in her role. She would make a bonny wife. *His* bonny wife if he were willing to admit the way he felt about her.

Catriona tilted her chin up, her blue eyes growing as dark as the sky. "And Fia?"

"Aye. If it were not for Fia, James would never have noticed me."

Catriona frowned at James. "I am sorry for delaying my journey to be with you. My favorite horse had become lame."

James noted the tone of her voice, as sweet as the honeyed mead he drank and the definite intimation was she wished to be with him, alone. Aye, a romp in his bed, to renew old acquaintances? To prove she still had what he desired?

"I see." James didn't believe she had a favorite horse that was lame. Nevertheless, he realized just how much her delay had bothered him, more than he'd wanted to allow himself to believe. And he realized just how much she was not the one for him. Would she smile at others who visited his abode like she did Keary after she and James were wed? Most likely. Just like his da fawned over other lassies while he was married to his mother.

None of it mattered now.

"When we return to Craigly, will you walk with me in the gardens, James?" Catriona asked.

"He has already asked me," Eilis said. "Although if it rains, he and I will have to find some other means to entertain ourselves."

The lass was quick. "A game, Eilis," James responded. "I have a Norman's chess game. Have you ever played chess?" Although why he offered was beyond his comprehension. He'd never known a woman who knew how to play.

"*I* have," Catriona said, looking hopeful that he'd ask her instead.

Eilis frowned, and he assumed she didn't know the rudiments of the game.

"Eilis?"

Although he preferred to best someone who could challenge him, James wished to find any means that he could to spend more time with Eilis before they exchanged vows. "I can teach you, if you have never played, Eilis." If the word reached his clansmen that he was teaching the lass the game, he'd never live it down.

"Mayhap I could watch you and Catriona," Eilis said.

Catriona gave a smug smile.

"Nay, I insist." He just hoped Eilis would catch on quickly as he didn't wish to embarrass her should she not be able to master the rules.

When they rode into the inner bailey, most of his people had already taken refuge inside the keep, except for a few stalwart men, speaking to each other in the blustery wind. James helped Eilis down from her mount while one of his men helped Catriona.

Eilis gave him an odd look, but she didn't say a word.

Fia and his mother joined them as soon as they walked inside the keep. Servants scurried to close the shutters over the windows.

"I have asked Father Rivers to stay with us the night. Did you have a nice ride?" his mother asked, looking from Eilis to Catriona then settling her gaze on James.

He knew she intended he and Eilis wed on the morrow. He had every intention of doing so also. "Cut short by the impending storm, my mother. But Eilis and I shall play a game of chess."

The strange expression Eilis and Fia shared made him again wonder what the matter was.

"Do you play well?" his mother asked Eilis while

they walked to the solar. "James usually only engages the very best in the game. Niall and Ian tend to challenge him the most. Although Dougald is the only other I know who has bested him."

James's stomach tightened.

Eilis's expression made her appear as though she was concerned. She looked at James as if waiting for him to release her from her nightmare but didn't say a word in reply to his mother.

He gave Eilis's hand a reassuring squeeze. "I am teaching the lady the rudiments."

His mother failed to hide a smile. Fia still looked as worried as Eilis.

As if the walls had ears, Niall appeared out of nowhere and smiled at James. "You are teaching the lass chess? This I have got to see."

James was certain the word would soon spread throughout the keep.

Once he and Eilis were seated at the gaming table in his solar, James carefully explained the rules of the game to her. As they played, he surmised she was either really adept at chess or she already knew it beforehand. Every move he made, she countered with speed and decisiveness.

Before long, several of James's men joined them and a few ladies also, but everyone watched in silence. Eilis captured a significant number of James's more important chess pieces, and every time she acquired another, several of his men studying their moves nodded. The room stayed quiet, until she grabbed another of his pieces in triumph. Then a murmur of comments rippled through his men.

Either in absolute awe or dumbfounded, the ladies

remained silent. He assumed Fia already knew something of Eilis's skill. Twice he caught Eilis looking up at him with the most woeful of expressions. Did she fear he'd be angry with her for doing so well?

He loved competing with those who had the ability and competitiveness to wish to beat him. Niall and Eanruig came close, but James had never played a lass before, and, therefore, he'd never thought one could come near to besting him. The idea was so novel he wondered if other lasses were just as gifted. What puzzled him was whether Eilis had picked up the game that quickly or if she'd known all along how to play.

Yet when he was showing her the rules, not once had she told him she already knew the rudiments of the game. Did she not wish to embarrass him?

He couldn't figure her out. In fact, everything about the lass intrigued him more. He found his desire to learn everything there was about her growing every minute of every day. Catriona no longer garnered his attention in the least.

He tore his gaze away from Eilis, as she concentrated steadily on her next move, her red-gold curls dangling over her shoulders, which were hunched forward. She made her move.

"Checkmate," Niall said, almost as giddy as a wee lad catching his first fish in the loch.

Eilis looked up slowly at James as if she were afraid he'd be angry.

He smiled at his good fortune to find so skillful an adversary, and he had every intention of besting her the next time. He bowed his head in acknowledgement of her prowess. "'Tis not oft anyone can beat me, Eilis."

"'Tis luck, my laird," she quickly said.

"Aye, luck." He didn't believe it at all.

Niall laughed. "If only I had that kind of beginner's luck."

Blinking her hardened blue eyes, Catriona crossed her arms. "I thought you did not know how to play."

Fia stood taller. "She beats all of our clansmen."

Aye, the truth of the matter then. "Why did you let me think you could not play, Eilis?" James asked, his voice gentle.

Fia supplied the answer. "The men do not like it that she can best them." She shrugged. "But they insist she play again and again when she visits Glen Affric just to see who can until my da makes them stop."

"I want to match my wits against you next, Eilis," Niall said, smiling broadly.

"The lady needs her rest; 'tis late," James countermanded.

Eilis relaxed her tense shoulders. It seemed James had rescued her from his cousin. Besides, James had it in mind that he, not his cousin, would play the nymph again. His pride would not allow otherwise.

James signaled to his people. "Please, leave us. I wish a moment alone with the lady."

The rest of his people took their leave while his mother said, "Remember the priest." She gave him a pointed look, then quit the solar.

Catriona glowered at Eilis, turned on her heel, and stalked out of the chamber.

"Think you I would be angry, Eilis, if you beat me at the game?" James asked.

"All the men I have ever played, except for my da, became angry with me."

"You played with your da?"

"Aye, he taught me the game."

"Did you beat him also?"

"Once, but—"

"You could have feigned the inability to play." James leaned back in his chair.

"No more than you could, my laird." She sighed. "In all seriousness, I see not how your actions will capture Catriona's heart. You should pursue her instead of me."

"Nay. You heard my mother. She has invited the priest to stay. We will be wed on the morrow."

"I must leave here. When my uncle learns I am here—"

"Do not speak further on the subject."

"I will, my laird. You do not seem to understand how dangerous my uncle can be."

"He has not promised you but Agnes to Dunbarton." James waved aside her concern. "He does not frighten me, lass."

Eilis's eyes were round and her voice soft when she spoke. "He frightens me."

James reached over and took Eilis's hand, wishing she could understand he would let no harm come to her. "You are safe with me."

She jerked her hand away. "Catriona is not here to see this, and I must insist you make some effort to court her."

Unable to fathom why the lass could not see that he would protect her, and she had naught to worry about, he narrowed his eyes. "You insist."

She clenched her hands and glowered back at him. "Aye."

"You will not dictate to me, lass. You will be mine

on the morrow."

"Your stubbornness will earn you a battle on two fronts, my laird."

"So be it, Eilis. I would not be honorable if I were to turn you over to either Dunbarton or your uncle. We have an agreement, you and I. That is what I will honor."

Eilis eyes filled with tears, and she gave her head a little shake. Without another word, she stood, whipped around, and stormed out of the solar.

Wondering how it had happened, James had the distinct impression he'd lost more than a chess game with the lady this eve.

\*\*\*

Mulling over the conversation he'd had with Eilis during the evening meal, James sat with Eanruig before the fire in his solar following the chess game.

James took a swig of his mead. "If Eilis was offered to Dunbarton as his betrothed, it seems the precious cargo that went down with the ship Dunbarton was waiting on was our very own Lady Eilis."

"Aye. As your seneschal, I must advise that offering the lady for your brother and Gunnolf's release may be enough to earn their freedom."

James downed the rest of his drink and shook his head. "The lady is not truly Dunbarton's betrothed. So no, I will not give her up in exchange for my brother. If Dunbarton learned her uncle had deceived him, no telling what he might do to her." On the other hand, James was concerned Dunbarton would want the lass anyway, as lovely as she was. More so than that, because James wanted her also. Would Dunbarton demand concessions from her uncle—for his attempted swindle—in regard to allying against the MacNeills in battle? Most likely. The question then: would her uncle agree to Dunbarton's terms?

"We have not had time to hear back from the messenger. Think you Dunbarton will want his son back?" Eanruig asked, breaking into James's grim ruminations.

"Truly?" James queried.

Eanruig nodded.

"Nay." James stared into the fire. "'Tis only wishful thinking that Dunbarton would change his mind about Keary."

Niall knocked on the door and poked his head in. "A word, James."

"Aye, come in."

Niall stalked in and took a seat. "Lady Akira is distressed that Allison is upset and wishes you would have a word with the lady to ease her concern."

"I will speak with her. But I am sure I will not ease her discomfort."

Niall nodded and poured himself a mug of mead. "One of Keary's companions attempted escape in a keg bound for the village. The gate guard checked it when one of our men discovered Keary's companion had slipped away."

"And?"

"He will stay below stairs until you say so, James. Mayhap the others will learn from the example. The worst of the matter is that Keary found something to write with and penned a missive to his father about Agnes being kept hostage here. I destroyed the missive, but I wanted you to be aware of the trouble Keary is trying to stir up."

"He knew who she was? Or assumed she was?"

"Seems so. Most likely he overheard something a servant said."

James considered Niall's rumpled appearance and the lines under his eyes. He looked as tired as James felt. "If you have no other news, you may retire, Niall. I need you well rested for the morrow."

"Catriona may try to send word to Dunbarton as well."

"Aye, you are right. Eanruig, see that none of Catriona's people leave the grounds until after we hear back from Dunbarton concerning the bargain over his son."

"Aye." Eanruig finished his mead and set the mug down. "I will see you on the morrow."

"Aye." James turned to Niall. "Get some sleep, Niall. No dallying with the lassies tonight."

Niall smiled. "Since Eilis arrived, I have had no interest. Remember that, should you not wed her. I will gladly take her to wife."

James rose and slapped Niall on the shoulder. "If she was not already spoken for, I would give her to you. Although I suspect you would have to fight Dougald for her also."

Niall chuckled and finished his mead. "When it comes to the fairer sex, he would beat me." He headed toward his chamber.

James went to speak with Allison, although the hour was late. The guard bowed his head, and James acknowledged him then knocked on the door.

"Aye, yes?" a lady called out.

"'Tis Laird James wishing to speak to Lady Allison a moment."

A faint light flared to life in the chamber, and women's hushed voices filled the air. Then after much time, Allison, very pale of face, opened the door and bobbed a curtsey. "My laird."

She wouldn't look at him and watched the rushes at her feet instead.

"What trouble were you in at Brecken Castle, and how was Eilis involved?"

"The lady was mistaken, my laird. I have already told Niall thus."

"Aye, and the lady's memory is returning. I would rather hear the truth from your lips before she recalls what had happened. When my brother and Gunnolf return, they will also be able to vouch that you were the one who released them from Dunbarton's stronghold. Try me, lady, and the situation will only worsen for you."

The lady's eyes filled with tears, and he believed his mother would not approve. What had Niall said? His mother wished James to lessen the lady's discomfort? Then Allison would have to be honest with him first.

She shook her head. "Eilis was wrong."

"Know you she is MacBurness's niece?"

Allison's eyes grew round. He couldn't tell if she had known who she was then and couldn't believe he'd found out or didn't recognize the name.

"Lady Allison?"

"Nay." Allison shook her head vehemently. "I knew only her first name, Eilis."

He tilted his head back. "I see. So you knew her."

Allison's cheeks even seemed paler if 'twas possible.

"Allison, how did you know her?"

She let out her breath in a tormented way. "A man...a man tried to have his way with me when I went to see to my horse in the stable. The mare was new and nervous. She seemed to enjoy my saying goodnight to her before I retired for the eve. One night, a man followed me into the stable unbeknownst to me. He...he forced me down hard on the stable floor. I bumped my head and was momentarily dazed. Eilis heard me squeak and came to my rescue. He...he took her from the stable, and I did not see her again. I had only seen her once before in Lady Anice's chamber speaking privately with her. She was a pretty girl but terrified of her family. 'Twas none of my affair, and I was not prone to gossip."

Allison trembled slightly, and her eyes remained downcast. "I...I wished to know what had become of her after the incident in the stable, but Lady Anice would not speak of it. Only said there had been trouble, and that a cousin had taken Eilis from the grounds. She had no choice. Her uncle wished her returned at once. I never inquired who her uncle was. I was afraid the cousin might have been the one who attacked me in the stable. Still, I feared whoever it was might try again, so I left there, seeking employment here instead. I have never had any trouble here, my laird. I do not wish to leave." She hastily brushed away tears.

"What about your connection to Dunbarton?"

She sniffled. "My half brother is one of his men, aye. Since I had lived there as a young girl, but most thought I still served Lady Anice, I was able to slip into the castle, ply the guards with a draught to make them sleep, and free your brother and Gunnolf. None, not even my brother, know I work here. I cannot risk returning."

"And there is no lady to serve there."

"Nay, my laird."

He took a deep breath. "Your secret is safe with me." She curtsied, and he left her at her chamber to see Fia. He would continue to have Allison watched, to ensure she had not lied to him.

\*\*\*

Furious, Eilis stalked across the guest chamber while Fergus remained outside their chamber door.

"He really cares for you, Eilis." Fia put her hands over her heart. "To be Laird James's wife."

For James's sake, Eilis had to leave Craigly. She wouldn't even hazard being his wife. Why couldn't he see how dangerous a game he played? Battles on two fronts? He'd never win, not with the difficulties he was already having with Dunbarton and his men even without her uncle's interference.

She had already fallen in love with James, his mother, his cousin Niall, even his brother Douglas and friend Gunnolf, and the healer Tavia, too. And so many more of his people. Nesta and her gabby ways, and Ian, the sweet lad that he was. Everyone's well-being was in her hands. She couldn't be the cause of their downfall.

"James and I have just fought," Eilis said to her cousin. "Even if that were not so, what will happen if our uncle learns I am here? He cannot. What if he and the rest of our kin deny I am Eilis? You know they will. Then it will be as before. I will have to wed Dunbarton. I must leave here at once. I would not wish you to share the same fate as me. Try for James's hand. Or return home to your family."

Fia's brown eyes studied hers, then she smiled. "James does not even know I exist. He only wished my presence to learn who you were. So no, I will not return home but journey with you instead. We have had adventures before. I would not wish to be left out of your next one."

"The door is guarded at night. I have a guard with me at all times when I am not in the guest chambers."

Fia raised her brows. "You think His Lairdship is not interested in you? Why not? If he cared naught about you, he would let you leave, not confine you."

Unsure as to what to do about escaping, Eilis sat down hard on the cushioned bench. "Would your brother aid us?"

"Ha! He would never go against our uncle."

"'Tis only a couple of lasses who will," Eilis said, disgruntled.

"He is a powerful clan chief."

"Aye." Eilis rested her head on her hands. "I tried to slip past the guard, but he does not sleep on duty."

Fia walked over to the window and looked out.

"If we had a rope—," Eilis said.

"Och, you know how I fear heights."

"Aye, after you took that tumble down the cliff." Eilis sighed. "I already tried to slip through James's chamber."

Fia turned and stared at her. "Nay." She elongated the word, emphasizing her surprise.

"Aye, I did. Ran right into him."

Fia's eyes widened. "Was he…was he dressed?"

Eilis shook her head at her cousin. "Of course he was, Fia."

"All the way?"

237

Eilis's cheeks heated.

"You are blushing. He was not dressed all the way?"

"He wore breeches." Eilis had no plans to tell her about the other times.

Fia smiled. "Did he kiss you?"

If Eilis said no, her cousin would know the truth of the matter. Instead, she looked at her embroidery.

"Oh, Eilis, he must marry you if he has compromised you in any way. You must tell me what happened." When Eilis wouldn't speak, Fia smiled at her and touched her arm. "I...I think you love him. 'Tis the best thing that could have happened to you."

"Nay, 'tis not," Eilis said sharply.

A knock sounded on the door, and both looked in that direction.

"Laird James is here to see Mistress Fia," Fergus said.

Eilis swallowed hard. "What does he want?" she whispered.

Fia patted her arm. "To know more about you, I suspect." To Fergus, she called out, "I am coming."

"You must not say anything."

"Aye, I will be careful."

As soon as Fia left the chamber, her eyes wide as she joined James, Fergus shut the door, and James began questioning Fia in earnest. "Tell me what happened when Eilis was at Brecken Castle. About the incident in the stables." James drew her away from Eilis's chamber so she did not overhear their conversation.

"I know naught about it, my laird." Fia seemed sincere, bothered even as she glanced back at the chamber and wrung her hands.

"Lady Allison told me about an incident there. Who was the cousin who took Eilis from Brecken Castle?"

"I promise I do not know. Eilis was quiet about what went on in the family. I tried to get her to tell me, curious as I was because her da had been the clan chief before his death. Then her uncle took over. I lived such a simple life on a farm near a village, far from castle life. Yet she loved to be with me, weaving, feeding the chickens, gathering eggs, spinning yarn, anything to get away from our uncle. We have many cousins so I do not know which it would have been. Nor did she ever tell me of a time when she visited Brecken."

James considered Fia's sincerity and nodded. "Think you could learn what happened?"

"Most likely, no. Even if I can help her to remember, she might not wish to speak with me about it. Can I ask you something, my laird?"

He nodded.

"Do you intend to wed Eilis? She loves you if she has not told you. She fears our uncle more than anyone, but if it were not for that, she would gladly be your wife."

"Did Eilis put you up to this?" James asked, although he already knew the answer to his query.

"Nay, my laird." Fia smiled. "She would strangle me if she knew I had told you thus. Is that all you wished of me?"

"Aye, lass. Eilis will be my wife. One way or another."

Fia smiled and kissed him on the cheek. "Praise be to thee, my laird. You will be good for her." Then Fia

239

curtseyed and hurried back to the chamber.

James stared after her, wishing tonight when he returned to his bed, Eilis was once again snuggled underneath the covers. Only this time he would know 'twas her. And he would do more than just kiss the lass's sweet lips.

# CHAPTER 17

Early the next morn, Eilis and Fia went to the hall to break their fast, but James seemed in a strange mood. He leaned over to Catriona. "How was your eve? Did you sleep well?"

At first, Catriona pushed out her bottom lip in a pout. "My chamber is not as nice as some, and I did not sleep well. Did you, my laird?"

Eilis bit her tongue. Was Catriona intimating that she needed James's company last eve to make the night pass more quickly? And why was James ignoring Eilis and only speaking with Catriona this morn? Had he taken her advice, not advice, but command to seek Catriona's interest rather than Eilis's?

She should have been satisfied. So why was her stomach bunching into knotted hemp?

By the time the meal had ended, Eilis could not wait to quit the hall. Not once had James looked Eilis's way, nor had he spoken a word to her. Fia looked on sympathetically, and like Eilis, had not much of an appetite.

When Eilis and her cousin left the hall and, with Fergus guarding as usual, they took a walk in the herb gardens. Fia cleared her throat. "Laird James mentioned to me you had been to Brecken Castle."

Eilis looked sharply at Fia but said naught.

"Do you remember?"

"Aye. That is where I met Lady Allison."

"And the trouble you had there? A cousin took you away?"

Eilis stared at the flowers in the garden, vaguely remembering Allison had been in trouble in the stable. "Aye...oh, Fia, a man had...had attacked Allison." Eilis closed her eyes then looked again at Fia. "'Twas the cousin I had taken such a fancy to."

Fia's eyes widened. "You do not mean Fann, do you?"

"Aye, 'twas he. The devil was in the drink. He had been in his cups and had tried to take advantage of poor Allison, but I...I heard her scream and raced in to see the matter, thinking a horse had nipped her. When I saw it was our cousin, I seized a pitchfork and poked him soundly in the arse. He turned his fury on me, but then realizing the trouble he might be in, he forced me to leave Brecken at once so I would not reveal his identity. Allison had no idea who he was."

"Och, Eilis, why did you never tell me?"

"He was out of his head with drink, and he never did it again that I know of."

James stalked into the inner bailey and spoke to a couple of his men across while Catriona practically was tied to him like a saddle to a horse.

"I cannot believe he has a guard watching your

242

every move." Fia folded her arms and gave Fergus the evil eye.

"'Tis not that he needs me here any longer. Look at the way Catriona fawns over him. And how he talked only to her at the meal this morn." Eilis took a heavy breath. "He has finally realized his mistake in wishing me for a bride."

Catriona reached for James's arm, but he sidestepped her.

Then one of the men he was speaking to looked Eilis's way, and when he did, James caught sight of her watching him. He smiled and took Catriona's hand and kissed it.

Eilis's mouth gaped before she caught herself. So did Fia's.

"Did you see what James just did?" Fia asked.

"Aye. You see why I say he has no more need of me?"

"But..." Fia clamped her mouth shut, and she and Eilis glanced back at Fergus. The guard watched them, his face expressionless.

Two men approached James and pulled swords from their scabbards, and Eilis's stomach clenched. "What is His Lairdship doing now?"

They challenged James, and he spoke to Catriona then she moved a safe distance away.

"What is happening?" Eilis tried to mask the alarm in her voice but failed.

"Practicing sword fighting," Fergus said.

"Two against one?"

For the first time since she'd known him, Fergus smiled. "Our Laird likes more challenging odds in case he is bushwhacked some day."

The two men thrust at James, and every time he swept their swords away from his chest with a clang.

At first, James stepped back from their thrusts. Suddenly, he slashed at one, then the other, forcing them to retreat. With a decisive blow, he knocked the sword from one of the men's hand, and charged like a wild boar at the other until he struck the man's sword and it flew into the air.

His people clapped.

Catriona quickly made her move to congratulate him, but after he resheathed his sword, three young boys approached him, wielding wooden swords. One handed a spare to James then they all attacked him with a vengeance, growling and yelling.

James sounded just as fearsome as he whacked their swords with his, but not once did he strike hard, nor did he wound them in mock battle. Instead, he groaned whenever one of the junior warriors slashed at his leg or hit his arm.

Then in a dramatic final bout, the tallest of the lads knocked James's sword from his grasp. The courtiers cheered.

Eilis asked Fergus, "Does he oft practice with the lads?"

"Aye. They must learn to protect themselves. Our laird is one of the best swordsmen around."

Again, Catriona moved in close to James to get his attention.

"I have seen enough, Fia. Let us retire to our chamber, shall we?"

"Och, you cannot let her have him. The poor man." Fia hurried beside her as they entered the keep.

"He wanted her, Fia. My only purpose in being

here was to ensure she saw the error of her ways. Now that she has, my obligation to him has been fulfilled."

Eilis glanced back at Fergus and frowned. "I hope you do not repeat everything I say to His Lairdship."

"Only that which His Lairdship wishes to hear."

'Twas good that she spoke of naught that James would be interested in hearing in Fergus's presence. Eilis entered the guest chambers with Fia and waited for Fergus to shut the door. Once the latch clicked, she said to Fia, "Our best chance at escape is to climb over the wall they are rebuilding."

"They have a guard or two there every night. But, Eilis, you must consider James wishes to wed you."

"We had a fight last night, I tell you. One little fight, and he sees me as too much of a challenge and returns to the woman he wanted in the first place? There are bound to be more disagreements after marriage. What then? Would he seek another woman's arms for comfort? Mayhap he wouldn't even need that excuse if he becomes anything like his sire."

Fia wrung her hands, her brow wrinkled in thought. "I know you well enough to believe this has more to do with worrying that our uncle and Dunbarton will join forces and destroy the MacNeills. That is has nothing to do with your concern that James no longer desires you." She sighed. "I have to agree with you about our uncle and Dunbarton's combined forces and how brutally they could deal with the MacNeills. But what if James offers a bigger bride price to our uncle for you? Mayhap this is all for naught."

"Think you Dunbarton will give up that easily? That our uncle will agree to receive anything less from James than the sun and the moon and the earth, too?"

Fia snorted softly. "Aye, once he learns James loves you, our uncle would stop at naught to get the most out of the bargain."

"All right then, 'tis agreed. Where the wall is still being rebuilt is the only place we might be able to climb over. The gate is closed tight in the eve," Eilis said, feeling less decisive about this than she wanted to be. In fact, deep in her heart, she had the traitorous hope she and Fia wouldn't succeed. She had to at least make the effort to protect the MacNeills in any way that she could.

Fia stared out the window. "How are we to get past the guard at our room?"

"We go through James's bedchamber."

Fia's eyes widened.

"*Before* he has retired this time. His door is slightly beyond the bend in the wall. All we need do is slip out of here after we finish the evening meal."

Fia looked back out the window and gasped.

Eilis hurried over to peek out and stared at the redheaded man astride his black horse, accompanied by several other hardy Highland warriors. "Who is he?"

Fia gaped at her. "Do you not recognize him?"

Alarmed at Fia's worried response, Eilis asked again, "Nay, who is he?"

"Och, you have not regained all your memories. 'Tis our cousin Broc. Uncle MacBurness's only son. His being here is not a good sign. Agnes's brother must know you are here, or he would not have come. Oh, Eilis, I fear we are doomed."

\*\*\*

James stiffened as he listened to Eanruig give him the grave news in the great hall. "You say he is Agnes's brother, Broc MacBurness?"

"Aye."

"And he believes we have his sister, Agnes, here?"

"Keeping her safe, my laird, and he wishes to take her off our hands now."

"He does, does he?" James ran his hand over his chin. "And you have told him?"

"That we have no lady like that here, my laird."

James glanced at his mother, standing quietly in the entrance of the great hall. He took a heavy breath. "My lady mother, please ensure the kitchen staff prepare meals for two of our ladies in their chamber for evening meal."

"You should have married Eilis already and not have been dallying with Catriona all morn." Frowning at him, she inclined her head and hurried off to the kitchen.

Mayhap, but he'd hoped if he'd shown no interest in Eilis this morn, she would realize the error of her ways, capitulate, and agree to wed him.

"You intend to keep the ladies' presence here secret?" Eanruig asked.

"Possibly Fia should come to the meal, although I am afraid she might be too nervous to face her cousin, Broc. He may know she is staying with us."

"Aye, the word must have reached his father that you have shown some interest in marrying Fia, and he wonders why."

"Or the word is out that she has come here to see her cousin, whom she cares for a great deal. I assumed it would come to this eventually but not as soon as all this." James sighed.

"How will we keep this Broc from taking Eilis

away with him?"

James raised his brows.

Eanruig smiled.

\*\*\*

A knocking at the bedchamber door made Eilis and Fia jump.

Tavia entered. Her face looked so grave, Eilis feared the worst concerning her cousin Broc, but she didn't speak a word.

"'Tis not good news I fear for you, my lady," Tavia said, wringing her hands.

Her heart sinking, Eilis sat down hard on the cushioned bench.

"What is wrong?" Fia asked.

"A Highlander has come to call. He says he is searching for his sister, Agnes MacBurness, and he described you, Eilis."

Eilis frowned. "Aye, because our mothers were twins, and Agnes and I looked verra much alike."

"He says," Tavia continued, her voice small and disconcerted, "that rumors abound in Glen Affric that Agnes survived the sinking of the ship she traveled on. He says he believes some kind family has taken her in. He wishes to bestow coin on the family who cared for her, but 'tis now time for her to return home to her own family."

"He wants naught of the kind! He intends to deliver me to Dunbarton and force me to marry the man who is betrothed to Agnes, not me!"

"He is waiting at the evening meal. Lady Akira has given instructions servants will bring food to you both in your chamber."

"James cannot hide me here forever."

"I am certain he does not intend to. I am sure he will come up with a plan that will work out well for all concerned. He is quite clever."

"Nay. My clan will say I am Agnes. No one will go against my uncle. Then my uncle will wage war against Laird James and his people."

Tavia looked at Fia, who nodded.

"James is an honorable man. For now, he is keeping quiet, but I am certain he is afraid someone will let it slip that you are here. He will do everything in his power to keep you out of Dunbar's clutches, but..."

"But?"

"What if 'tis the way you say, and your uncle does wage war against us? He would only have to gather Dunbarton's men as well and crush us." Tavia looked at the floor and then sighed as she raised her gaze to meet Eilis's. "Not only that, Catriona might tell Broc you are here if she can get word to him somehow."

Eilis's heart nearly stopped. Catriona would do everything to cause trouble for her.

Tavia took a deep breath. "I will help you to leave here now."

*** 

Broc strode into the great hall with his men, his walk confident, outwardly arrogant, as if *he* were laird of the manor. He greeted James with guarded respect, then sat beside him at the head table while his men took seats at one of the lower ones.

At once, James recognized the brutish Highlander with the scar across his face, giving him a perpetual scowl and realized just who was staying in the chamber next to his. The girl he'd searched for in vain until he'd left the Highlands to fight in the Crusade. No wonder he had felt some connection to her from the beginning. With the utmost restraint, he remained seated and glanced in the direction of her chamber abovestairs.

She was the sweet lass he'd rescued from drowning in the caves by the sea, weighed down by a wet gown and a bag of rocks. And Broc had mistreated her, as injured as she was. The girl James had wanted to kiss again, hold, protect, and never let go of. In that moment, he'd fallen in love with her, only to be teased mercilessly by his brothers over the matter.

Ah, 'twas a sign that he should rescue her first in the briny sea, and then a few summers later, his seneschal and cousin fish her out of the sea once more and return her to him. His prayers had been answered. Which proved she belonged with him. He would love her always, just as he'd promised her in his heart from the beginning.

James leaned back in his chair and eyed Broc with contempt. The whoreson would never touch Eilis in a brutal manner again. In truth, the lass would be his as soon as he could make the arrangements.

Aye, 'twas the only solution. She would never marry Dunbarton.

As a man served mead, Broc said to James, "You know I have come for my sister, Agnes."

"Aye." James carved off a slice of bread for Broc but did not comment further, waiting for Eilis's cousin to explain in his own words his mission—although 'twas all a lie.

Broc observed James's people. Counting the number of able-bodied men? Seeing if he had enough men of his own he could call up to do battle if

THE ACCIDENTAL HIGHLAND HERO

necessary?

"My sister is betrothed to Laird Dunbarton. He is anxious to have his bride at Lockton," Broc finally said.

"As any man would wish, to be sure," James said, disguising any hint of emotion. Although deep inside, he wished to fight Broc for treating Eilis so shabbily.

Normally filled with conversation, the hall was silent except for the clanking of goblets against the wooden trestle tables.

Lady Akira moved a slice of stag around on her trencher but failed to eat a bite. Lady Catriona, on the other hand, devoured everything in sight. When she wasn't stuffing her mouth with succulent morsels of deer meat, chomping on bread, or sipping leek soup, she was casting smug smiles at Broc.

At once, James knew what the woman had in mind. As soon as she could, she'd alert Broc or one of his men about Eilis staying with them.

An herbal draught that would make Catriona sleep was needed, but James noticed then that Tavia wasn't eating her meal at the hall. Was she dining with Eilis and Fia? He had the uncanny feeling something wasn't right.

In fact, ever since Eilis had arrived, his people had acted differently. Curious as to who Eilis was. Amused to see his attentions toward the lass, even though it had been purely a ruse in the beginning. Worried that this Broc might take her away. James had never seen his people so interested in anyone not of their own ilk.

Niall was sure to be upset about Broc coming for Eilis also. James glanced at the seat his cousin normally occupied, but he was absent also. That did not bode well.

"Where's Niall?" James asked his mother, knowing Niall would not purposefully miss a meal unless he had good reason and had already let James know of it.

His mother shrugged but avoided eye contact.

James frowned. His gaze swept over the length of the elevated table where he normally sat with his family, advisor, and special guests. *His advisor. Eanruig.* Where was he? Now that James considered the table where Eilis, Fia, his cousin, and Eanruig were absent, it looked rather barren.

"Where is Eanruig?" James asked his mother.

Again, she lifted a shoulder in resignation but wouldn't look at him.

If Broc hadn't been sitting beside him, James would have insisted on answers. The truth of the matter was he feared whatever they were up to had to do with Eilis. Again, as when they brought the lass half-drowned to his castle, they were hiding their dealings with her from him when *he* was the laird of the clan!

James motioned to a servant, and when the young man joined them, he said, "Find my cousin. I want him at the meal."

The man glanced at Lady Akira, who poked her spoon into her soup and ignored the look the fearful servant gave her.

Was everyone but James in on the conspiracy?

His head pounded with irritation. "Find him and have him attend the meal at once."

"Yes, my laird." The lad took off at a run.

"Having family troubles of your own?" Broc asked, his tone amused.

"My cousin sometimes forgets the time of day because he is so busy with other important matters."

"Yes, well, as to this business with my sister, word has reached me from Glen Affric that Agnes was rescued from the ship that sank. My cousin, Fia, is supposed to be here as a bride choice for you." Broc glanced at Catriona. "I am surprised she is absent from the meal."

"She had a hectic day, and sleep eluded her last eve. So the lass retired to her bedchamber early."

"She is Agnes's favorite cousin."

"Really?" James said. "She has mentioned how attached she is to her cousin, Eilis, but said nary a word about Agnes."

Broc's face clouded. "Really. Well, the lass is a bit willful at times."

"Eilis or Fia?"

Broc leaned back in the chair. "I am sorry. I suppose Fia has not heard. Eilis died of a fever the morn Agnes had to set sail. A terrible tragedy. Eilis was most disconcerted about having to leave after her cousin's sudden death."

"You mean Agnes was?"

Uncomprehending Broc, stared at him.

"You said Eilis was disconcerted. But she was the lass who died, so you said."

Broc stabbed another slice of meat. "Aye, I meant Agnes."

"I will make you a proposal."

Broc's calculating eyes widened some. "Aye, what have ye to offer then?"

James glanced at Catriona who hung on their every word. "In my solar we shall discuss the business. For now, eat and drink."

Catriona's eyes darkened. "You know Eilis resides

here, Broc?"

He gave a smug smile. "Aye, so I have heard."

James shoved his trencher aside, wishing now he'd seen this side of Catriona earlier, *before* he'd invited her visit. He supposed she'd always been this way, but he could not see it prior to this or she'd been on her best behavior in his presence.

"Eilis is well?" Broc asked, although he chomped on a piece of brown bread and washed it down with a mug of mead. He did not appear truly interested.

"She was injured in the shipwreck."

Broc's knife paused midair above his slice of deer meat. "Badly?"

"She looked more than well to me." Catriona sniffed.

James could imagine what Broc was thinking. If Eilis had been injured badly, she might not be worthy enough to marry to Dunbarton.

Unable to wait any longer, James ended the meal. "Come, we will talk." He motioned for Broc to join him.

Catriona glowered at James. 'Twas time to send the woman away. He would make his wishes known to her once he had made his bargain with Broc concerning Eilis.

*  *  *

Tavia hurried Eilis into James's bedchamber.

"What is going on?" Eilis asked, her skin prickling, hopeful that Tavia had a plan of escape that would truly work this time.

"Shhhh. Fergus is waiting beyond your door as usual. But here," Tavia said then moved a small chest, "there is a passageway to a tunnel that leads beyond the castle wall. 'Tis meant for the laird and his family's escape should ever the need arise and was built a hundred years ago when erecting the original timber castle."

Tavia lighted a candle while Eilis pulled the trap door open. The smell of damp earth rose from the dark pit.

"'Tis chilly and wet down there. Have a care where you step. Some stones have become dislodged over the years." Tavia climbed down the ladder first. "When I was a wee lass, some of the others and I would explore down here. We made a map on the wall to guide us to the tunnel that leads outside."

Eilis hugged her arms around her waist and shivered. "Where do we go from here, Tavia? Once we are beyond the castle walls?"

Turning, Tavia smiled, the candlelight flickering off her dark brown eyes. "Why I have told you Niall speaks of you every minute of the day. The ladies who normally catch his eye are driven to madness over his interest in you." She continued to splash through the ground water accumulated on the stone floor. "He is rescuing you from Broc."

"But what will James do? Will he not be angry with his cousin?" Eilis couldn't help worrying about the two of them. She'd never want anyone to hurt her relationship with her cousin Fia. Certainly, she didn't want to harm James's with his cousin.

"Niall is a grown man. He will do what he feels in his heart is right. And James, likewise."

"I do not want them to be angry with each other over me."

"'Tis not your concern, my lady. They have their

255

rows from time to time, and they always mend their ways."

Eilis didn't believe James would easily forgive Niall over this.

A light shown through a doorway, and Tavia handed the candle to Eilis then slipped a key into the lock. "Niall gave me the key as soon as he saw Broc arrive."

Tavia pulled the door open, and it creaked on rusted hinges.

The fading sunlight shown in Eilis's eyes, blinding her for an instant.

Niall hurried forward, while Eanruig held onto horses' reigns nearby. James would be furious, to be sure, that his seneschal was in on this also.

Another lad she didn't recognize stood some distance away, wringing his belt through his fingers.

"Tell His Lairdship you could not find me," Niall said to the lad, while helping Eilis onto a horse.

Eanruig assisted Fia onto another.

"Lock the door to the tunnel and return things the way they were," Niall said to Tavia.

"He will know I helped the ladies escape. Can I not come with you, Niall?" Tavia asked.

"Nay. Our clan needs you for your healing skills." Niall mounted his horse. "Besides, traveling with two women will be difficult enough."

Tavia reached up and squeezed Eilis's hand. "Godspeed, my lady. I pray thee find protection wherever you go. And you, Fia, as well."

"Thank you, Tavia, for everything," Eilis said, her stomach churning with nervousness as she glanced back at the castle tower looming above them.

Tavia closed the door to the tunnel entrance, then the four rode off.

"Where will we go?" Eilis asked, the hope returning that she truly would get away this time, away from her family, leaving James behind who would be glad someday that he was not faced with a battle on two fronts. Yet she couldn't help wishing she could be his wife, staying with him and his mother, with his kin, the first time she'd ever felt at home and cared for. Loved even, except when her mother and da had lived.

"To see Lady Anice and the new laird of the castle. Malcolm is James's next oldest brother. Broc and his father will not know you have taken refuge there."

Eilis tightened her hands on her reigns. "You cannot be serious, my laird. We will cause trouble for more of your kin."

"What would you have us do?" Niall asked, his voice couched in annoyance. "James wishes your hand, and he will be unbearable to live with if you wed Dunbarton."

Eilis closed her gaping mouth.

Niall raised his brows. "You think not, bonny lass? Why he says naught, but his feelings are shown in his actions. You are the only one he has ever acted thus toward. You are the one for him, no other."

"But Catriona..."

"Aye, Catriona. Did you see the way he switched the trestle tables on you?"

She couldn't fathom what Niall was speaking of.

"The way he kissed Catriona's hand to make you jealous? I nearly laughed when I saw his actions. He had been avoiding her all morning after you and he had quarreled last eve. Catriona continued to pester him like a sucker fish."

Eilis laughed.

"Aye. So what does he do? He spoke only with her at the meal, sees you watching him, and he kisses Catriona's hand. 'Twas a means to get your attention. I was standing atop the scaffolding, supervising the mending of the south wall when I saw him do it. Nearly fell off I was so shocked. I have never seen him desire any woman before like he wants you. When he discovers I have spirited you away…"

"He will be furious with you."

Niall smiled. "Aye. Teach him to show any interest in Catriona when he wishes her not and when he refuses to be more forceful in this issue concerning marrying you."

"He has good reason," Eilis said, annoyed.

Chuckling, Niall nudged his horse closer to Eilis. "And you care for him as much as he does for you. But, aye, he did not realize your cousin would be hot on your trail so soon after Eanruig discovered who you were."

"This is folly. Someone will warn my uncle, and I will be right back where I started."

# CHAPTER 18

Hurrying into the great hall, Ian joined James and spoke privately before he and Broc quit the meal. "My laird, a bairn rode with Broc's party. One of his men holds him in the barracks while our men guard them. One of our men perchance overheard the wee lad mention Eilis with tears in his eyes. He believes the sea took her. Mayhap he is her cousin, but what if he is her brother?"

James glanced at Brock, but one of his kin was keeping the man occupied. Turning to Ian, James said, "Bring the boy to me."

"But the man guarding him..."

"One man? Have my men take care of him. I wish to speak to the lad at once."

"If the lad is Broc's brother? Or mayhap even his son?"

"'Tis no matter. If the lad has a fondness for Eilis, I wish to set his worries asunder."

"Aye, my laird." Ian quickly hurried out of the

great hall.

James assumed the wee laddy had to be Broc's brother, or Eilis would have mentioned him. James reconsidered. What if the boy was Eilis's son? What if she had been married or had a bastard son? James watched the entryway in earnest. Could no one act in an expeditious manner?

Then he saw Ian's head as he towered over a serving maid but could not see a lad. Until Ian skirted the maid, hurrying forth with a small boy whose hand was clinging to Ian's. His green eyes round, the lad stared straight at Broc still standing behind the head table. Blond curls trailed down his shoulders, yet the laddy looked remarkably like Eilis and not Broc.

She had a son. Her innocence had all been feigned.

Broc suddenly spied the lad and roared, "What right have you in bringing the lad here?"

James faced Broc. "Sit and be still. I will have a word with the lad, alone."

Broc glowered at James as if he wished to do battle with him this very instant.

"Sit," James commanded. "You obviously brought the wee lad here for some purpose. I shall speak with him now."

For what seemed like an eternity, Broc stared James down. The hall remained deathly quiet, no one leaving until their laird did.

Broc slowly took his seat, but his hard gaze focused on the lad who had yanked Ian to a stop some distance from the head table, his eyes filled with tears, his lower lip quivering.

James motioned for his mother to come with him. He wouldn't have done so, but he believed the lad might need a woman's gentle touch to gain the truth from his lips.

Outside the hall, James crouched in front of the lad while his mother smiled at him with adoration in her gaze. After having raised four boys and a nephew, she looked ready to take on a new charge.

"Your name, laddy? I am James."

The boy's eyes grew huge. He whispered, "Ye are laird?"

"Aye, and you are?"

The lad looked at James's mother.

"I am Lady Akira. Laird James's mother."

"My...my mother is dead."

Which brought up the question again, did the boy think Eilis had died at sea? "Eilis is verra much alive, well, and—"

The lad let out a sorrowful squeak. His eyes rolled into the back of his head, and if James hadn't caught the boy's frail body, he would have fallen in a dead faint on the rushes covering the floor.

"Oh, my," James's mother said outside the great hall as James cradled the unconscious lad in his arms. She motioned to a servant to join James and her. "Fetch Tavia at once." As the man hurried off, James's mother said, "Let us take the lad to Eilis's chamber. Why did she not mention the wee bairn?"

"Her lack of memory?"

Or had she chosen not to remember? Mayhap that was the reason her uncle had not found her a suitable husband. She had a bastard son.

James carried the lad abovestairs while his mother chattered nonstop. "We must keep them both—Eilis and the boy. You must do whatever you can to bargain for them. The wedding cannot be put off any longer. You have compromised the lady's good name, and since she is not betrothed—"

James grunted. "And what do you call the bairn?"

His mother gave him a sour look. "A mistake? Mayhap she is widowed? Matter's not. You will wed her and return her honor, James."

In truth, none of it mattered. Taking the lady to wife would be his pleasure.

His mother knocked on the door to Eilis's chamber, but when no one opened it, James had a very bad feeling about this. Already his muscles were tensing for battle.

His mother pushed the door aside. She stood in the entryway and didn't move out of James's path, just stared into the chamber. "She and Fia are not here. Well, lay the lad down and I will…will check into the matter."

James cursed under his breath, stalked into the chamber, and laid the lad on Eilis's mattress. "You will stay with the boy while *I* look for the women."

His mother covered the boy with a coverlet and brushed a tangle of hair away from his cheek. "He will make a fine—"

Ian knocked at the chamber entrance, his face flushed, his hands clenched into fists. "I could not find Tavia, and a servant said she thought our healer aided Eilis's escape. That Niall is with her."

James stormed toward Ian. "I will…"

James's mother hurried after him and grabbed his sleeve. "She fears this Broc. And so does the lad. Take a care with your temper. She needs a gentle hand, as does the boy."

"I will wring Niall's neck, I was about to say, Mother," James growled as he headed out the door. "As far as the lady is concerned, you have ordered me to marry her, remember?" He cast a glance over his shoulder, his brows raised, as he and Ian rushed for the stairs.

"Aye." His mother smiled. "Because 'tis your heart's wish."

His mother's words could not be truer, and James was ready to thrash Niall for his rashness.

Ian cleared his throat. "What about Broc, my laird? He stews in the hall still where you commanded him to sit."

James gave a dark chuckle. "Have a servant take him to my solar and give him mead. I will visit with him shortly. Where are Eilis and Niall?"

"Beyond the castle walls, my laird, on the west side."

James headed for the outer bailey, saw Catriona walking his way, and gave her a look like now was not the time to speak with him.

"My laird—"

"Not now, Catriona." He motioned to a stable boy. "Get my horse."

The boy disappeared into the stable.

"My laird," Catriona said, hurrying to catch up with James's long stride. "I wish a word."

Fergus hurried out of the keep. "My laird, you wish me to come with you?"

"Aye, gather five more men."

"Aye." Fergus dashed off.

"My laird," Catriona said, reaching her hand out to caress James's arm. "You wished me to give you my answer." She looked up at him with an adoring look. "I will give it now."

The boy hurried James's horse out to him, and James swung into his saddle as Fergus and five men rushed out of the keep to join him. "Later, Catriona. This is not the time or place to discuss business."

"But…" She almost looked like she could cry. *Almost.* He'd never seen her weepy before, and even now, the expression didn't suit her.

"Later."

He kicked his horse to a gallop while his men rode out after him.

\*\*\*

Eilis, Fia, and their escort, consisting of Eanruig and Niall, headed in the direction of the village, but she kept feeling they would not get very far.

"We will solicit some of our kin there, who will ride with us for protection," Niall said. "'Twould not have been a sound idea to take any more of the staff at Craigly, or James would have suspected wrong—"

"Hold!" James shouted from the distance as he and his men headed toward them at a gallop from behind.

Eilis's heart sank, all her hope of escape shattered as she and her escort turned around.

Niall winked at Eilis. "No doubt my cousin has a plan."

"He will have all our heads from the look of the stern expression on his face," Eilis warned.

James slowed his horse to a trot and turned him around to walk beside Eilis, escorting her back to the castle.

She let out her breath in exasperation, avoiding James's harsh look. "Broc will give me to my uncle, who will turn me over to—"

"Me," James said, interrupting her. "'Tis the least I can do to repair your honor."

Eilis's face flushed with mortification. James had done nothing to dishonor her! And she didn't wish anyone to think he had.

Niall smiled. "I knew you would come up with a plan, cousin."

"You *are* marrying Eilis?" Fia asked, her eyes wide.

Eanruig shook his head, although he looked more thoughtful than anything. "What of Lady Catriona, my laird?"

"The devil with her. Eilis is the pearl I plucked from the sea before I went on Crusade. 'Tis the lass I was always bound to wed."

Eanruig shifted his gaze from James to Eilis. "The one you searched high and low for? The same lass your da was willing to pay any amount to have the girl returned to you as much as you wanted her?" Eanruig smiled broadly. "The sopping wet young lassie lying on the edge of the cliff Malcolm said you kissed but knew not. Och, you had the whole of our kin in an uproar for weeks. 'Twas a sign for sure."

"Aye," James said, sighing. "The very lass."

Eilis closed her gaping mouth, frowned, then said, "James? You said you were named James. I had taken a fever, and I did not remember much of that day."

"The kiss?" He raised his brows speculatively.

Her face heating, she touched her lips.

"Aye, you remember, as chaste as it was."

As Eilis recalled, 'twas the very first kiss a lad ever presented her with, and 'twas not chaste in the least. At least as far as it felt to her. And him between her legs as his head rested on her breast, listening for her heartbeat when she had fainted, he had said.

James gave Niall a pointed look. "I will have a word with my cousin concerning his absconding with my bride later. But I intend to wed you first, lovely lass."

"But Broc...he will put an end to your plans."

"Do you wish me as your husband, Eilis?"

"Not if Dunbarton and my uncle join each other to fight you and your kin."

"If we lived another thousand years, I surmise Dunbarton and I will never get along. As for your uncle, if he looks for alliances, he will have mine and more of a bride price than Dunbarton would ever pay. Trust me, lass, your uncle will not refuse this. Especially under the circumstances."

"Circum...oh." Her cheeks heated anew. "You mean because of Nesta's tales."

"She only embellished them, to be sure. Because of the uhm, circumstances she found us in, 'twould have been anyone's assumption who might have found us that I had already claimed you for my own, dear Eilis. So, aye, your uncle will be glad to have a son who honors his commitment." James smiled at Eilis.

Part of her was thrilled, but another part of her felt alarmed.

As they grew closer to the outer bailey, she saw Broc and his men mounting their horses. Had they learned Eilis had run away? She wanted James's solid, warm body wrapped around her for protection.

"There is one other important issue, though," James said to Eilis before they entered the outer bailey.

She waited breathlessly to hear it.

"A wee lad has come to visit. He is most anxious to see that you had not drowned in the sea." James gave her such a questioning look, but she had no idea what he was searching for.

She could think of no bairn who—

Fia gasped. "Ethan, God in heaven. Did Broc bring him here? You must give him refuge. He cannot be returned to our uncle."

"Ethan?" Eilis squeaked. "Lord have… How could I have forgotten him?" Tears filled her eyes.

"Hold," James gently said, stopped her horse, pulled Eilis into his lap, and held her close.

Niall took her horse's reins.

"Dear Eilis, your son will remain with us." James held her even tighter against his chest.

Fia sputtered something under her breath. Eilis smiled through her tears. "He is my wee brother." Why had Broc brought him here? To make her do her uncle's bidding, that's why.

James smiled, appearing relieved Ethan was not her son.

"I cannot believe I could forget him."

"He is here now, and here he will remain. With you and me and the rest of our clan. Worry naught more about it," James assured her.

As they reached the inner bailey, the messenger galloped to join them after his trip to see Dunbarton, with news concerning exchanging Dunbarton's son for James's brother.

"He does not look pleased," Niall warned.

Everyone waited expectantly, but James dismounted, then helped Eilis off her horse while Niall lifted Fia from hers. Several of James's men gathered outside, ready to do battle with Broc and his men should the need arise. All waited for a signal from James to begin the fight.

"Return the ladies to their chamber," James said, his hand on the hilt of his sword as Brock advanced.

"She comes with me now," Broc commanded. "The lad also."

"Eilis and her brother will remain here. If you wish to enjoy our hospitality longer, so be it. But they will not be leaving here tonight."

Broc jumped down from his horse and stalked toward Eilis, his expression intimidating for women and men of lesser fortitude as he scowled at James.

James drew his sword. "Hold, man. You will not touch the lady."

"She is my cousin, and for now I am her guardian until I return her to my da."

"She is my wife." Or at least she would be. Tonight. No further delaying the matter.

Broc stood slack-jawed and looked from James to Eilis. Broc's men appeared just as surprised. James hoped his people didn't also.

"Aye," Eilis said in a brave voice, although it still sounded meek to James's ears.

He slipped his free arm around Eilis's waist and felt her shiver. God's wounds, her beast of a cousin would never lay a hand on her again. "Come, wife, a word with the messenger from Brecken and then off to bed with you."

She drew closer to his side, her face flushing beautifully. James remembered the day when he wished to protect her from her cousin on the top of the cliff, the way she'd been injured and the whoremonger had treated her so roughly. If the man so much as took another step in her direction…

James tightened his hold on the hilt of his sword and steered her around Broc toward the keep.

"Ye have proof ye are wed?" Broc called after James, his voice threatening.

"Aye." Soon enough.

James's guards would keep Broc and his men in line in the meantime.

"What was the word?" James asked the messenger inside the keep, unable to wait until he reached the ladys' chamber, as Niall and Ian tagged along.

"Dunbarton said he would not exchange your brother for a son who was not his. He would exchange Dougald for his betrothed. Those were his only terms."

"Then someone sent word to Dunbarton concerning Eilis," James said, frowning.

"But as Agnes or Eilis?" Niall asked.

"Matters not at this point. Fetch the priest from his bed, Ian."

"Aye, my laird." Ian bolted down the stairs.

"What do we do about Dunbarton?" Eanruig asked.

Niall shook his head. "We ought to lay siege to his castle."

"If he promises to release your brother and Gunnolf," Eilis said tearfully, "I will be Dunbarton's wife."

"Nay, sweeting." James gave her a slight embrace. "We will come up with another plan. Come, you must see your wee brother. I am afraid I gave him a fright when I told him you were alive."

"Ethan," she whispered. "Dear God, he cannot be

269

returned to my uncle. If naught else, he must remain here in your care."

"Both of you will." James knocked on the door, and Tavia answered, her eyes rounding as she saw Eilis and Fia.

James's mother looked just as surprised.

"How is the lad?" James asked, not wishing to discuss the conspiracy of his people to ferret Eilis away without his permission.

Eilis rushed into the chamber before Tavia could say. Ethan jumped off the high bed and he, and Eilis ran into each other's arms. "El!" he cried out. "Ye are alive!"

"Aye, Ethan, my darling. Aye."

James's mother smiled, but her expression shifted as she looked at James's grim look.

"Dunbarton will not release Dougald," James said. "I did not have high hopes he would. I will come up with another plan."

James's mother paled. Tavia hurried over to her and held her arm.

"What is the rush? This is an ungodly hour to be taking a wife," the old priest grumbled from beyond the chamber. "What are we doing here and not in the chapel?"

Ian said, "Father, circumstances are such that the laird must wed at once to avoid bloodshed."

"Bloodshed ye say? Verra well. Where are you taking me then?"

"The solar," James said, intercepting them. "Come, we will have another ceremony where all of our people will celebrate, but for now, those of us here will witness the event in my solar."

His mother's pale face brightened slightly, but then she frowned. "Eilis should change out of the traveling gown."

"No time, Mother." He offered his hand to Eilis.

She hesitated while Ethan's arms were wrapped around her legs.

"Come, Ethan," Fia said, pulling him away and lifting him into her arms. "Your sister is marrying Laird James."

Ethan smiled shyly at him.

James inclined his head then turned to speak to Eilis. "Come, lass, and be mine."

"But Dunbarton…"

"The devil with him, Eilis." James softened his scowl. 'Twas not the way he wished to coax his bride to married bliss.

"If this is a mistake…" She took his hand, and he pulled her out of the chamber at a brisk pace, heading for his solar, not risking that she might change her mind.

The mistake was in letting Broc take the lass away from him the first time so many summers ago.

# CHAPTER 19

After the abbreviated wedding ceremony, Father Rivers grumbled something about marrying at a more decent hour while Fia carried a sleeping Ethan to Eilis's chamber. Lady Akira kissed Eilis again, bidding her a good evening with a look at James to be gentle, and took her leave. Niall, Eanruig, and Ian went below stairs to celebrate, though the bigger celebration would take place on the morrow.

James looked like he had won a battle, triumphant, a smile playing on his lips, yet when he escorted Eilis to his chamber, he seemed a little apprehensive. He stoked the peat fire, his back turned to Eilis so that she could remove her gown in privacy.

His sensitivity charmed her, and she cleared her throat to get his attention. He looked over his shoulder and raised his brows when he saw she had only removed her socks, garters, and shoes, her feet bare. "I...I need a maid to help me with my gown. Would you..."

He didn't wait for her to finish her question but straightened and stalked across the floor. She was reminded of the way he took charge of situations, regally, full of strength of purpose, his shoulders thrown back, chest out, his focus on her and nothing else.

And he was hers this night and always. She tried to ignore the nervous jitters twisting inside her belly, the way her heart fluttered when he drew close, the inane fear that suddenly shook her to the core.

He'd made love with Catriona, Eilis was certain, and the woman would be well versed in how to please a man. Whereas, Eilis had not a clue as to what she needed to do. He reached out to her, and she forced herself not to step back. She gave him a small smile of encouragement, but she was afraid it wasn't at all convincing.

He smiled even more and took her hands in his, brought them to his lips, and swept his mouth across them in the gentlest of caresses. "Naught to be afraid of, my siren from the sea. You have captured my heart, and I am yours now, this night and forever."

"I…" She straightened, looking up into his eyes, trying so hard not to appear as nervous as she felt, until a shiver rippled through her.

This time he leaned down and kissed her lips, his large hands gripping her shoulders, holding her fast so she would not melt into the rushes. For that is the way she felt with his lips on hers, heating her to the core, like the flame warming the tallow, slowly melting it into a puddle of hot liquid.

She barely remembered his lifting her gown over her head, except that his lips separated from hers for the

273

briefest of moments and then his arms were around her, holding her tight against his body, keeping her warm and protected.

He was still fully dressed, although he lifted her off her feet and carried her to his bed, his gaze sweeping down her nakedness, his look full of admiration.

With great anticipation, she waited for him to remove his clothes and hoped she would be as good as Catriona in bed, if only she could make the right moves.

She only got a glimpse of his nakedness, the powerful muscles in his arms and chest and legs, the lance that stretched out to her as hard as any spear, and the dark curly hairs surrounding it before he joined her in the bed.

She vaguely worried about what her uncle and Dunbarton's response would be to learn she had married the MacNeill.

Then James was on top of her, kissing her into submission, making her forget about anything but him. His powerful body pressed against hers in the chilled air. His mouth pressured hers for a response that effectively stole her thoughts. She wrapped her arms around his waist and kissed him back with enthusiasm. Her tongue danced with his, soliciting a groan from deep within him. The sensuous sound spurred her on, made her experiment more, touching his skin, exploring every inch of him.

"Siren," he huskily mouthed against her lips, his fingers sifting through her hair as if each strand was the most beautiful thing he'd ever experienced.

He made her feel precious, desirable, lightheaded, and awash with joy. He shifted lower and captured her breasts in his hands, massaging and suckling the nipples with his mouth. A new sensation instantly sprang up between her legs, a sweet ache that begged for relief. Please finish me off, she wanted to plead with him. But she said naught and moaned low with the pleasure he stoked deep inside her.

'Twas naught like anything she'd ever experienced, and she wanted to feel the same delicious pleasure over and over again. She reached down and seized handfuls of his satiny locks, gripping them as he kissed her belly, sending a thrill straight through her. When he inserted his fingers between her legs, she sighed—'twas the most sinfully exciting sensation she'd ever had. He was killing her.

"Please, James, do something to make the ache stop."

He groaned and pushed her legs apart, lowering himself slowly in between. "You might feel a wee bit uncomfortable in the beginning…"

She slipped her hands down to his firm arse and pressured him to get on with the lovemaking. He smiled, his dark eyes clouded with desire. "Marsali, my pearl."

He speared her with his lance, slowly, allowing her time to accustom herself to his size. Then a prickle of pain and he was inside her fully. 'Twas the most erotic pleasure, his entering her the way he did, his staff diving in, the friction pushing her to the top of the cliff, to a headiness she'd never felt before.

The heat of his rubbing against her, despite the coolness of the room, stoked a fire burning deep inside her, building until she felt she could take no more or would explode. Ripples of pleasure washed through her, and an exhilarating peace settled over her.

"I love you, James," she whispered, remembering the boy of her youth who had lain between her legs at the top of the cliff after rescuing her, only they'd both been dressed and soaking wet to the skin. Her James, partly a blurred memory from the past, now so real, she could scarce believe he was hers.

Yet a trickle of fear wormed its way into her heart. What if her uncle and Dunbarton vowed to kill her new husband?

\*\*\*

James feared his new bride would faint away she'd been so tense, shivering with expectation, partly because of the cold and partly because of never having been with a man. He was grateful his kisses had stirred up her basic primal needs, the desire to be loved and the need to love in return. Generous with her kisses and an eager learner, she was a bonny bride. Her touching him triggered his need to prove she had made no mistake in choosing him. He wanted to please her in the worst way.

Now, she gripped his shaft inside her tight, lithe body, her mews stirring him to completion, and with a final thrust, he spilled his seed deep. He rolled over and pulled her into his embrace, and she cuddled against his chest, her arm wrapping around his waist. "Hmm," she said, slipping her leg over his.

He knew he would get no sleep this eve, not the way the woman so innocent in his arms awakened his needs.

\*\*\*

Something vaguely stirred Eilis from her sleep, although she couldn't recall what. 'Twas James's fault she was so muddle-headed, waking her two more times, nay three, to make love to her again in the middle of the night.

She smiled as she ran her hand over her naked belly, thinking how even now she might have a babe growing inside her. She didn't know how many times he'd have to join with her to make it happen, although Fia had once told her one time could be enough. She should know because one of the milk maids had sworn she'd had only one transgression, and she was with child.

Eilis reached out to touch James, but her fingers only grappled quilts and furs. She frowned to learn he was no longer in bed with her. Why did he not wake her? Then she again heard the noise that must have disturbed her sleep.

"Our laird said to wake her and get her dressed."

"We tried to, and she shooed us away thrice already. Let the poor lady sleep."

Eilis didn't recognize the women's voices.

Someone pounded at the chamber door, and one of the women scurried to answer it, her feet hurrying across the floor. "Aye?"

"Lady Eilis, is she not dressed yet?" Niall asked, his voice perturbed.

"Laird James wore her out last night. We have tried to rouse her from the bed, but she is verra tired."

"Laird James's wife is needed at the celebration. I will wait here for her as I am to escort her to the hall."

"Aye, at once," the lady said, and the door squeaked closed.

Eilis groaned and ran her fingers through her tangled hair. She couldn't possibly get ready quickly enough to suit anyone.

One of the older women pulled the curtains aside
and smiled brightly at her.

"Where is Fia?" Eilis asked, trying not to grumble,
still too tired to move very quickly.

"She has taken the wee bairn down to break his
fast. Laird James gave him an amber rock that the lad
carries around like 'tis the greatest treasure," the
woman said, helping Eilis into a shift. "Lady Akira has
taken your brother under her wing. I have never seen
her so happy. Well, and also since she has you to call
daughter after all those boys to raise, Niall included."

Nesta hurried into the chamber and smiled. "I
brought you another gown. Lady Akira said we will go
to the village to find some new material and fashion
new gowns for you, my lady. His Lairdship also said he
left something on his chest for you."

Nesta brought the cloak over, the silver brooch still
fastened to it, the one Eilis had worn when he'd rescued
her from the sea. She touched it tenderly and
remembered that experience as if it had been yesterday.
She sighed.

But what about Broc? And Dunbarton? And
James's brother and Gunnolf? Although Eilis knew that
'twas important to celebrate life even when
undercurrents of danger lurked all about them. Life was
too short to focus only on adversity.

Then she wondered, what about Catriona? The
woman would want to poison her, to be sure.

"An amber stone?" Eilis queried.

"Aye, the tale His Lairdship tells is that he found
the most exquisite treasure fishing for stones at the edge
of the sea. Only he had to rescue the siren before she
retrieved the amber stone. When he went looking for

what she had tried to free from the rocky beach at low tide, once her cousin had stolen her away, he found the amber stone. He told the wee lad, Ethan, that 'twas from his sister, Eilis, a gift from her heart."

Eilis smiled.

"Think you our laird could be such a poet?" The old woman shook her head.

"Aye, 'tis the pearl from the sea that brought it out in him," Nesta said, helping to plait Eilis's hair. "My da was never one for poetic sentiments, I did not think. Until one day I heard him speaking alone to my mother. Hearing his sentimental words, I cried a few tears. 'Tis a bonny lass that will make men do the strangest things."

Eilis glanced at the other woman, strangely silent. She was busy with the linens, pulling each of the comforters back, the furs, the pillows. What a mess Eilis and James had made of the bedding in the throes of passion. She wished she could have straightened the covers before the women had to see such a shambles.

Then the woman pulled off two of the linens, whispered to the older woman, and scurried out of the room. Nesta seemed to have heard and smiled. "Mayhap Laird James did not realize where this would lead to. The servants knew from the moment he carried you from his horse and back into the keep, the way he held you close to his heart, although his face wore a scowl like when he was ready to do battle. But we knew he was worried more about your health and..." She sighed. "We knew. 'Twas all the talk amongst the servants, the betting going on as to when he would finally take you to wife. Although many of us believed he would have done so earlier and sent word to Lady

Catriona that she was already too late."

"Catriona," Eilis said.

"Aye, she is wanton. We guessed she would chase after Keary or some other, mayhap even your cousin, Broc. But what is she up to? Plying her feminine ways on our Laird James. Polecat. He should send her back whence she came now before new rumors begin to fly."

*And Nesta would be just the one to give them wing.* For once, Eilis was glad of it. "Then I must put a stop to her wicked ways."

"We will help," Nesta said, and the older maid nodded, her eyes smiling. "We serve you as well as we do our laird, and we know what kind of a woman Lady Catriona is to work for. Her servants are terrified of her. So we will help you in anyway that we can."

"Then come, ladies, before the rumors begin in earnest."

Nesta and the older woman giggled and followed her out of the chamber. Niall bowed his head to Eilis. "You are looking verra bonny this morn, my lady. Wedded bliss becomes you."

She tried to quash a blush, but as heated as her cheeks were, she feared she failed. "I understand Catriona is causing trouble."

"Fia is giving her a difficult time and so is Lady Akira. One of the servants burned Catriona's portion of the veal, and another gave her the sour mead at the bottom of the barrel. Most of all, James has been too busy speaking with your cousin, Broc, to pay the woman any mind."

Eilis let out the breath she'd been holding. She didn't think she'd be worried about the woman's attentions to James so soon after their marriage, but then again, what if he was just like his father? Taking a wife then finding any maid to satisfy his sexual needs beyond the marriage bed.

As soon as she walked into the hall on Niall's arm, everyone grew quiet. Her face flushed anew, and the heat spread all the way through her. Why didn't James wake her earlier this morn so she wouldn't be subjected to this humiliation?

He hurried from his chair and joined her, which helped somewhat. "You are looking lovely this morning, my beautiful wife," he whispered in her ear then kissed her cheek.

His kinsmen were smiling, and several raised mugs in salute. 'Twas only the sour-faced Broc, some of his men, and the dourest Catriona that dimmed the happy celebration.

"I understand Catriona is vying for your attention overmuch," Eilis whispered back and gave her husband a kiss on the lips, which caused a roar of cheers and mugs and knives tapping on the table.

James chuckled. "Once I found my siren, the woman lost the chance to be my wife. My mother and most of my people, even Niall, knew it from the beginning. I was the only one too thickheaded to realize it at first."

"Nay, my laird. You knew not who I was and could not make such a commitment, risking your people's safety. 'Tis your kindness and care for your people that made you hold back."

"Aye, my sweeting." He led her to the table and whispered again, "Did I disturb your sleep overmuch?"

She smiled at him. "'Twas for a verra good reason. But I apologize for arising so late."

"No apologies needed."

Catriona glared at Eilis as she took her seat. Ethan waved his amber stone at his sister and smiled as he sat between Fia and Lady Akira. Broc bowed his head to Eilis as if acknowledging she'd played her game well and won.

Catriona said, "Do you oft sleep away the day"

"Only when her husband keeps her up overmuch," James said with a gleam in his eye. He slipped his hand around Eilis's in her lap and squeezed.

She smiled at him. If it had been someone else he'd spoken to, Eilis might have been embarrassed. But Catriona deserved worse, the witch.

"Aye, and he promises much more of the same this eve." Eilis offered her a coy smile.

"If he is not away battling Dunbarton," Catriona said, her voice chilly and calculating. "Seems someone has told him that you are here, and he wishes you turned over to him at once. Then he'll release James's brother. I never thought James would prefer a woman over his blood relation."

Eilis stared at James in disbelief. "Is what Catriona says is true? Has Dunbarton ordered my exchange for your brother?"

"Eilis…"

"Oh, James, what are we to do?"

Broc snorted. "I have accepted James's bride price for you on my da's behalf, Eilis." He shrugged. "'Twas a much better offer than Dunbarton's. Since you are not Agnes, the betrothal was no longer valid."

Broc was standing up for her?

"My men and I will fight alongside MacNeill." Broc inclined his head.

Stunned speechless, Eilis glanced at James to see if what Broc said was true. James gave her a small nod.

Ian hurried over from the table where he'd been sitting beside Keary and spoke in private to James. Eilis strained to hear his words and picked up bits of the conversation—plan, fight, free Dougald. What had Keary in mind?

But would it be a ruse? To kill more of the MacNeill? Was Dunbarton's bastard son trying for a way to smooth over past difficulties with his sire?

James rose from the table and offered a toast. "To my bonny wife, Lady Eilis, also known as Marsali, pearl of the sea."

Everyone drank to the couple except for Catriona. Had she been the one to send a missive to Dunbarton, stating his betrothed was at Craigly?

"'Tis usual that the festivities continue throughout the day. But we have other matters that must be dealt with at present. Afterward, we will continue the feasting in celebration," James said to his people and his guests.

"What do you plan to do?" Eilis asked James, as he escorted her out of the hall.

"Worry not your bonny head, Eilis. Stay with Ethan and my mother and Fia. 'Tis time I fetched my brother home."

"What if 'tis a trick? What if Keary has sent word and his da plans to kill or capture you?"

"There is no other way, sweeting. Now that Dunbarton thinks you are Agnes or not and wishes you just the same, I have no choice. He will not release my brother or Gunnolf until I hand you over to him."

"But…"

283

"No more worries. Stay here. I will return before nightfall, and we will continue to celebrate our new beginning." He kissed her soundly and hugged her tightly against his chest.

She suppressed the tears threatening to spill.

"Now, now, my lady. You are to send your hero off with smiles and well wishes."

She smiled, but the tears began to roll down her cheeks anyway, and she hurriedly wiped them away. "I am sorry." She looked down, wishing to avoid seeing James's annoyance that she could not be cheerful for him when he went into battle.

He lifted her chin and gave her a wistful smile. "'Tis your tender heartedness that I love best. Take care of your wee brother, and I will return as soon as I can." Again, he kissed her, hugged the breath out of her, and then hurried with his men to the inner bailey, discussing their plans for the battle ahead.

What if she lost her Highland hero now, when they finally found each other, and she had a home, a mother, and her little brother to raise in a place where he would be loved and not terrorized into submission?

Tears filled her eyes again. How could she survive?

# CHAPTER 20

Ever since James had left to do battle with Dunbarton, Eilis couldn't hide her upset, and, although she tried to spend some time with Ethan, her brother was too excited about playing with his newfound friends below stairs.

Lady Akira had ordered a hot bath for her to help her to relax. James's mother had warned Eilis 'twould not do well for her to fret too much when she might be carrying James's child.

Eilis had never heard that worry could cause a woman to lose her baby, but she obeyed, since the lady had four sons and would know more than Eilis would about the matter. Ethan was having a great time playing with wooden swords with some of James's kinsmen's sons in the great hall while Fia watched with a protective eye.

Catriona had packed her bags and left with her servants and escort, vowing to ruin Eilis in any way that she could for deceitfully stealing James under her nose.

Nesta was busy talking nonstop as she usually did and despite the worry about James, the heated bath and not enough sleep was making Eilis drowsy.

Until Lady Allison came to the room and dismissed Nesta. "I will help the lady dress for bed. Go, Nesta. I can manage."

Nesta didn't immediately leave like she'd been ordered but waited instead for Eilis's word. "Thank you, Nesta. Mayhap you can bring me some goat milk later?"

Nesta smiled and curtseyed. "Aye, my lady." Then she hurried out of the room.

"Hurry, Lady Eilis. You must get dressed at once," Allison said, helping her out of the tub then hurried to dry her off.

"What is this all about?" Eilis sensed some mischief was at play, and her skin prickled with fresh concern. With Allison's help, she quickly donned her shift, a traveling gown, and her stockings and shoes.

"We go to Dunbarton's castle. I will get us in, and while the men are causing a distraction, we will free Dougald and Gunnolf."

"I thought Keary was helping James to get into the castle and free Dougald. And that you could not get in again without getting caught."

"Keary is not to be trusted. Aye, he wishes to overthrow his da and become the clan chief. But he does not wish to release James's brother. He will turn on James as soon as he has his da's people's support. He was the one who sent the missive to his da concerning you and how James was holding you here against his will. As for the rest, as I said, Laird James and those who rode with him will be enough of a distraction."

"How will you and I be able to slip in and free the men?"

"I told you. I was raised there. I know all the ways in and out. Also, I know the best way to get there from here. They say you slipped out of here without alerting the guards. We will have to use the same secret passage you used before. Since I'm not part of the MacNeill family, I do not know the secret passage."

"But Tavia had the keys to the door that leads out of the castle. It would be locked."

Allison pulled the key from the pouch hanging from her belt. "Let us leave before we are too late."

"But…why do you need *my* help?"

"The secret passage? I don't know the way. Also, I cannot take anyone else with me, and the two of us will be able to watch each other's backs."

"Should we not have an escort? At night, we would not be safe—"

"We cannot take an escort, Lady Eilis. No one will allow us to leave. I tried speaking to Niall, but he brushed me off. I fear no one will trust my words, despite that I have freed Dougald and Gunnolf at my own peril once already. The men are bullheaded and have only one thing in mind—a frontal assault. Come, hurry, my lady. We are wasting verra valuable time."

With a wariness that she had felt when Nighinn helped her escape, Eilis pulled her own cloak over her head this time and fastened the silver brooch, hoping she would not regret yet another hasty decision. Yet what if she and Allison could free Dougald and Gunnolf without any bloodshed? 'Twas worth taking the chance.

She had to know Allison's motivation though. "Why do you do this, risking your own life?"

Allison let out her breath. "Lady Akira took me in, has given me a home, and has been verra kind. I saw the way Dunbarton's men treated Dougald and Gunnolf when they first captured them. I could not sleep for knowing how brutal Dunbarton and his men could be. When he learns James will not give you up no matter what, he will kill them. If we can get to Dougald and Gunnolf first..." She spread her hands. "I can think of no other way."

She sounded as desperate as Eilis felt. "All right. But James will have my head no matter what the outcome."

Eilis and Allison shoved the chest aside that hid the trap door into the secret maze beneath the castle. Her hair still wet from bathing, she shivered as they entered the bowels of the maze.

If Allison was right about this and Eilis believed with all her heart that as soon as Dunbarton learned James had wed her, he would have James's brother and the Viking murdered before James and his men could breach the castle, she had to do her part to help. She just had to. Dougald was as much a brother as Ethan was to her now, and he'd saved her life. The pounding of her heart and her quickened icy breath in the chilled air beneath the castle warned her she might be the pawn in a dangerous scenario. Still, if she could help James and his brother, she would do anything.

But who to trust? Keary? Or Allison? Mayhap neither.

*** 

Dougald struggled with the manacles around his

wrists, clanking the metal from time to time.

"Any luck?" Gunnolf asked from his cell beyond.

"Nay. You?"

"Not me either. Think you another sweet lassie will come to free us?"

"Nay, 'twould be too dangerous for any to try again."

Gunnolf shifted on his straw. "Think you the guard was telling the truth when he said that James had taken Keary hostage and offered him in exchange for us?"

"Aye."

"But there has been no release."

"No doubt Dunbarton still refuses to acknowledge his bastard son."

"You would think since he cannot seem to have one by a legitimate wife, he would acknowledge one of his bastard sons."

"Aye. Think you James has Dunbarton's betrothed hidden away at Craigly?"

Gunnolf snorted. "Nay. Your brother would not do something so underhanded as that. Dunbarton lies."

Running feet headed out of the dungeon, and Dougald sat up and tried to discern what was happening. "There is commotion abovestairs. Think you James is coming to our rescue?"

\*\*\*

When Eilis and Allison arrived at Dunbarton's castle, the place was quiet. Guards walked along the wall walk while Allison guided Eilis to the south side of the castle. Eilis assumed James and his men had not arrived yet because Allison had learned a more direct route in all her travels back and forth between the two places.

"'Tis an escape route much like the one James has leading out of his chamber," Allison whispered.

"So we will be slipping into Dunbarton's chamber?" Eilis didn't like the plan. She had thought they'd be going straight to the dungeon beneath the castle and lead Dougald and Gunnolf out that way. Traveling all the way through the castle to the dungeon and out again, och, how could they manage without getting caught?

Allison lighted a candle, and they traversed the maze of tunnels, but she snuffed the candle out when they reached a small wooden door.

Eilis's stomach flip-flopped, and she feared her heart beat so loud, everyone in the castle would hear it.

Allison took her hand and led her into the chamber, the only light, one beyond the door leading into the rest of the castle. "Dunbarton's chamber," Allison whispered.

In the chamber of the devil himself. If he caught Eilis in here…

Men's voices caught their attention and Allison quickly traversed the floor to the door leading to another room then peered in. "Lady's chamber, unoccupied," she whispered.

"Think you the MacNeill will be pounding at our gates soon?" the man said, as he and another's boots tromped by the door.

"Aye, but what a surprise they will find when they get here."

Allison groaned softly and shut the door from the lady's chamber to Dunbarton's. "'Tis Dunbarton's advisor, but I do not know who the other man is." Then she patted Eilis's arm. "Stay here until I make sure the way is clear. I know my way around, and everyone knows me. You will be safe until I come back for you."

"Why did I really need to come, Allison? I am not a bargaining tool for you, am I?"

Tears filled Allison's eyes. "You saved me from your cousin once, my lady. I would not ask you to help if it had not been that no one else would aid me. I wish no harm to come to you. Stay. I will not be long."

Allison slipped outside the chamber and closed the door. Eilis had a very bad feeling about this. Why would Allison leave her here? In Dunbarton's wife's chamber where, if the situation had turned out differently, Eilis would have lived permanently? What if Allison truly intended to free Dougald and Gunnolf, only by using Eilis as the bargaining tool? Did she have feelings for one of the men?

After what seemed like hours, the door opened. Eilis barely breathed. A man entered the room, his large body shadowed in the light outside the chamber then he shut the door.

God's wounds, who was he, and would he find her here?

*** 

Delayed in arriving at Lockton by a band of thieves, not any of Dunbarton's men, James and his men quickly had made the brigands see the error of their ways...dead men no longer stole from unsuspecting folk.

Keary spoke to one of the guards at the gate, who reluctantly lifted it for him and *his* men. Dunbarton would kill the whelp if he knew Keary had helped James and his men to enter the bailey in the middle of the night. Worse, that Broc, son of MacBurton, would be aiding in the plot to free James's kin instead of siding with Dunbarton.

"Keary, how now," one of the guards said, greeting him with a slap on the back. Thankfully, the man was interested in seeing Dunbarton's son return and didn't pay any mind to his *friends*. "Dunbarton will have your head when he discovers you are back from the Crusade, but I for one am glad to find you well. Are the women as beautiful as they say?"

Keary smiled. "Aye, that they are. My friends and I will take our pallets for the night, although we wish a bit of mead before we retire."

"Aye, good to see you return. We were told you had died in battle or lost your way home."

"No' me. No one would keep me from home for long." He dismounted while a stable boy was rousted from the stalls to take care of the horses.

Keary motioned to James and the others. "Come, we drink, then sleep."

James and his kin and Broc and his men hurried to dismount, everyone eyeing the guards on the walk who stood with their bodies tense, hands poised to unsheathe swords. The guards glanced at them, somewhat curious, then went back to their posts.

James assumed the one who let them in was assured enough that they belonged. He hoped his own men were never that naïve. 'Twas something he'd discuss with Eanruig when he returned to Craigly.

Keary escorted them inside the keep as though he were laird and not Dunbarton's bastard son then motioned to the stairs that led into the dungeon.

While most of the men hovered around the stairs, waiting for a fight, James and two of his men and Keary headed down the stairs into the foul-smelling abyss. Torches let off a smoky light, and someone stirred, then heavy footsteps headed in their direction.

Keary greeted the lumbering, half-asleep guard. "Dunbarton wishes to see the MacNeill and Viking prisoners in his solar."

"Keary, ye back from Crusade? What does Dunbarton want them for at this hour?"

"He wishes to make special sport of them."

The man scratched his bearded chin, glanced at James, but didn't seem to recognize him, then shook his head. "Aye, whatever His Lairdship wishes."

He scuffled toward the cells, then after several long moments, a key ground open the door lock and then another. As soon as he shuffled toward them with Dougald and Gunnolf leading the way, their wrists and ankles manacled, the naked prisoners raised their brows in surprise then smiled. James circled around them in one fell swoop, jumped the guard, and knocked him senseless.

Dougald smiled and said to Gunnolf, "See, 'twas the plan. My eldest brother would rescue us."

"Ja," Gunnolf said, lifting his manacled wrists while Keary hurried to unlock them. "Could have let me know sooner, though. I was still trying to come up with my own." He motioned at his nakedness. "You have clothes and weapons for us, ja?"

Ian hurried down the stairs. "Aye, just procuring the items." He handed the ragged garments to Dougald, and he shared some with Gunnolf, who grunted.

"The man who wore these must have been no taller than your mother, Dougald."

Dougald laughed.

Ian said, "Lady Allison is abovestairs and has awakened her brother. Apparently, he is one of Dunbarton's bastard sons."

Keary ground his teeth and headed for the stairs. "My half brothers, all Dunbarton's bastard sons, plan a revolt then."

James shook his head. He wished to get Dougald and Gunnolf free of the castle before anything else untoward happened to them, especially as weakened as they had to be. "Hold, Keary, allow us to leave before you start your battle."

"Too late, my laird," Ian warned. "Lady Allison brought Lady Eilis here also. She is waiting in the lady's chamber adjoining Dunbarton's."

"Eilis, God's teeth, man, why did you not already say? What in the devil's name is she doing here?"

He rushed up the stairs with the men, but already swords had been drawn, and Broc and the rest of the men were fighting in the great hall.

\*\*\*

"Lady Eilis," the unknown man whispered, drawing closer as Eilis inched away from him in Dunbarton's lady's chamber.

She didn't recognize his voice. She moved away from him, desperately trying not to make a sound as her feet slid rushes across the wooden floor.

"My lady, come. We are to free Dougald," he said, his voice rushed but meant only for her to hear.

Who was he? She didn't trust the man, and now she didn't trust Allison. As quietly as she could, Eilis slipped under the bed, much relieved she didn't run into a chamber pot and make a lot of racket. She lay very still while the man's feet shuffled through the rushes as he searched for her in the dark.

The door opened again, letting in shadowed light from the corridor, and another man whispered, "Have you got her?"

"She seems to have slipped away."

"God's teeth, if only Allison had stayed here with her." The man paced then said, "All right. It cannot be helped. As long as Dunbarton's dead, then all we have to do is kill that meddling Keary and the others. Come, before James finds a way to free his brother. We may still find James's woman in the meantime and..."

Battle cries erupted below stairs, and Eilis squeezed her eyes shut and wrapped her arms around herself, praying James would be all right and she could slip out to meet him in due course.

Although she would hate to see his expression if she managed to get away.

"Come on. Seems we are too late."

The two men rushed out of the room.

Now what was she to do? Return alone in the dark to Craigly? If she stayed here, someone from the Dunbarton clan could take her hostage and use her to make James pay. If she attempted to help, what could she do but get underfoot?

"Lass?" someone said, his voice hushed as the door cracked open a hair.

She hadn't even heard the door open this time, but the voice sounded like James's. Heart pumping with relief, she whispered, "James?"

# CHAPTER 21

Eilis prayed that if the man was truly one of the enemy—and not James—who had just entered Dunbarton's lady's chamber where she was hiding under the bed, he would not locate her.

The man said, "'Tis Dougald, sweet angel. James was battling a man when he sent me in search of you. Where are you?"

"Dougald." She choked on tears and scrambled out from underneath the bed. "Are you all right?"

"Aye. Allison sent me here to get you. She tried to reach us, but her cousin caught her, and he forced her to tell him you were here—only she said you were in Dunbarton's chamber, hoping you'd hide before they searched the lady's chamber. When her cousin left her and headed for the laird's chamber, she managed to get word to Ian about your plight. James and our men, and even your cousin and his, are fighting Dunbarton's kin as we speak." Dougald seized her wrist. "Come, we must go at once."

"Is James all right?"

"Aye, although he is sorely vexed that Allison brought you here." Dougald lighted a candle and led her through Dunbarton's chamber. "Tell me where to go."

She pointed to a tapestry she thought covered the door they'd come through. "One of the men said Dunbarton is dead."

"Aye. Poisoned by one of his bastard sons. Hopefully, one that intends to live peaceably with us will rule." Dougald jerked back the tapestry and opened the door. He handed her the candle and readied his sword, then advanced down the stairs.

"How many sons are there? I thought only the one."

"Five. We will leave them to sort it out amongst themselves. If we aid one to take over, how do we know he will honor a peace between us? We do not."

"Where are we going? Surely we are not leaving by ourselves."

Dougald softly chuckled. "You were so quiet in the cave that eve. We will meet some of my kin outside the castle, lass. I will return you to Craigly, and James will follow shortly."

"What of Gunnolf?"

Dougald stopped to consider the passage that split into two.

"Left," she said. "'Tis the same path Allison showed me as we made our way here."

"Aye, lass. Gunnolf is of berserker descent. Once he starts fighting, best to let him finish the battle. I prefer rescuing fair damsels."

She gave him a small smile. Their footfalls echoed off the limestone walls and sounded eerie in the dark. "I am so sorry they caught up with you at the cave. 'Twas all my fault."

"How so, lass?" He peered over his shoulder at her.

"I had tethered my borrowed horse outside the cave."

"The horse must have run off in the storm. Dunbarton's men had searched all night for us, looking in every cave they could find." He raised his brows at her. "I understand James wed you last eve."

"Aye." Eilis only wished to see James again soon. Although she was relieved Dougald and Gunnolf were well.

Dougald shook his head. "Here Gunnolf and I had been arguing whether either of us had a chance to woo you. Although we would never have guessed the woman he wanted was the same one he rescued at the cliffs. Malcolm will be exonerated."

"Why?"

"Malcolm stopped him from rescuing you from your cousin. When James couldn't locate you afterward, he did not speak to Malcolm for weeks." Dougald grabbed the handle to the door. But when they heard men in the narrow passage behind them running to catch up, Dougald jerked the door open and pulled Eilis out into the chilly night air. He snuffed out the candle and helped her to mount the horse she'd ridden to get there, then he took Allison's horse. "Around front."

Before they could get very far, five men swooped out of the secret passage door, one holding a torch, all wielding swords, and no one Eilis recognized.

"Go, my lady!" Dougald slashed at two of the men, but another chased after Eilis and ran in front of her, making her horse rear.

She hung on for dear life and screamed.

Her scream brought other mounted men racing around the east side of the castle walls, and she feared she'd brought all the Dunbarton's men to battle.

When she saw James, her eyes filled with tears.

"Lady," he said, exasperated, and he and his men quickly dispensed with those who attacked Dougald. One other darted back inside the secret passageway maze to safety.

"We return home now," James said, motioning with his sword toward the MacNeill lands. He resheathed his sword and reached over to pull Eilis from her horse. Once she was seated in his lap, she rested her head next to his chest and snuggled tight, thrilled beyond words that he and his kin were unharmed. "The Dunbarton men did not fight us with much enthusiasm. Methinks they wished us on our way so they could deal with the battle between the sons."

"Allison said you needed our help."

"Allison could have gotten you killed. She had the best intentions, but she will no longer work at Craigly."

"I do not understand her thinking."

"Her half brother is one of Dunbarton's bastard sons. Working for my mother, Allison could not bear to see Dougald taken hostage, so she vowed to free him since she had the means to enter the castle at will, and she knew how to prepare a sleeping draught. She also wanted her half brother to have a chance to rule. Then when we stormed the castle with Keary's help, Dunbarton's four other bastard sons decided to fight for the chance to replace Dunbarton. Most are tired of the squabbles between our people and Dunbarton's iron rule and weary of the fact he would not recognize any of his bastard sons as his own."

"Two of the men said they wanted to keep you from freeing your brother."

"Aye. They learned Allison had brought you to the castle and apparently were loyal to a son of Dunbarton who does not wish to end the strife. Hopefully, he will not take power."

"I still do not understand why Allison wanted me there."

James tightened his hold on Eilis and kissed her forehead. "Dear Eilis, her brother heard of your charms—how you had returned to Craigly at great risk of your family's discovery to warn us about Dougald and Gunnolf being taken hostage again, how you had defended the goat herder's livestock against the wolves, how you rescued Allison from her assailant at Brecken, and were betrothed to the old Dunbarton. Her brother, Finbar, wished to take you for his own wife. He hoped I might not survive the skirmish at the castle. And Allison would be your sister. She much admires you, Eilis, but no one can as much as I do."

"But Lady Allison—"

"Will stay with her brother. Blood comes before friendship."

Dougald rode up beside them and winked at Eilis. "Here Gunnolf and I were betting which one of us would have a chance at wooing the fair maid. Neither of us can believe you had her locked up in the castle tight and still managed to lose her. Twice, so it seems."

James grunted. "And you, my brother, how did you manage to allow Dunbarton's men to catch you not once but twice?"

"Gunnolf and I had to fight the swine for stealing our livestock. The other time?" He smiled at Eilis. "'Twas a bonny lass we were protecting." Then he shrugged. "Besides, we had no weapons and were outnumbered six to one." He let out his breath in a huff. "Is mother well?"

"Aye, she has taken in another lad, Eilis's wee brother. Of course she is delighted I have taken Eilis to wife. She was not happy to hear Malcolm wed Lady Anice without inviting her to the celebration. And that in taking the lady to be his wife, he had not received King Henry's permission first."

Dougald cleared his throat. "Aye, well, I will give you the details in private."

Eilis yawned and snuggled tighter to James. "Then James will have to tell me what you will not."

Dougald laughed.

"We will speak of it on the morrow, my brother," James said.

Dougald shook his head. "Just like Malcolm."

"You should try married life sometime, Dougald. Priorities change."

"Aye, as well they should."

Broc came riding up from behind, his face red, his sword bloodied. He shoved the steel into its scabbard. "I had come for a fight, but..." He inclined his head to James. "I thought my quarrel with you, not Dunbarton's kin. Should be interesting to see which of his sons win out. I understand this is your brother, Dougald. If no one in your family is interested in the fair Catriona..."

"Broc, you cannot be serious. The woman is a witch," Eilis said.

"A witch?" Broc asked, his brows raised.

301

"Aye."

Broc rubbed his jaw and nodded. As superstitious as he was, she knew that would be enough to dissuade him. There was no way that she wanted Catriona in the family, even married to her cousin, whom she didn't hold in high regard and deserved such an ungrateful woman.

Near the wee hours of the morning, they arrived back at Craigly. Except for the guards on duty who greeted the warriors returning home, the castle was quiet.

Then Niall rushed out of the keep. "God's knees, Lady Eilis. Lady Akira herself is ready to lock you in the dungeon. She has been worried sick about you and the babe."

Everyone looked at Eilis. Her skin heated as if the sun had baked it all day. "I am all right, as well you can see." How wouldd anyone know if she was yet with child? Although she secretly wished it with all her heart.

"And going no where further unless I say so," James said, as Niall helped Eilis down.

James dismounted and handed his reins to Niall. "The celebration for Dougald and Gunnolf's safe return and the wedding celebration may begin without us when everyone arises to break their fast. Unless the castle is under siege, the lady and I do not wish to be disturbed."

Gunnolf smiled at Eilis. "Ja, Dougald told me we had no chance with you if Laird James took a fancy to you."

Bleary eyed, Fia hurried out to greet Eilis and gave her a resounding hug. "You are all well, dear cousin.

Lady Akira nearly had a stroke. Thankfully, Ethan slept through everything."

James swept Eilis up in his arms. "On the morrow, ladies, you may visit. On the morrow." With that he hurried into the keep, greeted his smiling servants with a courteous nod, and hastened abovestairs.

"Wish you a bath before we retire?" James asked Eilis.

Ian greeted James outside his chamber. "I rode ahead, my laird, and had a hot bath prepared. Greetings, my lady."

"Ah, Ian, I thank you," Eilis said smiling.

His cheeks flushed, Ian smiled broadly and bowed low. "My lady."

James shook his head and carried Eilis into his chamber. "The lad will be impossible to live with now."

Before he could enter the room, Lady Akira hurried to intercept them. "Eilis…" Tears choked her, and she couldn't say anything else.

James set Eilis down on the floor, and she hugged her new mother. "I am fine, my mother. All is well."

Lady Akira embraced her back. "Fergus will have to continue to guard you if you do not stay put," she scolded. "Dougald, is he well?"

Dougald rushed up the stairs. "Aye, my mother." He enfolded her in his arms, although she wrinkled her nose at the smell of him, and he released her.

James motioned for his faithful guard to leave. "Retire, Fergus. We will not need your services any further. The lass now knows her place."

Lady Akira smiled. "Aye, with us, her kin." She sighed. "I must away to bed so I can get up at the first hint of dawn and make sure your wee brother has plenty to do to keep him occupied. Take a bath, Dougald, or you will chase away our staff." She gave him a loving look. "I am well pleased you are home again." He opened his arms to give her another hug, but she waved him away. "After you have bathed." She gave Eilis another loving embrace. "Sleep well, dear, and take a care with the babe."

She toddled off to bed, and Dougald winked at Eilis. "She will spoil your brother and your bairn terribly. Not like with us, eh, James?"

"Aye." James lifted Eilis back into his arms and headed into the chamber, while Dougald reached for the door.

"Malcolm ordered a bath made to accommodate two. Mayhap you wish to also?"

Eilis's mouth dropped, and James quirked a brow at his brother.

Dougald saluted them with his hand. "See you on the morrow." Then he shut the door with a clunk.

James set Eilis down next to the bath and touched her face with a tender caress. "You are well? No one harmed you when you were hiding at Dunbarton's castle?"

"Nay, James. I was fine. Scared a little, but I am fine." She reached down to slip off her shoes.

James was quicker, and after he removed his weapons, he reached down to untie her shoes, then slipped his hands up her legs and unfastened the garters.

She closed her eyes and rested her hands on his head, loving how kind and giving he could be when he should have been angry with her for leaving the safety of Craigly to venture to Dunbarton's domain.

"You have no regrets that you took me to wife

instead of Catriona?"

He snorted. "I have always desired to find my treasure from the sea, sweet Eilis. 'Tis no other like you."

He rose his hands up her thighs then released her and pulled her gown over her head. "None other can ever compare." Through her thin chemise, he caressed her breasts and leaned over to kiss her lips.

Her body reacted to his persuasive touches, the ache growing between her legs, the tips of her breasts tightening, peaking, wanting more.

"Hmm, sweeting, in the bath with you, and after we have bathed…" He lifted his head. "You are not too sore, are you?"

"To make love again? Nay."

James quickly dispensed with her shift and lifted her into the bath, then removed his own clothes. "What say you about a bath built for two?"

She splashed her hand in the water and reached for the soap. "The servants will not like it."

James leaned over the bath, naked, his chest beautiful, bronzed, kissable. He relieved her of the soap and began to run it over her breasts, her neck, down her stomach, between her legs. She squealed. He chuckled.

"The servants will not mind as long as I am pleased and show them my gratitude."

"May…may Fia stay here?"

"Aye, as your lady-in-waiting. And to help raise your wee brother. Aye."

"Can you join me in the bath?" she asked, curious whether it would work.

"Nay, we would get stuck, and Nesta would love to tell the tale."

But it didn't take much coaxing, and Eilis crouched between James's legs while she soaped his chest and arms. He closed his eyes, and she feared he was falling asleep, but when she touched the rigid staff between his legs, his eyes shot open. "'Tis a willful water sprite who has snagged me."

He smiled and hauled her out of the tub, both dripping wet. Briskly, he dried her off and then himself, and before she could utter a word, he swept her through the bed hangings and joined her in the bed.

"I was about to give up my title and lands to Dougald to avoid marrying a woman I wished not, but, my sweet lassie from the sea came home. And rescued me."

Ha! He had done all the rescuing to her way of thinking.

She kissed his upturned lips, saw his eyes drowning with want. Aye, she was home at long last—with the hero of her dreams.

# ABOUT THE AUTHOR

Bestselling and award-winning author **Terry Spear** has written over sixty paranormal romance novels and seven medieval Highland historical romances. Her first werewolf romance, *Heart of the Wolf,* was named a 2008 *Publishers Weekly*'s Best Book of the Year, and her subsequent titles have garnered high praise and hit the *USA Today* bestseller list. A retired officer of the U.S. Army Reserves, Terry lives in Spring, Texas, where she is working on her next werewolf romance, continuing her new series about shapeshifting jaguars, writing Highland medieval romance, and having fun with her young adult novels. When she's not writing, she's photographing everything that catches her eye, making teddy bears, and playing with her Havanese puppies. For more information, please visit www.terryspear.com, or follow her on Twitter, @TerrySpear. She is also on Facebook at http://www.facebook.com/terry.spear. And on Wordpress at:

Terry Spear's Shifters
http://terryspear.wordpress.com/

# ALSO BY TERRY SPEAR

**Heart of the Cougar Series:**
Cougar's Mate, Book 1
Call of the Cougar, Book 2
Taming the Wild Cougar, Book 3
Covert Cougar Christmas (Novella)
Double Cougar Trouble, Book 4
Cougar Undercover, Book 5
Cougar Magic, Book 6

**Heart of the Bear Series**
Loving the White Bear, Book 1
Claiming the White Bear, Book 2

**The Highlanders Series:** Winning the Highlander's
Heart, The
Accidental Highland Hero, Highland Rake, Taming the
Wild
Highlander, The Highlander, Her Highland Hero, The
Viking's
Highland Lass, His Wild Highland Lass (novella),
Vexing the
Highlander (novella), My Highlander
**Other historical romances:** Lady Caroline & the
Egotistical Earl, A Ghost of a Chance at Love

**Heart of the Wolf Series:** Heart of the Wolf, Destiny
of the Wolf, To Tempt the Wolf, Legend of the White
Wolf, Seduced by the Wolf, Wolf Fever, Heart of the
Highland Wolf, Dreaming of the Wolf, A SEAL in
Wolf's Clothing, A Howl for a Highlander, A Highland
Werewolf Wedding, A SEAL Wolf Christmas, Silence

of the Wolf, Hero of a Highland Wolf, A Highland
Wolf Christmas, A SEAL Wolf Hunting; A Silver Wolf
Christmas, A SEAL Wolf in Too Deep, Alpha Wolf
Need Not Apply, Billionaire in Wolf's Clothing,
Between a Rock and a Hard Place, SEAL Wolf
Undercover, Dreaming of a White Wolf Christmas,
Flight of the White Wolf, A Billionaire Wolf for
Christmas, All's Fair in Love and Wolf, Wolff
Brothers: You Had Me at Wolf, Night of the Billionaire
Wolf, Red Wolf Christmas
**SEAL Wolves**: To Tempt the Wolf, A SEAL in Wolf's
Clothing, A SEAL Wolf Christmas, A SEAL Wolf
Hunting, A SEAL Wolf in Too Deep, SEAL Wolf
Undercover, SEAL Wolf Surrender
**Silver Town Wolves:** Destiny of the Wolf, Wolf Fever,
Dreaming of the Wolf, Silence of the Wolf, A Silver
Wolf Christmas, Alpha Wolf Need Not Apply, Between
a Rock and a Hard Place, All's Fair in Love and Wolf,
Silver Town Wolf: Home for the Holidays
**Wolff Brothers** (New to Silver Town): You Had Me at
Wolf
**White Wolves:** Legend of the White Wolf, Dreaming
of a White Wolf Christmas, Flight of the White Wolf
**Billionaire Wolves:** Billionaire in Wolf's Clothing, A
Billionaire Wolf for Christmas, Night of the Billionaire
Wolf
**Highland Wolves:** Heart of the Highland Wolf, A
Howl for a Highlander, A Highland Werewolf
Wedding, Hero of a Highland Wolf, A Highland Wolf
Christmas
**Red Wolves**: Seduced by the Wolf, Red Wolf
Christmas
**Heart of the Jaguar Series:** Savage Hunger, Jaguar

Fever, Jaguar Hunt, Jaguar Pride, A Very Jaguar
Christmas, You Had Me at Jaguar
**Jaguar Novella:** The Witch and the Jaguar
**Romantic Suspense:** Deadly Fortunes, In the Dead of
the Night, Relative Danger, Bound by Danger
**Vampire romances:** Killing the Bloodlust, Deadly
Liaisons, Huntress for Hire, Forbidden Love
Vampire Novellas: Vampiric Calling, The Siren's Lure,
Seducing the Huntress
**Other Romance:** Exchanging Grooms, Marriage, Las
Vegas Style

**Science Fiction Romance**: Galaxy Warrior
**Teen/Young Adult/Fantasy Books The World of
Fae:**
The Dark Fae, Book 1, The Deadly Fae, Book 2, The
Winged Fae, Book 3, The Ancient Fae, Book 4, Dragon
Fae, Book 5, Hawk Fae, Book 6, Phantom Fae, Book 7,
Golden Fae, Book 8, Falcon Fae, Book 9, Woodland
Fae, Book 10
**The World of Elf:**
The Shadow Elf, The Darkland Elf
**Blood Moon Series:**
Kiss of the Vampire, The Vampire...In My Dreams
**Demon Guardian Series:**
The Trouble with Demons; Demon Trouble, Too;
Demon Hunter
**Non-Series for Now:**
Ghostly Liaisons, The Beast Within, Courtly
Masquerade Deidre's Secret
**The Magic of Inherian:**
The Scepter of Salvation, The Mage of Monrovia,
Emerald Isle of Mists (TBA)

Made in the USA
Las Vegas, NV
01 October 2023

78367986R00194